Siste

Flapp

By day, the three Dryer sisters, Betty, Patsy and Jane, are dutiful and obedient daughters, doing chores insisted on by their tyrannical father.

But what their father doesn't know is that his daughters lead secret lives—as flappers who dance all night in Hollywood's speakeasies!

Their father insists they will marry wealthy men of his choosing, but these independent sisters are determined to find love on their own terms!

Read Patsy's story in

The Flapper's Fake Fiancé

And look out for Betty's and Jane's stories coming soon!

Author Note

Welcome to the first story in the Sisters of the Roaring Twenties series! Patsy, Betty and Jane are innocent sisters by day and fun-loving flappers by night.

This is Patsy's story, who finds herself caught up in the mystery of an escaped convict along with the story's hero, Lane Cox.

The roaring twenties brought us many things, including slang. Here's a short list of some words and phrases that became popular during that time:

Alarm clock: chaperone

Baloney: nonsense

Beat one's gums: idle chatter

Bee's knees: terrific

Charlie: a man with a mustache

Chin music: gossip

Choice bit of calico: attractive young woman

Ducky: very good

Flat tire: a bore

Juice joint: a speakeasy

Oliver Twist: a skilled dancer

Squirrel: to hide

I hope you enjoy Patsy and Lane's travel to happily-ever-after!

LAURI ROBINSON

—

The Flapper's Fake Fiancé

HARLEQUIN®
HISTORICAL™

Recycling programs
for this product may
not exist in your area.

ISBN-13: 978-1-335-50542-2

The Flapper's Fake Fiancé

Copyright © 2020 by Lauri Robinson

This edition published by arrangement with Harlequin Books S.A.

For questions and comments about the quality of this book,
please contact us at CustomerService@Harlequin.com.

Harlequin Enterprises ULC
22 Adelaide St. West, 40th Floor
Toronto, Ontario M5H 4E3, Canada
www.Harlequin.com

Printed in U.S.A.

A lover of fairy tales and history, **Lauri Robinson** can't imagine a better profession than penning happily-ever-after stories about men and women in days gone past. Her favorite settings include WWII, the roaring twenties and the old west. Lauri and her husband raised three sons in their rural Minnesota home and are now getting their just rewards by spoiling their grandchildren. Visit her at laurirobinson.blogspot.com, Facebook.com/lauri.robinson1 or Twitter.com/laurir.

Books by Lauri Robinson

Harlequin Historical

Unwrapping the Rancher's Secret
The Cowboy's Orphan Bride
Western Christmas Brides
"A Bride and Baby for Christmas"
Married to Claim the Rancher's Heir
Diary of a War Bride

Oak Grove

Mail-Order Brides of Oak Grove
"Surprise Bride for the Cowboy"
Winning the Mail-Order Bride
In the Sheriff's Protection

Brides of the Roaring Twenties

Baby on His Hollywood Doorstep
Stolen Kiss with the Hollywood Starlet

Sisters of the Roaring Twenties

The Flapper's Fake Fiancé

Visit the Author Profile page
at Harlequin.com for more titles.

Dedicated to an amazing fan who
loves the roaring twenties.
This one is for you, Tambra!

Chapter One

August 1928

An escaped convict! Imprisoned for robbing a train seven years ago. That's the real cat's meow!

And whiskers!

Patsy Dryer's heart thudded as she quickly folded the newspaper article and tucked it inside the suitcase that held various other articles she'd saved over the years. This was it. The story that would get her name in the byline. She'd be the reporter. The one to get the scoop on the news overtaking Los Angeles.

Father wouldn't be able to keep her locked up then. She'd become rich and famous on her own—without having to marry a man he handpicked. He was adamant that his daughters marry well and kept them all under lock and key until he found a suitable man for her and her sisters.

He'd already picked out a man for her oldest sister, Betty, so it was only a matter of time until he found one for her and Jane. Which meant time was running out.

Right next to the articles Patsy had snipped out of the

newspapers was a stack of articles she'd written, about all sorts of things, along with a rejection slip for each one.

But this. An escaped convict. That's exactly what she needed. Everyone would be interested in that and when her version of the story hit the editor's desk, it would be printed for sure.

Then she'd have a real job, and wouldn't have to worry about being forced into a marriage, or stuck in the house cleaning all day, day after day.

With that thought encouraging her, and her mind spinning with images of a man dressed in black-and-white stripes, she closed the suitcase and shoved it under her bed.

Gathering all the information she could before another reporter beat her to the scoop was a priority, and she knew just the place for that to happen.

The Rooster's Nest. Everyone knew whiskey loosened lips. If there was news to be heard, that's where it would be heard first. The crowd at that speakeasy was full of tough guys—mainly dockworkers who were certain to know more about an escaped convict than anyone else.

The docks were full of chin music. And criminals. At least that's what she'd heard. Well, read. The newspapers were always full of stories about people being shanghaied.

Oh, maybe that's what happened to the escaped convict!

She had to find out more information right away.

The morning sunlight filling the room sent a river of discouragement clear to her toes. It'd be hours before she could get to the Rooster's Nest. Before she could sneak away. Today was wash day. So those hours would be filled with washing everything from rugs to linens, hanging it all out to dry and ironing each and every piece before putting it all away.

Patsy pushed up her sleeves and huffed out a breath while walking to the door of her bedroom, past the vanity table with its round mirror and matching bench seat, both painted bright pink to match the rest of her bedroom furnishings. Her life had been painted pink since the day she was born because she was the baby of the family. Daddy's baby girl.

Despite graduating high school, and secretarial school, everything was still painted pink. When she had her own house, her own life, nothing would be pink. She wouldn't be anyone's baby girl, either. She'd be a reporter. A woman of means.

Shopkeepers already thought of her as a woman of means because she was Patsy Dryer, William Dryer's youngest daughter, but they didn't know the half of it. Her family hadn't always been rich. Father hadn't started making money until ten years ago, and most of his wealth had been acquired in the past few years, since the houses he'd had built started selling. Those houses didn't sell on their own, either. They had to be cleaned from top to bottom once they were built, and that was what she and her sisters had been doing, besides keeping their own home in tip-top shape all the time.

She and her sisters had decided some time ago that they weren't going to do this forever. They weren't going to be like Mother, either. Being told when to get up, when to go to bed, when to eat and what to do all the time.

"I'll wash today," Betty said as Patsy stepped into the hallway. "Jane will run the wringer."

Betty, being the oldest, kept track of rotating everyone's household duties. Everything from washing day to shopping day, Betty was in charge, per Mother's orders, of course.

Mother, of course, was following Father's orders.

That was the golden rule of the Dryer household.

Father's orders.

The Dryer household was a prune pit. So old-fashioned it felt as if she was being smothered every day, living in the last century, long before women were given the right to vote. Father threatened he'd send them to a convent if they didn't follow his orders. Well, living here was nearly as bad.

It was not that she wasn't grateful. She was thankful that she always had plenty to eat and new clothes to wear, but what was the fun in having new clothes if you were never allowed to go anywhere? Not allowed to do anything? Father's strict rules kept them practically imprisoned in their own house.

She wasn't the only one to feel the way she did. Her sisters were as starved for freedom as she was.

"And I'll rinse," Patsy replied to Betty as Jane stepped out of her bedroom and joined them in the long hallway that would take them downstairs of their big Hollywood-land home.

Theirs had been the first home built in the hills that now hosted several dozen large and elaborate homes. When Father had inherited the land that was too hilly for farming years ago, he'd decided to plot it off and build houses to sell. Like everything else, he had very specific building requirements and very specific requirements as to who could purchase any of the homes—only the rich and famous. Because that was what he wanted to be. He wanted the Dryer name to ring with recognition.

His words, not hers.

"So I'm on the wringer?" Jane asked.

They all three had inherited their mother's blond hair and their father's blue eyes, and as if Father had control over their size, too, they were like stair steps. Betty the tallest, then Jane and then her, the baby of the family. The shortest.

Betty nodded at Jane. "Yes. It's your turn."

Jane nodded in agreement, accepting things were as they were, because that's what they were required to do.

Or did.

Until the day Father had made them visit a convent. That night, six months ago, Jane had snuck out and visited a speakeasy.

Patsy had been floored to learn what Jane had done, but upon hearing about the fun and adventure her sister had experienced, Patsy had joined her the next night, and had the absolute time of her life!

Betty joined the two of them the night after that.

That night, they'd all agreed if they were going to have to live in a convent the rest of their lives, they'd better have fun now, while they could.

So they'd become flappers. Real, live flappers.

They wore short skirts, fancy hats and feathered headbands and makeup, listened to the new fast-paced music, danced with any man they chose and didn't care if others thought their behavior was acceptable or not.

And it was so much fun!

Excitement filled Patsy from head to toe. She loved their secretive flapper life. "We're going to the Rooster's Nest tonight," she whispered, even though Father was already at work and Mother was down in the kitchen.

A short time ago, after breakfast, she and her sisters had returned to their rooms for half an hour of "digesting time." What *was* that? Digesting time? To her, it was nothing more than another one of Father's rules. However, it was one that she didn't mind because it gave her time to sneak articles out of the newspaper her father had finished reading up to her room.

"Haven't been to the Rooster's Nest in a while," Jane said. "I heard they have a new piano player that is really the bee's knees."

"Hush," Betty hissed as they started down the long, curved staircase. "Wait until we are on the back porch."

"Read something interesting this morning?" Jane whispered.

Betty shot them both a glare, but there was a hint of an enthusiastic gleam in her eyes.

Patsy pinched her lips together and nodded at Jane.

The excitement in her sister's eyes nearly matched hers, and with new enthusiasm to get their chores completed, they all increased their speed down the wide steps.

Hours later, after the beds had been stripped and re-made, they were finally in the back porch, where the hum of the washing machine motor, the sloshing of water and the constant high-pitched squeak of the rollers on the wringer gave them the opportunity to talk without the fear of being overheard.

"Why the Rooster's Nest?" Jane asked, feeding a white sheet between the rollers on the washing machine, filling the air with the smell of bleach.

Patsy waited until enough material rolled out of the wringer for her to grab and guide the sheet into the rinse tub before answering, "There's an escaped convict on the lam."

"Really?" Jane flipped the arm of the wringer around so it was in position to squeeze the rinse water out of the sheet.

"Yes," Patsy answered while swooshing the sheet about in the water. Her sisters knew about her desire to be a reporter. Jane wanted to be in showbiz, and Betty… Betty just wanted out of Father's house, to move to Seattle, where she'd once visited their grandmother before she'd died. "I read about it in the *Gazette* this morning. It appears the convict robbed a train seven years ago, and escaped from prison just last week. The article warned people to keep their doors locked."

"The Rooster's Nest will be the place to go, then," Jane said, feeding the rinsed sheet into the wringer so it could drop in the basket to be hung on the line. "If there are any goods to be had, that's where you'll hear it."

Patsy nodded. "That's what I figured, too."

"The Rooster's Nest means we'll have to take a streetcar." Betty pulled a sheet out of the washer and waited for Jane to flip the arm of the wringer back over the washing machine tub. "The red line."

Patsy bit her bottom lip, waiting for Jane's reply. Both she and Jane knew that if Father ever learned about their nighttime excursions, they all would be in trouble, but Betty would be in the most trouble. He forever pointed out that she was the oldest and the one responsible. For everything.

"We've done that before," Jane said.

"I know." Betty looked at both of them with a serious gaze. "We just have to be more careful when taking the streetcar."

Patsy nodded. The Rooster's Nest wasn't that much farther away than some of the other joints they visited. It was just located on a busier street, which meant they had to be more cautious about not being spotted by someone who might know them, or their father.

Jane nodded. "You don't have to tell us twice. If we ever got caught, we'd be locked upstairs like Rapunzel for the rest of our lives."

That was the real malarkey. They all knew it. "With our hair cut off," Pasty added. "So we couldn't throw it out the window to be rescued by a knight in shining armor." That was the one step none of them had dared take. Cutting off their long hair. Father thought all women should have long hair.

Jane laughed, but Betty didn't. Her blue eyes grew sad. Patsy knew why. Their father had announced last month that Betty would marry James Bauer, a man whom none of them liked. He was the owner of one of the companies building houses for their father, and most certainly was not a knight in shining armor. But James was what Father looked for in a man. Rich. That was all he cared about.

"We'll leave at eight thirty," Betty said as she pulled out another sheet.

"Eight thirty it is," Jane said, feeding the sheet through the wringer.

Patsy grinned at both of them and nodded while swooshing around the sheet in the rinse tub. Eight thirty was hours away, but excitement filled her nonetheless. Despite the fact that she was nineteen, Jane was twenty-one and Betty twenty-two, they were sent to bed at seven thirty every night just like they had been when they were small children. She'd hated that for years. Right up until Jane had showed them what could happen after their parents were sound asleep. Now she was glad that Father lived by such a strict schedule. One that included his own bedtime, as well. And that their big house meant their parents had a large bedroom downstairs, while the three of them had the upstairs rooms all to themselves.

By 8:31 that evening, Patsy had climbed down the ivy-covered trellis that extended to the second floor, right outside the upstairs bathroom window. Jane climbed down next, and then Betty. They all had their blond hair tucked up beneath floppy brimmed hats, bright lipstick shimmering on their lips and thick layers of mascara on their eyelashes. The shin-length, long-sleeved, paisley-print dresses they'd worn all day had been changed into fashionable A-line sleeveless dresses with hems that stopped above their knees.

Her dress was dark blue with two layers of fringe on the hem, Jane's was red-and-white-striped and Betty's was deep purple with silver lace on the hem and neckline. Sewing was another household skill they were well versed in, and one they each put to good use regularly. Their parents only ever saw the simple paisley-and-gingham-print dresses each of them sewed. These ones, their flapper dresses, were made of silk, satin and other enticing materials that had been secretly slipped in the house and sewn in secret for this. Their late-night excursions.

Once on the ground, Betty gave both Patsy and Jane a thorough once-over, then, upon her satisfied nod, they were all three off, running across the backyard like the house had just been raided.

They darted through the line of trees that separated the backyard from a dirt road that led up the hill, where houses would someday be built, and then followed the road downhill, all the way to an abandoned house on the edge of the development. It was a fairly new house that had once been owned by the mob, but the government had confiscated it. Their father had tried to buy it, because it butted up to property he already owned, but it wasn't for sale. That suited them fine because they could walk through the yard without the fear of being seen, and then onto the street where the red line of the streetcars rolled by.

"Perfect timing!" Jane exclaimed as they all hurried

to the edge of the street where they could climb aboard the city trolley ringing its bell. "I can't wait to hear that new piano player."

Patsy agreed, mainly to be nice. She enjoyed music, but Jane loved it. Jane even dared sneak into the living room and listen to the radio. Of course, that was only when Father wasn't home, but Mother was home. So far, she hadn't gotten caught, and Patsy hoped things stayed that way.

"We have to leave before midnight," Betty whispered once they were aboard the streetcar. "No later than eleven forty-five or we'll miss the last car home."

Patsy and Jane agreed with nods. Other than that, they didn't speak to each other, or do anything to draw attention to themselves or each other. There were hundreds of thousands of people in LA and the chance of their running into someone who knew them was unlikely, considering other than shopping and church on Sunday mornings, they rarely left the house, but they'd agreed long ago to be extra cautious on their excursions.

They leaped off the streetcar as it stopped a block away from the Rooster's Nest, which was located beneath a laundromat. Others were going that way, too, and the sisters walked along with the others as if they didn't even know each other.

The entrance was in the front of the building, except that once they were in the entranceway, everyone took an unmarked brown door on the left that led down a lighted flight of stairs. Jane was several steps ahead and Patsy grinned at how her sister's head bobbed to the music emitted into the stairway.

At the bottom of the stairs, the first person in line knocked on another door. The small sliding peephole opened, and upon hearing the password, the door was opened for all of them to enter. The password was simply the speakeasy's name, but it was still a security measure. If the person who opened the slide saw a police officer's uniform, he would signal the bar, and all of the alcohol would be dumped or hidden so the place couldn't get busted for selling it.

Patsy's grin increased as she stepped through the door at the bottom of the stairs and rounded the corner. The large room was full of bright sparkling lights, music and people. All sorts of people.

She loved the thrill that filled her every time she entered a room like this. It was as if she was instantly transformed into an entirely different person.

Tonight that thrill was even bigger. This was it. Her chance to write an article that would get printed and launch her into the world she read about every day. She wanted to see all the things written about in the newspaper, from the ostrich rides at Lincoln Park, to the jazz bands playing music along the beach boardwalk and a gazillion things in between. Being a reporter would allow her to do all that, and there wasn't a thing her father could say about it.

She rubbed her hands together, ready to learn all she could about the escaped convict. Rex Gaynor was his name. The newspaper had said as much. Her attention zoned in on a trio of men sitting at the end of the bar. No fancy jackets covered their work shirts or the wide suspenders holding up their britches. Hot dawg! Those were the type of men who talked, a lot, once they drank enough, especially to a flapper.

Happiness bubbled inside her. She loved this. Being someone other than dull, boring Patsy Dryer. Here, she was anyone she wanted to be.

That had been scary at first, to break out of the quiet,

shy girl she'd been her entire life, but once she had, an entire new world had opened up for her.

Tonight, she was going to be Libby, short for Liberty. That was her favorite, the name she used the most, because that's what she was, liberated.

Libby wasn't shy, or quiet, she was bold and vivacious, and knew how to get what she wanted.

She glided up to the bar, planted one foot on the rail near the floor and an elbow on the bar. Cupping her chin, she winked at the men. "Hello, fellas. What's the news on the dock today?"

All three laughed, and the one closest to her, an older man with thinning gray hair, asked, "Don't know, bearcat, you got any chin music?"

She giggled, loving everything about being a flapper, about being Libby, and laid a coin on the counter to order a fruit drink without alcohol. Betty had warned them all, numerous times, about how dangerous some homemade alcohol could be, and how they shouldn't drink it. The Volstead Act prohibited the manufacturing and sale of alcohol, not the consumption, which meant people who wanted to drink, drank anything. And people wanting to sell alcohol made it out of anything at hand.

She had tasted several types of cocktails over the months, but ultimately, agreed with Betty. Most of it tasted awful and burned her throat. So did cigarettes, which she had also tried, and decided she didn't need either whiskey or cigarettes in order to have a good time.

Once her drink arrived, she took a little sip and set the glass back down. "Well, the only chin music I've heard is from the newspaper, something about an escaped convict."

The man farthest away from her, wearing a squat leather hat and boasting a big, black mustache, shook his head. "Ain't read any papers lately, doll, but that guy over there is who I'd talk to if I wanted to beat gums over what's printed in them."

Patsy glanced across the room, toward a table where a man with brown wavy hair, parted on the side, sat alone.

"Why?" she asked.

"That's Lane Cox," the mustached man added. "He owns the *LA Gazette*."

The air locked in Patsy's lungs. Lane Cox. The very one who had sent back every article she'd submitted to his newspaper. He not only owned the *Gazette*, he was the best reporter in LA. She tilted her head to see past people mingling about, to get a better look at him. Odd. She'd expected him to be old, and gruff looking. Not young and dapper. However, seeing him meant she was at the right place. He must be investigating the Rex Gaynor story, too.

"If you want the news on the dock, ask that man."

Patsy turned back toward the three men. It was the middle one who'd spoken this time. A younger man, with short-cut black hair. He was looking across the bar, at a man wearing a red shirt and black suspenders and puffing on a cigar. That man had a mustache, too, and therefore instantly earned the nickname Charlie. After Charlie Chaplin, a very popular actor with a black mustache. "Who is that Charlie?" she asked, loving being able to use popular lingo.

"Don't know his name, but if something is going on at the docks, he knows about it," the middle man answered.

"How do you know that?" she asked.

The man shrugged and took a long draw on his drink. "He's been cruising the docks for weeks."

That cigar-puffing Charlie wasn't dressed like a dock-worker, which meant something, that was for certain.

Letting things settle for a moment, Patsy picked up her drink, and while sipping on it, glanced across the room, toward Lane Cox, wondering if he knew who that Charlie was. But Lane was no longer at the table. A scan of the room said he wasn't anywhere to be seen.

She pinched her lips together to keep her smile secretive. If that Charlie knew anything, she'd find out before Lane Cox even. She could almost see the little drawing that would be printed along with her article, that of a man in a striped suit being hauled back to jail. She'd be a hero and a reporter.

Bee's knees, this was so exciting!

She set her glass on the bar and sashayed along the length of it, to the other end where the man was talking to the bartender. Without waiting for the conversation to end, she laid a hand on Charlie's arm. "Hey, big-timer, care to cut a rug?"

The man turned and looked at her with a cool eye.

He wasn't very handsome. In fact, the long scar next to his left eye was rather frightening.

Patsy would have run from this man, but being Libby from head to toe, she brightened her grin and batted the lashes she'd carefully coated with black mascara. "One dance to please a gal?" She patted his arm. "Please, a handsome man like you?"

The man grinned. "Who can say no to a little billboard like you?"

Her heart thudded at how well she could play the part, and she whirled about, looking at the man over her shoulder, knowing he'd follow her to the dance floor.

The man at the piano was pounding on the keys, filling the room with the fast tempo of the ragtime song.

Charlie followed her, all right, and took a hold of her

hands to pull her to his side as he started to move along the dance floor.

Being Libby and not Patsy, she controlled the icy shiver that rippled her spine at being so close to the man, and told herself that the Peabody was one of her favorite dances. It truly was and she was good at the fast one-step, as well as the long gliding strides that went along with quick steps. It was also a dance that kept enough space between partners.

As they circled the dance floor, he asked, "You come here often, doll?"

"Every so often." She pulled up her best frown. "But I guess I'll have to stop."

"Why?"

"Because of the escaped convict." She looked across her shoulder at the man, hoping her expression made her look scared. "The chin music is that folks should stay home and keep their doors locked. That's frightening. He could be anywhere."

The man let out a barrel of a belly laugh. "Don't you worry that pretty little head over Rex Gaynor. He's only after the stash of cash he stole."

Her heart skipped a beat. So did her feet. "Stash of cash? From where?"

Charlie got her back in rhythm with the music and led her all the way across the end of the dance floor, and then back the other way before he answered, "The train robbery. He hid it before getting caught, and broke out to go get it."

She kept her feet moving when they wanted to stop again. "The paper didn't say that."

He laughed. "Papers don't know everything, doll."

Patsy had grown breathless, but dancing had nothing to do with it. Her heart was racing, stealing her ability to breathe, because of the information she'd just gained. "I wonder where he hid it."

The man laughed again. "Only Rex knew that."

The music ended and so did their dancing. She was about to ask him for another one, in order to learn more information, but he nodded at someone behind her.

"Sorry, doll, but I gotta blow this joint." He winked. "Don't be a squirrel."

Libby was never a squirrel. She didn't hide from anything. Didn't have to. Spinning about, she looked to see whom he'd nodded at. The only person over that way was walking out the door located beside the end of the bar. All she saw was the back of a brown shirt. A moment later, Charlie walked out that same door.

Patsy considered following him, but she and her sisters had a rule. None of them could leave, not even step outside, without the other two—until it was time to go home. Then they left one at a time, but right behind each other.

She twisted left, then right. Jane was leaning on the piano, talking with the piano player, who was taking a break, and Betty was sitting at the far end of the bar, near where the three men she'd spoken to earlier still sat. Betty glanced at her, and then at the drink Patsy had left on the bar. Which meant she most certainly could not follow Charlie out that door.

She walked over, drank the drink and then set the glass on the bar again. "Is the powder room that way?" she asked as if Betty was a stranger.

Betty gave a slight nod. One that said *I'll be watching you come out*.

Patsy knew the rules, and wasn't going to jeopardize their double lives. But it was hard at times, having to follow so many rules that got in the way of her truly becoming a reporter. That was never going to happen if she could write only about mundane things.

She used the powder room and applied another layer of bright red lipstick before returning to the bar and ordering another drink.

Her mind was still spinning, but now, besides an escaped convict dressed in white and black stripes, there were images of bags of stolen money floating around in her thoughts. She scanned the room. There had to be someone else she could talk to. Someone who might know more about Rex Gaynor.

The room was full of people, those sitting at tables, laughing, drinking and smoking, and those on the dance floor. The piano man was pounding on the keys again, and the dance floor was full of men and women kicking up their heels. That's what she usually did, too. There was nothing like the fun of that. Dancing beneath the bright lights, completely free of all the restrictions she normally lived by. It was hard to sit on the sideline.

As the idea of hitting the dance floor filled her, the music stopped and a man next to the piano announced they were starting a dance-off.

She loved dance-offs more than anything.

"Five dances. The foxtrot, the Charleston, the Lindy Hop, the shimmy and the tango!" the man yelled. "The best pair of dancers to finish all five dances will win these here trophies!"

The crowd cheered as he held up two glass mugs.

"Full, of course!"

The crowd cheered louder.

"Berries!" Patsy shouted along with others. She couldn't care less about the mug; it was the dance-off itself that excited her. Tugging her hat down to make sure it was good and tight so her long hair wouldn't fall out while dancing, she glanced around the room, looking for a man who might be able to really cut a rug. An Oliver Twist.

To her surprise, Lane Cox rounded the corner near the door right then.

"Copacetic!" Learning a bit more while dancing would be absolutely perfect!

She didn't waste a step in getting across the room to grab a hold of his arm. "Come on, you're my partner."

He tried to pull his arm away from her, but she held on and stepped closer to his side.

"Don't be a killjoy," she said, batting her lashes. He was not only far younger than she'd imagined, but also very handsome up close.

"I'm sorry, miss, but I'm not here to dance," he said.

She laughed. "I am."

He gave a slight nod that caused a section of his slicked-back wavy hair to fall over his forehead. "You'll have to find someone else."

This was a first. Men never refused dancing with Libby. He was the person who would know more about Rex Gaynor than anyone else. She hooked her arm fully around his. "I don't want to dance with someone else." Giving him a solid tug and a big smile, she took his profession into consideration as she added, "You can tell me more about Rex Gaynor and the stash of cash he's looking for while we dance."

Chapter Two

Lane Cox prided himself on rarely being surprised. He'd seen too much, heard too much, knew too much to let that happen, but right now, his breath was locked in his chest. It could be because the little blue-eyed flapper, batting her eyelashes at him, was about the cutest doll he'd ever seen.

But it wasn't.

He knew that.

Women. Any woman didn't affect him. One had at one time, but that would never happen again.

It hadn't this time, either.

Her looks weren't what stalled his breathing. It was her words. *Stash of cash*.

Very few people knew Rex Gaynor had broken out of prison to locate the money he'd stolen off the train he'd robbed seven years ago.

The train robbery that had changed Lane's life. His wife had been on that train. And their baby daughter. Both had perished.

"Come on, Oliver," she said. "It'll be fun."

He almost took a step, but stopped himself before that happened. "Oliver?"

Her giggle literally floated on the air. "Yes, as in Oliver Twist. You do know how to dance, don't you?"

He'd heard the term before, but hadn't gotten over her "stash of cash" comment, and wondered if she'd thought he was someone else. How could she know that about Gaynor? It wasn't public information. He gave her a solid once-over gaze from head to toe. Starting at the floppy blue hat that hid her hair, blond from the few stray hairs popping out near her neckline, to her slim neck and dainty chin, the blue fringe dress, the lanky legs, and ending at the tips of her toes inside the black-heeled shoes. She certainly didn't look like the type to be mixed up with an ex-con, but looks could be deceiving. "Yes, I know how to dance," he said, lifting his gaze back to her blue eyes partially hidden by the brim of her floppy hat.

She tilted her chin up and looked him square in the eyes. "Then prove it."

A challenge? From a flapper who should be home being tucked in bed by her mother? She was young. Now that he could see her face, he'd guess she was not twenty yet. Maybe younger even. A family member of Gaynor's? Sent here to get him off the scent of the story he'd been following? That was his life. Had been for years. Sniffing out the next story, and he was good at it. Very good. It had been said he never left a stone unturned, and this little flapper was definitely a stone he needed to look beneath. Find out how she knew about the cash, and anything else in that pretty little head of hers about Rex Gaynor.

Nothing excited him more than getting the scoop, and this story meant more to him than all the others had put together. He'd been there when Rex Gaynor had been put behind bars and was willing to do whatever it took to make sure the man was put back there again. "All right, doll, let's cut a rug."

She let out another lifting giggle as they headed for the dance floor.

Although the Rooster's Nest was located downtown, the clientele was made up of dockworkers and construction workers, with a few shady characters thrown in here and there. Which made her stand out like a blue jay flying with a flock of pigeons. This wasn't the kind of joint where a choice piece of calico was going to find herself a sugar daddy. Add that to the fact she knew more than she should about an escaped convict and he was in 100 percent.

A dance-off was a small price to pay in order to put an end to this story.

Pieces of paper with the number twelve were pinned to the backs of their clothes. A total of twenty couples got numbered pieces of paper pinned to their backs while judges were being chosen from the hundred or more bystanders. As they waited, he asked the flapper, "What's your name?"

Her eyes lit up like flames on candlesticks freshly struck with a match. "Liberty, but you can call me Libby."

That wasn't her real name. He'd bet every wooden nickel in LA on that. Still, he gave a slight nod. "All right, Libby. It's nice to meet you."

"You, too, Mr. Co—" She laughed. "I don't know your name. What is it?"

Yes, she did, but had caught herself before saying it. Which was only one of the questions he needed answered. "Lathan," he answered, and watched her expression. No one knew his real name, his legal name, except his lawyer.

She lifted a brow and then gave him the tiniest of nods. "It's nice to meet you, Lathan. Which of the dances is your favorite?"

He didn't have a favorite. Hadn't danced a whole lot the past seven years, and not much before then, either. Hadn't had time back then, still didn't. However, he wasn't inept, and knew he'd be able to keep up with her. Instead of answering, he asked, "Which is your favorite?"

Her smile grew even brighter. "The Lindy—no, the shimmy. Definitely the shimmy."

The dance that was banned in some of the high-class establishments for being too provocative. Why didn't that surprise him? He'd be lying if he didn't admit a piece of him wanted to see her shoulders twist and shake like she was trying to shimmy out of her chemise. That's what made it too provocative for other joints—because that's exactly what looked like was about to happen when women danced the shimmy. Or it could have been banned because others complained that watching flappers dance to the shimmy caused too many men to get more robust than usual.

"They are all cherries," she said. "Have you ever won a dance-off?"

"Can't say as I have," he answered.

She grabbed his hand and pulled him into the center of the dance floor. "Until tonight!"

The words had no sooner left her mouth when the piano player struck the first chord. The atmosphere in the room instantly spiked. Something spiked inside Lane, too. Recognizing the common tune, he curved one arm around her waist and settled his hand on the small of her back while grasping her palm with his other hand. The foxtrot was similar to the waltz, just a four-four rhythm instead of a three-four, and to his favor, didn't require any body contact.

He started out slowly, gliding her around the floor and through the several dance sequences. She was graceful, light on her feet and quick to catch on to each twist and turn.

"Attaboy, Oliver!" she shouted.

Her excitement had him picking up the pace, leading her faster around the floor. People on the sidelines cheered, shouting out the number of their favorite couple.

"Do you hear that, Oliver?" she asked. "They are cheering for us. Number twelve."

"I hear," he answered. "And the name is Lathan, not Oliver." It didn't bother him, but, for some reason, he wanted to get credit where credit was due.

Tossing her head back, she laughed, and then squealed slightly when she had to let go of his shoulder long enough to push her hat back down on her head.

"You should take that off," he suggested as they rounded the corner of the dance floor.

"Can't."

"Why not?"

"Because I didn't wash my hair today!" She laughed. "Or yesterday!"

Her answer was as unexpected as the enjoyment filling him. He didn't know a woman who would have admitted that, in public, to a virtual stranger. Most were far too vain to share such information.

Information. That's what he needed.

"So, what do you know about that escaped convict? Rick Gaylord, was it?"

Her smile never faded, nor did her steps falter as she shook her head. "You know his name is Rex Gaynor, don't pretend you don't."

"I wasn't pretending," he answered, gliding them around another corner. The bright overhead lights shined down on her like a spotlight, and it seemed fitting. She was lovely enough to be under a spotlight. With her looks, she could be on the silver screen. Maybe that was what she was hoping, why she was here.

No, if that was the case, she'd have chosen a classier joint than the Rooster's Nest.

"Then why did you call him Rick Gaylord?"

"To see if you really knew his name," Lane answered. It was an old trick, but one that rarely failed to work.

Her chin lifted in a prideful way. "I do know his name. It's Rex Gaynor. Seven years ago, he robbed a train running between LA and San Diego. He was sentenced to prison for the rest of his life, but escaped last week."

All that had been in today's paper. He knew because it had not only been printed in his newspaper, he'd written the article. Seven years ago, he'd owned the *Gazette* for only a year, and had been working day and night to get it into every newsstand, into the hands of every person living in Los Angeles.

His hard work had paid off. It was now the number one, most trusted source of news, not only in LA, but in the surrounding area that stretched over a hundred miles in all directions. Copies were also mailed across the nation every day. The president himself received the *Gazette*.

That was more than he'd dreamed at one time, but, as he'd told himself many times, he'd sacrificed a lot to make it happen. Naomi and Sarah were casualties of his work, of his dedication. At times, he wondered why he continued because of that, losing them, then he'd remember. It was because of them that he continued to work so hard. After they'd died, the paper had been all he had. Still was.

This time around, he was not too busy getting things off the ground to put his full attention on his family, on making sure the man who was responsible for their deaths paid the full price. Sarah had been only four months old when Naomi had contracted the flu. Naomi had recovered, but had still been exhausted, and taking care of Sarah wasn't allowing her to get the rest she needed. The rest, and help, that he couldn't give her because he was at the paper day and night. So he'd sent her to visit her parents, down in San Diego. They'd been gone for over a month, and her final letter to him had said that she was fully rested and ready to come home.

They'd been on their way home when Gaynor had robbed the train. With dynamite. The explosion caught the passenger car on fire, and Naomi and Sarah had died. Just five miles south of Los Angeles.

"Lathan? Lathan! We have to keep dancing or we'll be eliminated!"

He shook his head, dispelling the cobwebs that could grow so thick, so quickly, that there wasn't room for anything else, and increased the speed of his footsteps. She was leading now, this flapper who called herself Liberty. Libby for short.

He had no idea how long she had been leading, and quickly took over again, making a full round of the dance floor before the music stopped.

There was barely time to catch a breath when it started up again. This time it was a quicker, snappier tune that filled the room with a roar from the crowd of bystanders.

"It's the shimmy!" she shouted. A moment later, she was in a crouched position, shaking her shoulders while holding her hands at her sides as she slowly rose upward, then leaped into the air, spun around and crouched down again.

Not only were her shoulders shimmying, her entire torso was, and her waist and hips. The fringes of her dress were flipping and flopping in all directions.

He joined her in the moves, but unlike her, this was not a favorite of his. It may be fun to watch, but not fun to do. Not for him.

Until she grabbed his hands and leaped forward, pressing against him. Her shimmying body lit a fire in his. Before he knew it, he was shimmying along with her, up against her.

"You really are an Oliver Twist, Lathan!" she shouted. "A real hoofer!"

She'd make any man a hoofer. The girl had moves like no other. "Who taught you how to dance?" he asked.

She released his hands and did a shimmy show for him, crouching and then slowly rising while shaking her torso so hard he was sure she would shimmy right out of that blue fringed dress. She leaped into the air and spun around, shaking her backside at him, before leaping back around.

"No one taught me!" She grabbed his hands again. "I learned it all on my own!"

She certainly had learned it, and he wondered what else she'd learned. Thankfully, that thought brought him back to the business at hand. "What else do you know about Rex Gaynor?"

Pressing herself against him, she said, "Your turn. I already answered a question. What else do you know about Rex Gaynor? Something that wasn't in today's newspaper."

He knew plenty that wasn't in the article he'd written, and that's why it hadn't been in the paper, he didn't want to share any of it. He had a very good relationship with law enforcement because they trusted him to not share any information that might hinder an investigation. They also knew he'd share anything pertinent with them before printing it, and that he couldn't be bought off, not even by the mobs. That alone had helped him grow the newspaper as much as everything else. Knowing she wouldn't wait long for a response, he answered, "Gaynor wasn't from California."

She leaned back enough to look at him. Eagerness, more than before, shone in her eyes. "Where's he from?"

"Out east."

"Everything is east of California."

"Hawaii isn't."

Her laughter made him chuckle.

"You are quite a bird, Lathan, quite a bird."

Very few people considered him funny. Then again, very few people who knew him personally would believe he was dancing the shimmy with a flapper like this. He was normally too reserved to dance more than an obligatory dance with a hostess now and again.

"Where is he really from?" she asked. "More specifically than east."

"I believe it was Missouri," he answered, waiting to see how she reacted. Gaynor was from Missouri, and if she was family, she might be surprised he knew that.

"Missouri?" She nodded and then let go of him to crouch down.

Lane almost groaned aloud at having to watch her do her shimmying all over again. He could look away, but there would be no fun in that, and despite all, he was having fun.

More than he should be having.

When her display ended and they were close together again, she said, "Lots of Old West outlaws came from Missouri."

"How do you know that?" he asked, truly wanting to know. Then, his mind clicked. Liberty, Missouri. The town where the James-Younger gang was from, and others. She really could be a relative of Gaynor's. Some claim there was a connection between Gaynor and the James-Younger gang of yesteryear.

"I read," she said. "A lot."

The dance ended. Lane let her go and took a step back. This time he truly needed to catch his breath. He wasn't given much time to do so. Within a cat's heartbeat, the next song started.

The tango. Which meant full-body contact.

Lane drew in a deep breath, hooked her around the waist, grasped her other hand, and they were off, chest to chest, gliding across the floor with large, lavish steps. At the edge of the dance floor, he dipped her, then simultaneously, they spun and started back in the other direction.

"Your turn," he said. "What else do you know about Gaynor?"

"That he stashed the cash he'd stolen, and is now looking for it."

"Where?"

She laughed.

It was time to dip her again, so he did, and while holding her a mere few inches off the floor asked, "Do you know?"

"Do you?" she countered.

She was as good at questioning as she was dancing, and in all honesty, he admired her for that. "No," he answered truthfully, lifted her up and started back across the floor in the other direction. He truly didn't care about the cash. He just wanted Gaynor behind bars again. Where he belonged.

"Me, neither," she said, to his surprise. "But I intend to find out."

"Why?"

The music stopped. She took a step back and shook her

head while planting her hands on her thighs and bending over, as if to completely catch her breath. "Hear that?" she asked, looking up at him under the brim of her floppy hat. "They are still shouting number twelve."

He gulped in air. Thoroughly needing it. He hadn't danced three dances in a row in a very long time, but had to admit that keeping up a conversation with her while dancing chest to chest was taxing his reserves more than the fast steps.

The piano player struck a chord and she snapped upright. "The Lindy Hop! I love the Lindy Hop!"

"I think you love dancing, no matter what the dance is," he said, holding out his hands for her to grasp.

She grabbed his hands and, despite gasping for air a moment ago, she was instantly kicking up her heels. The swift twists, turns and numerous pirouettes made talking through this dance rather impossible.

Lane was certain he'd never seen someone enjoy dancing so much. The fast tempo proved to be too much for several couples. They bowed out, stumbling to the sidelines, or danced right off the floor and onto chairs. One couple collapsed right in the middle of the other dancers.

Right beside them.

Seeing the couple go down, he spun Libby in the other direction just in time. Two other couples weren't as lucky and tripped over the couple sprawled on the floor. Bystanders acted quickly, coming to the rescue of the fallen dancers, helping them off the floor before anyone else tripped.

The competition was down to six couples when the Lindy Hop dance ended, and no one had even a moment to catch their breath before the next song started.

"They saved the best for last!" she shouted. "The Charleston!"

She was already kicking up her heels and crisscrossing her feet at the ankles. He joined in and soon the final six couples were in two lines, facing their partners and attempting to outdance one another to the fast tempo of the music by every means possible.

The crowd was cheering and shouting out numbers.

He was competitive by nature, but the excitement in her eyes increased his competitive streak tenfold. Suddenly, he wanted them to win this dance-off.

She followed his every move like she knew exactly what he'd do next, from arms swinging to knees knocking, up and down the floor, around and back. The crowd was roaring, shouting their number, when suddenly, the woman on Libby's left lost her balance and stumbled into Libby.

Lane leaped forward, catching her before she fell, but the man beside him had the same idea with his partner, and the four of them ended up on the floor, arms and legs tangled amid each other.

His heart locked in his chest at the feel of Libby's supple body lying atop his, granting him full-body awareness like he may never have known.

The crowd erupted, and bystanders were instantly there, separating them. He shoved aside the hands attempting to help him, leaped to his feet and pushed the men away who had hoisted Libby off him.

"Are you all right?" he asked, guiding her away from the others.

"Yes, I'm fine." Her blue eyes were still shining as bright as when they'd been dancing. So was her smile. "Are you?"

"I'm fine." He guided her into a vacated chair. Amazed at her stamina and cheerfulness. Kneeling down in front of her. "Are you sure?"

"I'm sure." Her eyes narrowed slightly as she eyed him closely. "Are you sure?"

"Yes." He was fine, but disappointed. More for her than for him. He wanted them to win for her. "I'm afraid we lost," he said somberly.

"Oh, Oliver." She giggled and patted his cheek with one hand. "It wasn't about winning, it was about dancing, and neither of us lost at that!"

Something warm and unusual flooded his chest. She had to be the most remarkable woman alive. He didn't even mind the way she called him Oliver again. "I suspect you're right." Another unusual sensation filled him and he shot upright. He hadn't wanted to kiss someone in years. A lump formed in his throat. He didn't want that now. Couldn't. It was just the atmosphere. The dancing. The fun. He hadn't done anything like this for a long time. Stepping back, he said, "I'll get us something to drink."

She grabbed his arm. "You can't go now. The dance is almost over. We have to see who wins." She stood and wrapped both hands around his forearm. "I do hope it's number three."

He had no idea which couple was number three, and couldn't look. His eyes wouldn't leave her face. The enthusiasm still glowing on her face held him captive.

The music ended while he was still staring at her, and he was still hypnotized when she flung her arms around his neck.

"They won! Number three won!"

The sweet floral scent of her perfume, the same that he'd been smelling the entire time they'd danced, filled his nostrils as she hugged him. Everything about her seemed to be a weapon. A dangerous one.

"They won!" she squealed again and released him to clap her hands. "Cherries! Cherries!"

"You sure are happy for them." People had rushed onto the dance floor to congratulate the winners, but she hadn't. Just stood there beside him clapping.

"Of course I am," she said. "They won. I'm sure they would have been just as happy for us had we won."

She did have a downfall. Innocence. That wouldn't last long. Never did. Someday she would discover just how selfish the world was. Everyone wanted to know what was in it for them. A hint of guilt struck him because that described him, too. What's in it for him was the very reason he'd danced with her. "How about that drink now?" he asked.

With a nod, she hooked her arm through his. "I am parched after all that dancing. It sure was fun, though, wasn't it?"

He couldn't admit that, not even to himself. Fun wasn't in his life, hadn't been for a long time. Work was all he'd known. All he'd lived for, and it was time to get back to it. "Let's sit over here." He gestured toward a table somewhat separated from the others.

A cigarette girl arrived as soon as they sat down. They each selected a drink off her tray. He paid her and downed his drink in nearly one gulp. The cheap whiskey burned all the way down, which was exactly what he needed. It cleared his sinuses and gave his body something else to react to. He needed the respectable distance the table put between them, too.

Setting his glass down, he asked Libby, "How do you know that Gaynor hid the money he'd stolen off the train?"

She'd selected a sugary cocktail that didn't contain any alcohol. He'd made a note of that when she'd made her selection. She took another sip from her glass before setting it down.

"Someone told me," she said.

"Who?"

The smile she flashed him was as coy as the one the cigarette girl had given him while noticing the tip he'd included in his payment.

Shaking her head, she leaned across the table. "A good reporter never reveals her sources."

"Reporter?" He knew every reporter in the city, and many of the want-to-be ones who sent in articles on a daily basis, hoping to get them printed and their name in the byline. He swore there was as many want-to-be reporters as there were want-to-be actors in Hollywood right now. Some of the articles he received showed promise, but not many. Even those showing promise would need work, and that took time that he didn't have. Writing a good article took more than just facts and perfect spelling. There was an art to making facts compelling enough that people read it all the way to the end. "You aren't a reporter."

"How do you know?"

A shiver of recognition struck him. She was still smiling, but he'd seen the look in her eyes before. From nearly every person who had personally handed him an article they wanted printed in his paper. It was a form of being starstruck. He completed a quick search in his mind, trying to recall if she'd ever been in at the newspaper office, trying to sell an article she'd written. He'd had a slew of articles written for women about sewing curtains and cleaning ovens, things that just wouldn't sell newspapers.

He couldn't find a hint of memory, and she was too unique to forget. Running a finger around the rim of his empty glass, he said, "I know every reporter in this city."

She lifted her glass to her lips, and tipping her chin down, looked at him from under her lashes. "Not every single one." She took a drink and set the glass down. "I know that for a fact."

No, she didn't, but that wasn't a point he was going to argue right now. "What facts do you know about Gaynor?"

Her gaze left him. He glanced behind him, to where her eyes had briefly gone. The crowd had dispersed off the dance floor and the piano player was taking a break. He scanned farther around the room, wondering what had stolen her attention. There was nothing out of the ordinary. No one looking at them.

He turned back to her.

She'd lifted her glass again, and emptied it. As she set it down, she stood. "Thanks for the dancing, and the drink, but I have to mooch."

He stood. "Leave? Why? It's not that late."

Walking away from the table, she flashed him a grin over one shoulder. "Don't take any wooden nickels, Oliver."

He rounded the table. "Wait!"

Weaving through the people and tables, she grinned again, right before she slipped around the corner that led to the front door.

His shout had drawn attention, but he truly didn't care. Making his way across the room, he shot out the door, ran up the stairs and out onto the street, which was empty.

Completely.

In all directions.

Chapter Three

Patsy held her breath, watching Lane spin about, scanning the street in all directions. Her heart was thudding almost as fast as it had been while dancing. She felt as if she was playing a game of hide-and-seek. It was as exciting as dancing with him had been. Almost. She'd never enjoyed dancing with someone as much as she had with him tonight. Ever.

"Who is that?" Jane whispered in her ear from behind.

Patsy bit her lip to keep from speaking. Voices carried in the dark. There were other noises, cars driving on the streets and horns honking, but she couldn't take the chance he might hear because she was only a short distance up the street from the laundromat. It was where they always met up. Betty had been the first to leave, then Jane, who had given Patsy the signal right before she'd slipped around the corner leading to the outside door.

Patsy was never excited about leaving, and tonight was no different. However, if they hadn't had to catch the streetcar that would be coming along any moment, she might have considered staying just a bit longer inside, talking with Lane.

He started walking.

Toward them.

Betty grabbed her arm, and Jane's, to lead them down the narrow space between the buildings.

Patsy shot a final look around the corner of the building, at Lane, who was looking into the breezeway of the building, as if he expected her to be hiding, before she spun around and hurried along with her sisters.

"This leads into the alley," Betty whispered. "We'll catch the streetcar at the corner on the next block."

It was very dark between the buildings, but once they were in the alley, the moon lit their way and they ran toward the street. This, escaping, was more fun than it should be, too, and Patsy couldn't help but feel alive with the thrill of it all.

"That was the man you were dancing with," Jane whispered. "He was looking for you."

Patsy attempted to quell the smile that grew on her lips.

"Why?" Jane asked.

"Because we weren't done talking, but you signaled it was time to leave," Patsy explained.

"Talking about what?" Jane asked.

"The escaped convict," Patsy answered. She hadn't found out nearly as much as she was hoping to about Rex Gaynor, but that didn't deter her enthusiasm. In fact, it made it grow. Sleuthing, gaining bits and pieces of information here and there, was even more fun than she'd imagined. She was going to love being a reporter. A real reporter. The fact she'd danced with Lane Cox, the best reporter ever, was thrilling in itself.

The bells of the streetcar jingled in the night air.

"Hurry," Betty said.

"We'll have to jump on at the end of the alley," Patsy said. The constant clang and bang of the car on its rail

indicated it had rolled past the corner since no one had
been standing there waiting, and would roll right past
them, too. They'd jumped on while it had been rolling
past before. The trolley didn't move fast, so it was a rela-
tively easy feat. People did it all the time. Getting to the
end of the alley was their first issue. "Run!"

"We are already running," Jane said. "And these shoes
aren't made for running. I'm going to have blisters."

"It won't be the first time," Patsy said. They'd all had
blisters from their nighttime excursions, and had never
complained about something so minor. "Dancing in them
is no different than running!"

They shot out from the alley just as the streetcar rolled
near, and still running, Patsy grabbed a hold of the rail
near the front step. Jane grabbed a hold right next to
her, and Betty caught the rail by the steps on the back
of the car.

Patsy hurried between the rows of seats to peer out the
back of the car. Her heart skipped a beat at the sight of
Lane standing on the corner of the street that led to the
Rooster's Nest. He may not have seen her leap aboard,
but she had a keen sense that he had.

She plopped down on the seat and drew in a deep
breath, hoping that would slow her racing heart. What a
night! What an amazing night!

As usual, she and her sisters didn't speak to each other,
or anyone else, until they were off the trolley and walking through the abandoned house's yard. Her heart rate
had returned to normal, somewhat, but the thrill of the
night was still living inside her.

"Where are you going to hide that?" Jane asked Betty
as they walked through grass of the abandoned property
so tall it tickled their ankles.

"I'm not going to hide it," Betty said, looking at the glass beer mug she'd won.

"I was so excited when you won!" Patsy said. "I swear, tonight was the most fun we've ever had! It was beyond bee's knees!"

"It was," Jane said before turning to Betty. "If Mother or Father sees that mug—"

"I'll say I bought it to hold my hairpins." Betty wrapped both hands around the mug and held it to her chest.

Patsy frowned. The mug was too large for a hairpin holder, but that wasn't the confusing part. Betty was their alarm clock—their chaperone—the first one to say they could never keep anything from their nights on the town. If she or Jane had won, the mug would have been left at the Rooster's Nest, or already tossed into a bush along the way home. They all sewed pockets in their dresses, and never carried anything that couldn't fit in a pocket, due to climbing up and down the trellis. "That could still get you in trouble," she said.

"Serious trouble," Jane agreed.

Betty shrugged. "It's mine, and I'm keeping it."

Patsy caught Jane's eye, which held as much disbelief as she felt. That certainly didn't sound like the Betty they knew. "Who was the man you danced with?" Patsy asked.

Betty let out a long sigh. "Just a man."

Just like the look in Jane's eye, Patsy felt the longing in Betty's sigh. That's how she felt about dancing with Lane. She wasn't sure why. She'd danced with plenty of men the past few months, but dancing with any of them hadn't been nearly as thrilling as dancing with Lane. She wasn't sure why he'd told her his name was Lathan, either, but figured it had to be because he didn't want her to know who he was, which was silly because everyone knew who he was.

Well, maybe not. She had known that Lane Cox owned the *Gazette*, but she had never seen him before. She had tried to call him Lathan, but it just didn't fit, and knowing she couldn't call him Lane, she'd stuck to Oliver. That fit him better because he really was a good dancer. She'd felt as if she was floating during some of their dances, when he was sashaying her around, and twirling her about beneath his arm. Right now, just thinking about it, made her feet become lighter.

"Who was that guy that you danced with?" Jane asked.

Patsy grinned. "Lane Cox."

Jane's mouth fell open. "The owner of the *Gazette*?"

Betty made a hissing sound. "Patsy! What if he recognizes us?" Betty clutched the mug to her chest tighter. "We can't get caught. Not now!"

Patsy shook her head. "We won't get caught and Lane won't recognize us." Still too happy and lighthearted to let her sister's worry bother her, she added, "No one knows us. Besides, I told him my name was Liberty. No last name. Just Liberty."

"But he's a reporter. The best reporter," Betty said. "It's said he leaves no stone unturned while researching a story."

"We aren't a story he's researching," Patsy said. "He's far more interested in finding out where Rex Gaynor hid the money he'd stolen off the train he'd robbed seven years ago."

"Who's Rex Gaynor?" Jane asked.

"The escaped convict." Patsy huffed out a breath, exasperated. "How many times do I have to repeat myself?"

They were now walking up the road that led to their backyard, and Jane flipped around to walk backward, looking at her sisters. "You aren't repeating yourself. You never told us the convict's name." Jane frowned. "Isn't Lane Cox one of the editors you sent articles to, and he rejected them?"

A nerve snapped in Patsy's spine. It had been more than one article that Lane Cox had refused to publish. She had several rejection notes from him. Notes, not letters. He just mailed the articles back to her with a note scrawled, in red ink, across the top of her typewritten article that said *Not suitable for the Gazette at this time.* Followed by his initials: *L.C.*

Those little notes had hurt at first, then they'd started to irritate her, and made her try harder. She'd sent him articles about everything from sewing curtains to ruts in the roads caused by a bad thunderstorm, only to get the same note every time.

Not suitable for the Gazette at this time.

Finally she'd figured out that the articles she'd written weren't suitable because the *Gazette* printed real news. Which was where her troubles lay, as she wasn't able to get out and investigate any real news. Not until she'd read about Rex Gaynor.

That was the story Lane would print of hers. It would be so good that it would be a headline story. It would be so good he'd probably give her a full-time job rather than just buy that one story.

And that would be the beginning of the rest of her life.

Both of her sisters were looking at her, Jane still walking backward and Betty walking beside her.

"That was him, wasn't it?" Jane asked.

"Yes," Patsy answered. "That was him, and that's why I danced with him, to get as much information about

Rex Gaynor as I could." The fact she'd enjoyed dancing with him didn't change anything. Unlike that first Charlie who'd made her skin crawl. More information about Gaynor had been the reason she'd asked Lane to dance. It was the reason they'd gone to the Rooster's Nest.

"Patsy." Betty had one hand on her chest. "Lane Cox knows Father."

Something in her stomach dropped. Just the other day Father was complaining about how expensive it was to put advertisements in the *Gazette*. Really complaining. Still, she couldn't let that stop her. This truly could be her only chance to write a story that had a chance to get printed. "That doesn't mean he knows us. No one knows us." Reading the look her sisters shared and not wanting to hear anything they might have to say, she changed the subject. "Why didn't you dance in the dance-off, Jane?"

Jane shrugged. "Because I didn't want to."

"Or because you couldn't find a partner?" Patsy teased, not wanting the subject to switch back to Lane. She truly was only teasing, because just like Betty was the oldest, and the smartest, Jane was the prettiest and the most personable. She didn't even have to pretend to be a flapper. She was naturally outgoing—when able.

Jane spun around as they left the road and entered their backyard. "There wasn't anyone I wanted to dance with. I enjoyed just listening to the music. That new piano player is the real McCoy."

Patsy hadn't paid that much attention to the music, and was sure that Lane was what had made dancing fun, but it was only fair to admit that the dancing wouldn't have happened if not for the piano player. "He sure did a fine job of playing the songs for the dance-off. It was the best one ever." She looked at Betty. "You have to agree. You won."

"I agree," Betty said, then she put a finger to her lips as they entered the tree line.

The fun for the night was over. Now they had to be extra quiet and careful while crossing their backyard and climbing up the trellis into the bathroom.

Half an hour later, they were all three in their bedrooms, and Patsy was pretty sure that just like her, Jane and Betty were probably still holding their breath. She did until she had her blue fringed dress, hat and shoes tucked in the trunk in her closet, had her nightgown on and was lying between the sheets she'd washed, dried and ironed earlier today.

The sigh she let out was a mixture of relief and enjoyment of the absolutely most wonderful night. All of their night-out excursions were fun, but tonight, the enjoyment was greater than any other night.

She closed her eyes, remembering how delightful it felt being led around the dance floor by Lane. The smile that formed was so big, she had to lick her lips at how hard it pulled on them. The only thing that would have made it better was if she'd learned more about Rex Gaynor. Other than he might be from Missouri. That wasn't much help at all.

She'd learned more from that other guy, the one with the black mustache, who'd given her the heebie-jeebies.

Lane had made those go away. That other guy hadn't been half the dancer that Lane had been.

A giggle bubbled in her throat.

Oliver.

She'd loved calling him that. This truly had been the best night of her life.

And tomorrow night was going to be just as wonderful. They were going back to the Rooster's Nest. She'd find a way to convince her sisters they had to go again tomorrow night.

She glanced at the clock ticking away beside her bed and stifled another giggle. It was after midnight so she didn't even have to wait until tomorrow. It had already arrived. Therefore, tonight, they would be going back.

Still smiling, she closed her eyes and pressed the covers to her lips to cover yet another giggle she could no longer hold in.

Half an hour later, she was still too full of excitement to sleep, so she clicked on the light beside her bed and pulled a pad of paper and pencil out of her nightstand, then, sitting cross-legged on the bed, she wrote an article about the latest craze hitting speakeasies. *Dance-offs!* That would be perfect as a headline, and while writing, she closed her eyes every so often in order to remember minute details that would engage readers.

Lane's eyes went from his watch to the door and back again so many times he had to lift his wrist to his ear. His watch was ticking. Was working. He ran the tip of one finger in a figure eight in the condensation his cold drink left on the table, wondering if he was wrong. Libby may not show up again tonight.

He was sure that had been her, along with two other flappers, who'd run out of the alley and jumped onto the street trolley. It had taken only a few minutes for him to run to his car, round the corner and follow the route of the red line, but it must have taken longer than he'd realized, because he hadn't seen them get off. He'd followed the streetcar past several street corners. She must have jumped off at one before he'd started following the line. All three of them must have.

They must have come to the Rooster's Nest together, and left together.

Even though he'd watched her walk out alone, and hadn't seen her talk to anyone.

Then again, until she'd dragged him onto the dance floor, he hadn't noticed her at all. He'd come to the Rooster's Nest last night to talk with Harley Maus about a possible story concerning some activity down at the dock. Missing dockworkers. A woman was hounding him to find out what had happened to her brother, saying he'd never come home from work one night. That, people coming to him, looking for assistance, happened as often as want-to-be reporters mailing in articles they wanted printed in his newspaper. Folks who didn't get the answers they wanted from the police came to him, expecting him to uncover the truth. Trouble was, just like those sending in articles, they often didn't like the answers he provided, either.

Lane was half placating the woman because young men not coming home wasn't that unusual, especially dockworkers. Many went to work on the docks merely for the chance to get a job on an ocean liner and leave on the next tide. However, men had been shanghaied from the docks for centuries, and that's why he'd asked Maus to meet him.

Maus had arrived, and they'd stepped outside to discuss things, but the lead had not really gone anywhere. Maus hadn't heard anything about a young man missing, or being shanghaied. He had mentioned that someone had started up a distillery in the roughest of sections. That wasn't unusual, either, and Lane figured he'd check that out later. He felt bad for the woman, but the Rex Gaynor story was where he needed to focus his time.

He had just walked back inside the Rooster's Nest,

planning on having a nightcap before going home to bed, when Libby had appeared last night. The events that had occurred after that had kept him awake half the night.

She'd been right there, in his thoughts, keeping him awake, and she'd been in his dreams when he'd finally dozed off. She'd been in his thoughts all day, too. Wondering how she knew about the stolen money. That information had never been released to the general public. Not years ago, or recently.

Which was why he was here, waiting to see if she walked through the door again tonight, and find out exactly what she knew, and how she'd acquired that information. His sleepless night had left him with many other questions, too. Who was she? What was her real name? Where did she live? Would she be here again tonight or not?

He glanced at his watch again. It was getting late. Almost nine.

The wave of disappointment that washed over him was surprising. She was nothing more than a source. Just like any other. However, this story meant more to him than others. Not the story in itself, but the outcome. He wanted Gaynor back behind bars, paying for his crimes. His family hadn't been the only ones killed on that train, and they deserved to have Rex Gaynor pay for his deeds as much as him.

Could that be it? Could a member of her family have been on that train?

Lane picked up his glass and emptied the contents in one swallow. The table he was sitting at wobbled slightly, and he shifted his gaze from the door to the chair opposite him.

Raymond Klein had pulled out the chair. "Didn't expect to see you here, Lane," Raymond said while sitting down.

Lane set his glass on the table. "Just having a nightcap before heading home." The Rooster's Nest wasn't the sort of place he and Raymond ran into each other. Klein was known as one of the best screenwriters in Hollywood. All the big names, studios and actors, wanted him writing their scripts—work for only them—yet, his success had allowed him to remain independent—he wrote for those he wanted to, and when he wanted to. Lane respected Raymond for that. Having covered Hollywood news for years, Lane knew the good and the bad, and walked a fine line in what he reported. He let the gossip magazines print the chin music and rumors that the mongers wanted to read about like love lives and pocketbooks. He focused on the real news, and let the studios pay him well to print ads in the *Gazette* about their latest and greatest movies. His hard-earned readership gave the studios a good return on their money.

Raymond slapped the table. "This saves me a trip, or a phone call, which is how I would have invited you."

"Invited me to what?" Lane asked.

"I'm throwing a party tomorrow night." Klein took the flat hat off his head of unruly blond hair. "A real shindig."

"What's the occasion?" Lane asked, even though most people didn't need a reason to host a party or to invite him. There was a party, several of them, every night in the city, and he had an open-door invitation to almost every one of them. People, famous or not, wanted their names in the *Gazette*.

Raymond grinned, nodded and glanced around as if contemplating his answer. The full-fledged smile that appeared when he ended his scan of the room had Lane wondering if this time there truly was a reason for a party. One that had Raymond happier than Lane had ever seen him.

Raymond, his face aglow, leaned across the table. "I asked Ruby Lancaster to marry me yesterday." He slapped the table again. "And she said yes."

Ruby Lancaster was an actress who had been billed as "America's Sweetheart" by all of the Hollywood magazines. She was a black-haired beauty, and as friendly as she was lovely, leastwise, she had been on the few occasions Lane had met her. "Well, then, congratulations are in order." He picked up his empty glass. "I'd toast you, but..."

Raymond laughed. "You can do that tomorrow night. We're heading to New York the next day. That's where we'll get married."

"Are you moving there?" That would surprise Lane, considering both Ruby and Raymond had built their reputations here, not out east.

"No. Just the wedding will take place there. It's where Ruby is from. Her family still lives there. Then we'll be back. She just finished shooting a movie, so we have to act now, before production starts on the next one." Raymond gestured toward the bar with his head. "Needed to stop in here to order the whiskey. The Rooster's Nest is the only place to get Minnesota Thirteen anymore. Those prohibition boys are hitting the makers and those transporting it, hard."

Lane had heard that about that, how federal agents were burning barns, sheds, homes and even churches, across central Minnesota, and infiltrating communities with informers, which was making an impact on the bootlegging capital. However, like here in Los Angeles, overall, police forces and sheriff departments didn't side with the federal agents. With the support and, at times, help from local authorities, the makers of the highly popular Minnesota Thirteen found ways to keep on brewing, and had started sending their shipments up through Canada by rail and down the coast by ship.

The Rooster's Nest had a close connection with the docks, and was known as the best distributor of Minnesota Thirteen. None of this information would ever be printed in the *Gazette*. It may be newsworthy, but he didn't need prohibition agents hounding him. Furthermore, like the majority of the population, the readership of the *Gazette* was heavily against prohibition, but there were some who were for it, and they were also influential. Therefore he was careful to tread lightly on all aspects of the subject. Politics, leaning one way or the other, could kill a newspaper like a bullet to the head.

"No one will ever say they drank coffin varnish at one of my parties," Raymond said. "Especially this party."

Coffin varnish was a very appropriate name. Bootlegged liquor was made out of anything folks could get their hands on, and more oftentimes than that, it proved poisonous, especially when bootleggers took to using car radiators to distill it in.

Minnesota Thirteen was known as a premium, twice-distilled and properly aged corn whiskey that many claimed was better than what they used to get prior to prohibition. It was not only served at all the elite parties in Hollywood, its distribution was well guarded by the mob. "A party of this magnitude calls for only the best," Lane said.

"Yes, it does," Raymond agreed. Once again, he leaned closer and lowered his voice. "Gotta be honest with you, Lane, I've never been so happy. I was scared out of my wits to ask Ruby to marry me. More afraid than I've ever been before."

Lane's mind shot off track for a moment, back in time, to when he'd asked Naomi to marry him. He couldn't remember being afraid, but he could remember being happy. Very happy. That had been so long ago. They'd met while he'd been researching a story down there, and he traveled down to San Diego several times after finishing that story, to see her. She'd been the one to say they should consider getting married, before he went broke traveling down to see her. The next trip down, he'd asked her, she'd said yes, and they were married and she'd moved to LA with him within weeks.

Raymond laughed. "That's why the party is tomorrow night and we are leaving the day after. I don't want her to change her mind."

Drawn back to the present, Lane nodded. He had a finger on most things happening, but hadn't been aware of a budding romance between Ruby and Raymond. "Have you been dating long?"

Raymond shook his head. "That's just it. I didn't know her, not until a few weeks ago, when I had to make some script changes for the big brothers."

The Wagner Brothers, who owned one of the largest and well-established studios, were two of the biggest cheeses in Hollywood. They played the parts well, and played others just as well. There had been a lot of flak floating around about how their business dealings had been pushing the little studios out of the business by forcing movie theaters to show only their films. It had been happening for some time, but the smaller studios were gaining ground on the brothers. Some claimed it was due to mob involvement, which was completely believable. The mob was involved in nearly every business, and show business was too big of an asset right now for them not to be in it. Furthermore, he had on good authority the mob was who had built the latest and grandest theater downtown, and that theater had shown one of Jack Mc-Carney's movies at their premiere opening night. Jack's Star's Studio was one of the smaller guys, and certainly gaining ground since that premiere.

"We'd spent a couple of evenings going over the script and the changes she had suggested, and I was not only impressed by her insight, I was, well, smitten by her. Things went from there, and now we are getting married." Raymond laughed again, slapped the table and stood all at the same time. "I have a lot to do before tomorrow." He plopped his hat on his head. "My place. Tomorrow night. I'd appreciate if you're able to make it."

Raymond lived in a newly built apartment complex in the middle of LA. He'd been one of the first to buy into the idea of buying an entire floor of the building and turning it into a luxurious apartment. What had sounded like a shady deal, a fad, had become a reality. Celebrity and starlets were buying up shares in buildings and creating lavish living spaces all over downtown.

Their apartments now paralleled many of the homes being built up in Hollywoodland. That was also causing William Dryer, the developer of Hollywoodland, a good case of indigestion. He'd thought he'd had the market on luxurious living cornered, and had been raking in some good money. Dryer was a contentious man, set in his ways, and as ornery as a cornered bull, who, like many others, thought Lane should be giving him free advertising on a regular basis. Dryer was just bolder than most, had been in the newspaper office last week, demanding either an article or free advertising. He'd left without getting either. A hint of disgust rose inside Lane recalling how the man had even suggested that Lane should consider marrying one of his daughters.

He wasn't interested in ever getting married again. Especially to one of William Dryer's daughters. He didn't know the daughters, but he knew Dryer, and that was enough to turn him off.

"I'll be there," Lane said, standing up to shake Raymond's hand.

Raymond pumped his hand. "Thanks, Lane, I do appreciate it." He walked around the table, but then stopped long enough to say, "Bring a date, why don't you."

Lane didn't answer. It wasn't really a question, more of a friendly gesture. Although few knew he'd been married at one time, because it had been long ago, before he'd built up his reputation of fair and honest reporting, most knew he didn't date. On purpose. He was married to the *Gazette* now. There was no need for dates, or anything that dating led to.

He turned to watch Raymond leave, and his heart damn near stopped at the sight of who stood near the corner leading to the door.

She was wearing an orange dress with a scooped neckline and what looked like flecks of gold in the material by the way the light caught it, and a matching hat complete with gold feather, but it was the impish smile on her face that kicked his heart back into beating. How had he forgotten about those two little dimples that appeared in her cheeks when she smiled? They were adorable, and made him grin in return.

Nibbling on her bottom lip, while still smiling, she walked toward him.

He kept his eyes on her, and raised a brow as each step brought her closer. She didn't seem quite as confident as she had last night.

Until she stepped closer. Then she twisted her head

slightly, shooting him a playful wink as she rounded the table next to his.

His mouth was strangely dry by the time she stopped next to him. He spoke to people from all walks of life, but suddenly couldn't think of a thing to say.

"Hello, Oliver."

Her voice sounded like music.

"I was hoping you'd be here tonight."

He drew in a breath, and nodded at her honesty. "Hello, Libby, I was hoping you'd be here tonight, too."

"Is that why you are here?" She tilted her head back to look him in the eye. "To see me?"

Honesty was one thing, but there were times when it needed to go only so far. "Could be. Is that why you are here?"

She giggled slightly. "Oh, Oliver, I don't know why you do that."

"Do what?"

"Answer my question with a question."

"Did I do that?"

She giggled again. "Yes, and you know it."

She was right. He nodded at his table. "Care for a drink?"

Her nod may have been subtle, but there was nothing subtle about the shine in her eyes. "Would you?"

He laughed. "Sit down, Libby. We'll each have a drink."

She sat, planted both elbows on the table and propped her chin on her clasped hands. "Why isn't there any music tonight?"

Lane glanced at the empty piano bench. He couldn't say if anyone had been playing earlier or not. "I don't know."

"I thought they always had music here." Eyeing him, she asked, "Is the piano player taking a break?"

He waved over a cigarette girl. "I don't know that, either." Taking a cocktail without alcohol off the tray, he set it in front of Libby and then chose a glass of watered-down beer for himself. A dozen questions raced around in his head faster than his new printing press rolled out perfect copies of the *Gazette*.

"Thank you, Oliver." She picked up her glass and took a tiny sip.

He should insist that she called him by his name, but she seemed to enjoy calling him Oliver so much that he didn't want to stop her. She was enchanting. So enchanting that his next thought was to stand up and walk out of the Rooster's Nest. Forget he ever met her.

Chapter Four

Patsy wished she knew what Lane was thinking. He was staring at the door and there was a look about him. One of longing. Like he wanted to leave. The sip she'd taken of her drink welled in the back of her throat. Wouldn't go down. She'd been so happy to see him sitting at the table, and had decided to wait until he was done talking to another man before approaching him. Not because she hadn't wanted to interrupt him, but because she liked being able to stand there, looking at him. It was like looking at a sunrise. She couldn't figure out why it held her attention, other than because it was pure splendor. That's what looking at Lane had been.

Now she couldn't even swallow. It had been that way when she'd first seen him, too, and it had taken her a few moments before she'd been able to think, to remember she was Libby and not Patsy. Patsy would be nervous to see him again, but Libby wouldn't.

His gaze slowly shifted to her and though she still wasn't sure what he was thinking, the glimmer in his eyes as he lifted his drink allowed her throat to work again.

She swallowed and then set her drink down, afraid to test fate by taking another sip. "So," she said as she let her hand linger around her glass. "How was your day?" Her mind didn't seem to want to fully function and that was all she could think to say. It had been so easy to talk to him last night, yet, suddenly, she felt as if she was tongue-tied.

"My day was fine." He set his drink down. "How was yours?"

"Fine. It was baking day, but we got most of it done before the heat of the day became too great."

"Baking day?"

Her throat locked up again. Had she really said that it had been baking day? She'd never done that before. Normally she held her tongue, never told anyone anything about her real life. Why was she having a hard time being Libby tonight and not Patsy?

"What did you bake?" he asked.

What was she going to say? What could she say to cover up her blunder? She reached across the table and grabbed his glass, knowing the bitterness of the beer would open her throat. She took a big gulp and forced it down before handing him back his glass.

She wasn't sure if that gave her any sense or not, but now she really had to answer his question because her throat was certainly open. "Bread." She let out a cough to ease the bitterness in her throat. "We—I baked bread, and pies, and several dozen cookies. Because I have to eat. You have to eat, too, don't you, Oliver?"

"Yes, I have to eat."

She nodded. Everyone has to eat. There was nothing wrong with admitting that, or with admitting it was baking day. "What did you do today?"

"Worked."

She bit the tip of her tongue to prevent it from working until her mind was ready. "Oh, and where do you work?"

"Downtown."

"Where downtown?"

He took a swig of his beer, and then held it out to her. She shook her head.

He nodded and set it down. "You know where I work, Libby. You know who I am."

A shiver rippled up her spine. "Do I?"

"Yes, you do."

She tried her best to keep anything from showing on her face, but had no idea how to answer that. She did know, but didn't want him to know she knew.

"That's why you asked me to dance last night, so you could learn what I know about Rex Gaynor." He leaned back in his chair and crossed his arms. "What I want to know, is why? Why are so you interested in an escaped convict? Most young women would be afraid to know a criminal of his caliber is on the loose."

Patsy bit the inside of her cheek, contemplating exactly how she should answer. The one thing she had learned by living a dual life was that honesty, as much as possible, was the best route. One lie could easily lead to another, and soon it was hard to remember whom she'd told what to. That was the reason she never wanted to go back to the Green Door, a speakeasy a few blocks from here. She'd used two different aliases there, in the same night, and trying to keep things straight had proved to be more work than fun.

Not quite ready to admit to anything, she leaned back in her chair. "Well, now, Oliver, that is an interesting theory."

He lifted an eyebrow. "Theory?"

Keeping her chin up, she nodded.

He let out a low chuckle. "Let me assure you, it's not a theory."

Taking her chances at being as believable as possible, she leaned forward and released the smile tickling her lips. "I asked you to dance because you were the only man I wanted to dance with last night."

Slowly, as if deliberately making her watch his smallest movement, he uncrossed his arms, planted his hands on the table and then leaned nearly halfway across the table, until they were almost nose to nose.

Her heart was thudding excitedly. He smelled so good. The same spicy cologne as last night, and his eyes were shimmering. He did believe her. Thankfully, because that would make getting more information easier. A good reporter never shared their secrets, and Lane was the best.

"I don't believe that for a moment," he said.

She caught herself before her shoulders slumped, and locked her lips together to keep her mouth from falling open.

"Not, a single moment," he added.

The disappointment filling her was too great to keep completely hidden. She planted her elbows on the table, something her father would have frowned upon if she were at home, and rested her chin on one palm. It was the truth. He had been the only man she'd wanted to dance with last night, but she had a feeling that wasn't exactly what he didn't believe.

"Why are you so interested in Rex Gaynor?" he asked. "And please, tell me the truth."

She let out a sigh. This was certainly not how she'd imagined events playing out this evening. Another dance-off, with the opportunity to learn more about Rex Gaynor, was what she'd been thinking about all day. That and how handsome he was. Perhaps more than she remembered.

"Is that possible?" he asked.

Her heart leaped up to her throat. He couldn't possibly know her thoughts. "Is what possible?"

"You telling the truth? You are capable of that, aren't you?"

They were still practically nose to nose, but now her heart was pounding for a different reason. His rash tone that implied she couldn't tell the truth. "Yes, I'm capable of telling the truth."

"Then do so."

Not only was his statement a challenge, it was in his eyes. They were saying she wouldn't tell him the truth. The entire truth.

She stiffened and leaned back slightly, needing the space between them to keep her thoughts as straight as possible. "Fine. I asked you to dance in order to learn more about Rex Gaynor."

He nodded slightly and sat back. "Why?"

Huffing out a breath, she admitted, "You know why."

"I do?"

"Yes, that's what every good reporter does."

His expression turned stoic, and the chuckle in his tone bitter. "You are not a reporter."

He'd told her that last night, but this time, it bothered her more. "Yes, I am," she insisted.

"Tell me who you work for. One article you've written."

She clamped her lips tight as a wave of disappointment washed over her. This was not going how she'd imagined, not at all.

"You haven't written anything, have you?"

"Yes." She locked her back teeth together to keep from saying more. It was the truth. She had written several articles. Half a suitcase full. And one that was burning a hole in her pocket right now. She'd brought it along tonight, thinking about somehow slipping it in his pocket, so he could see how good she was. A foolish idea for sure.

"Published where?"

"They haven't been published because—" She stopped herself before saying he was the reason none of her articles had been printed. Him and his *Not suitable for the Gazette at this time* notes, written in red ink.

His expression was almost smug as he picked up his beer.

She slumped back in her chair as he drank. Fine, she wasn't a real reporter, but that doesn't mean she can't become one . A wave of determination filled her. She could still get all the information he had on Rex Gaynor. It would just have to happen in another manner. Not on the dance floor. And she could still write the article, her best one ever. And she'd send it to a different newspaper to print.

There was an odd dullness in his eyes as he set down his empty glass. "Where did you learn about the money?"

Patsy shook her head. She was here to gain, not give. "A source."

"What did the source say?"

"Why should I tell you? So you can publish it in your newspaper?" Although she'd already told him all she knew, she couldn't let him know that. A real reporter wouldn't. In fact, a real reporter would... What would a real reporter do? She balled her hands into fists. She didn't know any real reporters. Other than him.

"I might put it in my article, that is if I can prove it's true," he said. "That is the first rule of order of reporting, fact checking."

"I know that." At least she'd heard that.

"Then you verified your source," he said.

He wasn't asking, just assuming, and she chose not

to comment, even though she hadn't verified anything. But why would that Charlie say that last night if it wasn't true?

"That's good to know," he said.

Guilt at not having confirmed to verifying anything rolled across her stomach.

"You'd be amazed by how many articles people send into the *Gazette*, wanting to have them published, only to forget that one detail. The verification of facts. I can't print anything that hasn't been fully confirmed. Readers of the *Gazette* have come to expect that, and that's what they will get. The truth."

Confused, Patsy said, "But reporters don't reveal their sources." She wasn't exactly sure where she'd heard that, but she had, and she believed it.

"That's true, and that's also why they have an editor. My reporters, those who write regularly for the *Gazette*, turn in verification along with every article they write for me, everything from dates and times of when they met with sources, to pictures of being at the scene of the crime. As the owner of the paper, it's my call in the end, and I only print the truth. The verified truth."

She'd never thought of that, of having to verify all the information in an article, or of its importance. "Is that why you turn down so many articles?"

The briefest hint of a grin appeared before his face became somber again. "No, the majority of them aren't well written enough for the *Gazette*, but for those that are, the absence of verification is the main reason I won't, or can't, print them."

"Do you tell the people sending them in that?"

"No. If they are true reporters, they would already know that."

She let that settle. It made sense. The *Gazette* had a

reputation. Everyone relied on the articles being truthful. Not like some of the magazines that were full of stories about movie stars. Her parents never allowed them to read such magazines, but Jane snuck them into the house. They made Hollywood sound outlandish, including Hollywoodland, the very neighborhood they lived it. She and her sisters often laughed at how the magazines made it sound as if the streets were made of gold. They weren't. Most of them weren't even paved.

It appeared as if she had some things to learn about being a reporter. Perhaps more than she realized. However, it was still her way out of her father's house, her only way out. "If they don't know, and you don't tell them, how are they going to learn?"

He shrugged. "If I were to spend the time telling every person what they needed to know, I wouldn't have the time to publish a single copy of the *Gazette*."

That, too, made sense. If only she was allowed to visit the library again. Father had seen one of the books she'd checked out, claimed it indecent and refused to allow her to check out any more. The only reason she was able to read the newspapers was because it was her job to cut them in squares to use in washing the windows with vinegar and water.

"How did you find the source to confirm your information?" he asked.

Her mind shifted between the truth and, well, fibbing. It didn't take her but a moment to figure out which way she needed to go. "I haven't totally confirmed it." She shrugged. "Yet."

"You haven't?"

"No."

"Then how do you know there was any money?" he asked.

She didn't for sure, but was going to find out. Spinning around, she looked at the bar. Another shiver of excitement zipped up her spine. The three men who'd been there last night were there again.

Lane balled his hand into a fist to keep from reaching out and catching her arm as she pushed away from the table and stood. Last night, he'd been convinced she was somehow connected to Gaynor, until he'd seriously thought about it. Then he'd come to the conclusion that she was merely doing the same thing as him, looking for information.

Curious as to what she was up to, he didn't stop her as she turned away from the table. So far, he'd played his cards right, uncovered some of the truth and needed to continue doing just that.

She was a want-to-be, and from some of the expressions on her face while they'd talked, he'd guessed she'd sent an article to the *Gazette* at least once, if not more than once. That really shouldn't surprise him. Other want-to-bes had sought him out. They just usually weren't flappers with big blue eyes and matching dimples.

Or had a backside that made the hem of her dress sashay back and forth over the backs of her legs as she walked away from the table, straight to the bar.

He watched as she planted a foot on the foot rail and leaned against the varnished top of the bar. The grin she gave the three men sitting there was all it took to start up a conversation. They were more than willing to answer whatever she'd asked. His instincts were going up against something else inside him. He couldn't say exactly what, but that other part of him was ready to walk over to the bar and...

And what? Haul her out of here? To where? He still

didn't know her real name, or why she was researching the Rex Gaynor story.

He leaned back in his chair and noticed something on the floor. An envelope. He glanced around, and then scooped it up.

His name was on the front of it. He glanced around again, looking to see who might be watching him. For a moment, he wondered if Raymond had dropped it, until recalling the man had said he'd have called.

Lane opened the envelope, and grinned at the title neatly written across the top. Shifting his gaze between her and the paper, he scanned the article about the dance-off. He was impressed. She had an attention to detail, and the writing flowed well, all the way to the end. Even if he hadn't been a part of the dance-off, he'd have been able to see it in his mind by the way she'd recreated it.

He glanced up at her again, how she was interacting with the men at the bar. She may not be a seasoned reporter, but he now had to admit, she had the makings of one. What she was doing remarkably well, starting up a friendly conversation with virtual strangers, wasn't easy for everyone, yet she had a knack for it.

The men at the bar laughed at something she'd said, and another, odd sensation rippled in his chest. He couldn't call it jealousy. Didn't know her well enough to be jealous of her talking to other men. He wasn't the jealous type, not of anyone or anything.

However, he would like to know what she and those men were talking and laughing about. They were average dockworkers and he had a gut feeling that they'd tell her far more than they'd ever tell him.

Lane folded the paper, tucked it in the envelope and slid that into his pocket. As her lilting laughter hit his ears again, another sound filled the room. The notes the

piano player struck gave him an excuse to get her away
from those dockworkers. Not because of the information
they might give her, but because of what they might expect from her for the answers they gave her. There was
a give-and-take when it came to information gathering,
and he'd bet she knew nothing about that.

He stood, walked over to the bar and took a hold of her
elbow. "Excuse us, fellas, the lady promised me a dance."

She shot him a quizzical look.

He grinned and didn't give her a choice but to ac-
company him to the dance floor. The song playing was
a waltz, on the slow side, and he led her through a series of spins to carry them to the other side of the floor,
where it wasn't quite so crowded. She was as graceful
as last night. Her smile was as bright, too. A fact that re-
lieved him. He wasn't in the habit of forcing women to
dance with him.

Glancing behind them, toward the bar, she said, "I'll
have you know, I wasn't done speaking with those gen-
tlemen."

"Yes, you were." He considered telling her about the
envelope, but decided not to, just yet. "You won't get any
more out of them."

"You don't know that."

He spun her around beneath their clasped hands, and
then drew her so close the hem of her dress brushed
against his pants. He ignored how that sent a tingle down
his legs. Mixing business with pleasure was something he
never did, mainly because pleasure was not something he
engaged in, and wasn't this time, either. This was business. Pure business. "Yes, I do."

She stepped a mite closer and peered up at him from
beneath those long lashes. A warm flush filled his chest

cavity, forcing him to draw in a breath of fortitude. Business. This was business.

"What if I told you they know the source who told me about the money, and where I can find him?" Drawing closer still, she whispered, "To verify the fact of the stolen money."

Air locked in his lungs as her breath tickled his neck. The effect she had on him was distracting, and it was a moment before her words settled in his mind. "What man? What's his name?"

"I was about to find that out when you dragged me onto the dance floor."

"I didn't drag you," he corrected.

"You would have if I hadn't followed you."

That may be true. Needing space to think clearly, he stepped back and twirled her beneath his arm, but that, watching her swing around, looking at him with that charming little dimpled grin, consumed every thought he had.

Enchanting. That described her, and he'd bet she'd charmed those men at the bar as easily as she did him. She could charm a rabbit from its hole. Before he had a chance to contemplate the thought fully, he asked, "Are you busy tomorrow night?"

"Why?"

He pulled her close again. His entire body tingled at the nearness of hers. "Because I'd like you to attend a party with me."

"A party?"

The excitement on her face, in her voice, and the little skip she added to her dance step made him chuckle. "Yes. A party that a friend of mine is hosting downtown, in his apartment."

With a flurry of keystrokes, the piano player ended

the song, and as the final note sounded, she wrapped her arms around his neck. "I'd love to attend a party downtown!"

Both his hands had grasped onto her waist, holding her against him. The full-body contact caused an outbreak of desire inside him. Things he hadn't desired in years.

Years.

It took all his restraint to keep from acting on those desires, to keep from kissing her. He released his hold on her enough to walk her off the dance floor as the battle of wills going on inside him became closer to a full-fledged war. What had he been thinking? Asking her to Raymond's party was dangerous. That would set chins flapping with gossip. But, at the same time, he needed to keep an eye on her. The way she'd charmed those dock-workers was proof. Her snooping out information about Rex Gaynor could sets chins flapping just as fast. If the wrong people learned about the undiscovered money, it could hamper the authorities and their ability to catch Gaynor.

The article in his pocket was also concerning. It was rough, but it was good, and if she did that, wrote about Gaynor like she had the dance-off, another editor would snap it up.

Once at their table, he gestured to a serving girl, needing a drink more than ever.

Patsy was sure her heart would leap right out of her chest at any moment. A party! A real party! She knew exactly what she'd wear. Her black-and-white-striped dress, with her black beaded hat and pearls. Definitely a long set of white pearls and matching earrings and black shoes. No, her white shoes. The ones with the pearl buttons on the sides.

"Thirsty?"

She glanced up at Lane, and saw nothing but stars. The brightest stars in the universe. After a couple of blinks, they dulled enough to see the glass in his hand. She took it, drank half of the sweet cocktail and sighed. A party. A real party. With Lane Cox.

Bee's knees! She'd been wrong! Tonight was going better than what she'd imagined. Far better!

She set the glass on the table, barely recalling having sat down. Her mind was still on the dance floor, in his arms, being asked out on a date. A real date.

It was…

Oh, dear, what had she done? She couldn't go out on a date. She wasn't allowed to date. Her parents didn't permit dating. Even Betty, who had been told she'd marry James Bauer, soon, wasn't allowed to date him, not until they were officially engaged.

It didn't make sense, but many of Father's rules didn't make sense to any of them.

"What is your address?" Lane asked.

Having barely heard, she asked, "My what?"

"Your address, you know, where you live?"

"Why?"

He frowned slightly. "So I can pick you up tomorrow night."

No, no, no, no! He couldn't pick her up. Couldn't know where she lived.

Patsy swallowed the lump in her throat and searched her mind for a solution. "I'll meet you here," she said as the thought formed. "At the Rooster's Nest, at nine o'clock."

Frowning deeper, he said, "The party starts at seven."

Horsefeathers! She could never sneak out by seven. She couldn't even sneak out by eight. Father was never asleep until eight thirty. Disappointment flooded her. "I—I have commitments until nine."

"Commitments?"

She held her breath, trying to keep her frustrations hidden. "Yes, commitments." It would be impossible to get away any earlier than eight thirty. Impossible. But if she hurried... Biting her bottom lip, she looked at him. "I could be here by eight forty-five."

Lane cast her a thoughtful gaze, and for a moment she was afraid he'd say no, that would be too late.

"All right, eight forty-five it is."

Her heart leaped all over again. "You mean it?"

He grinned. "Yes, I mean it." Shrugging, he added, "The good parties don't get started until ten anyway."

She pressed a hand to her lips to stifle the squeal that rose in her throat. She would be here by eight forty-five, even if it meant she had to run all the way to the street-car stop. Bubbling with anticipation, she asked, "Whose party is it?"

"Raymond Klein."

The name didn't ring a bell, but still she nodded. "He's a friend of yours?"

Lane nodded, but looked at her oddly. "Have you heard of him?"

"No, not that I know of." It truly didn't matter; she was simply excited to experience a world she'd only dreamed of, but also knew she had to remain cautious.

"He's a screenwriter who has written several motion pictures and rewritten many others."

Another wave of excitement washed over her. "Will there be movie stars there?" she asked, thinking more about Jane than herself.

"Considering he's marrying Ruby Lancaster, yes, there will be movie stars there."

That name she did know. The actress had been in Jane's magazine last week. "Ruby Lancaster?" She was beyond beautiful. Her coal-black hair was sleek and shiny and cut in a bob that angled to points near her chin.

"Yes, Ruby Lancaster. Raymond will really be putting on the Ritz for this party."

She couldn't wait to tell Jane that! Growing a bit tentative, she asked, "You aren't razzing me, are you, Lane?"

He tilted his head and looked at her with a very serious expression for a long silent moment. "No, Libby, I'm not razzing you. Everything I've said is the absolute truth."

Then, there was just one more thing she had to know. "Why?"

"Why?"

She nodded. "Why did you ask me to go with you?"

He was quiet for so long, her insides started to shake. Then, when he reached into his pocket, her stomach hit the floor as she recognized the envelope. For no feasible reason, because it clearly was in his hand, she checked her pocket. Her empty pocket.

"This shows promise, Libby. Talent. But if you're serious about becoming a reporter, you'll have to get out and meet people, because that's what people want to read about. Real people."

Chapter Five

This had to have been the longest day of her life. Cleaning day had never been her favorite, especially when it was her turn to dust. Father insisted that even the light-bulbs were dusted, and this time of year, with all the windows open, they needed it. Dust from the dirt road filtered in and covered everything. Truth be, during the summer months, they could dust twice a week and still not keep up with the fine silt that clung to everything.

The good thing about the heat during the summer months was that Father went to bed as early as possible, and kept a fan blowing on him all night. Not that it made escaping any less dangerous.

Patsy glanced at the clock again. It wasn't even four yet. She had stolen some time while dusting upstairs to take her black-and-white dress out of the trunk in her closet and press it smooth. She had made the dress last month, and had worn it only once since then. As she and her sisters did as often as possible, she had sewn an apron out of the same material, so if her mother noticed the striped material on the line during wash day, that's what she'd think was hanging out to dry.

She still wanted to polish her white shoes and had to

ask Jane where the pearls were that she'd worn the other night. Now would be the perfect time. Her sisters were outside beating the dust out of the large rug from the living room. She also had to tell them where she was going tonight.

Her stomach grew queasy at the thought. She'd considered telling them last night, but the walk home had been silent. By the time Betty finally met up with her and Jane between the buildings, they'd missed the streetcar. That had made Jane angry and she'd become even angrier when Betty wouldn't tell them why she had been so late meeting them.

Patsy hadn't been overly happy herself. She could have stayed and danced and talked with Lane. He'd liked her article about the dance-off, had praised her for it, and she understood so much more about being a reporter. They'd danced several times last night, too, up until Jane had signaled that it was time to leave.

Lane hadn't followed her last night. There had been no reason. She'd see him tonight.

Patsy bit her lips together as she collected her dusting cloths. She'd been trying very hard to remember tonight was about becoming a reporter and not about going out with Lane, but it was hard. The more time she spent with him, the more she liked him, and liking any man wasn't in her plan. Especially one who might eventually give her a job. She hadn't thought about that aspect. Of working for a man. Bosses could be like fathers, and husbands, telling her what to do and when to do it.

Like dusting.

Sighing, she carried the rags into the kitchen to rinse out.

"Finished dusting?" Mother asked from where she sat at the table, peeling potatoes for supper, along with the roast that was already seasoned and ready to go in the oven. Although she and her sisters helped with the meal preparations, for the most part, Mother preferred to do all the cooking. She loved preparing meals, and was an excellent cook. At least it appeared that way.

"Yes," Patsy answered, carrying her cloths to the sink. "Do you need any help?"

"No, thank you, dear." Mother truly was a lovely woman. Her blond hair was still as yellow as sunflowers and her skin smooth and peach-colored. "I've already peeled the carrots."

"Candied carrots?" Patsy asked, hopeful. Mother's candied carrots were one of her favorites.

Mother grinned. "Of course. You and your father love them."

"They are so delicious." Patsy turned on the faucet to rinse out the rags. "I'll hang these dust cloths on the line, but first will see if Jane and Betty need any help with the rug."

"All the traffic on the road has really filled the house with dust this summer. I do wish your father would talk to the city council about having the road paved."

"I thought he had," Patsy answered, wringing out the dust cloths.

"That was last year, dear. There are several more homes up here now."

Patsy nodded. That was true, but after how angry her father had been at the city council last year, they might not allow him to attend another meeting this year. Whether there were more homes in the hills or not.

"Please ask your sisters to help you set the dining room table after your other chores are completed," Mother said.

"I will." That was another one of their chores, things they did every night, and that had her wondering,

"Mother, do you ever feel…" She searched for an appropriate word. "…cooped up?"

"Cooped up?" Mother smiled. "How could I in a house this large? This beautiful?"

How indeed?

"You'll understand someday how wonderful it is to dedicate your time to taking care of your family," Mother said. "Your father works very hard to provide for us, and we need to work just as hard in showing him how much we appreciate that."

Patsy nodded, although a part of her wondered if there was something wrong with her because she wanted more than to simply take care of her family. She wanted a life. The freedom to do what she wanted, when she wanted to. Her sisters wanted that, too, so how could all three of them be wrong?

From the time they'd been born, they'd had chores to keep them busy before school and after school, and all day long since their schooling had ended. They'd never been allowed to do fun things like other children had, except for the few times when she'd been young. She remembered going places and doing things then, but that had happened only when her grandmother had come to visit. Her mother's mom, from Seattle, and mother's sister, Aunt Joan.

She carried her damp cloths through the back door, across the back porch and then out into the yard, all the while thinking about Aunt Joan, and why no one had mentioned her for years.

Betty and Jane were beating the big red-and-gold oriental rug, one on each end. Patsy shook out her cloths and hung them over a line not being used for the rug. "Do either of you know why no one ever mentions Aunt Joan?" she asked.

Her sisters looked at each other, then at her.

"Because she had a baby out of wedlock," Jane said.

Patsy was stunned. "When?"

"Shortly before Grandma died," Jane said. "That's why we are kept under lock and key, so we don't follow her footsteps."

Patsy shook her head. "Father has always had strict rules."

"They became stricter after that," Jane said. "And Joan was forced to give up her baby and was sent to the convent."

"The convent?" Patsy's insides quivered. "Why don't I remember any of this?"

"Because we were in school and never told any of it, and aren't supposed to know now, either, but that's what happened," Jane said.

Patsy looked at Betty, who nodded and gave the rug a solid whack with the wire beater.

Patsy felt sick to her stomach about what happened to her aunt, and about never knowing a thing about it.

"We are going to the Rooster's Nest again tonight," Betty said, almost as if the earlier conversation hadn't even happened.

Jane gave her end of the rug a solid whack while it was still waving from Betty's hard hit. "Yes, we are."

Patsy looked at both of them before replying, "We need to leave early. Before eight thirty if possible."

Betty shook her head and whacked the rug again. "That's not possible. We can't chance being caught."

"No, we can't," Jane said, swinging her metal rug beater at the rug.

Patsy held a hand up to stop the rug from waving. The dust had long ago been beaten out of it. "I know we can't chance being caught," she said. "But I have a date."

The beater in Betty's hand stopped midswing. "What do you mean? A date?"

"A date." Patsy's heart skipped a beat at using the word *date*. "Lane Cox is taking me to a real Hollywood party. Downtown."

"What?" Jane asked, her beater hanging at her side.

"That's impossible!" Betty hissed. "We aren't allowed to date."

"I know." Lane hadn't specifically called it a date, so she may have jumped to a conclusion on that. "It might not really be a date. Lane read one of my articles and liked it, and said that if I want to be a reporter, I need to get out and meet people, and invited me to a party."

"You can't get out and meet people," Betty said. "You can't go downtown! We can't—"

"I know we can't risk getting caught," Patsy interjected. "That's why I told Lane I'd meet him at the Rooster's Nest, and I'll make sure I'm back *before* the last streetcar so we won't have to walk all the way home."

"It's too risky," Betty said. "Way too risky. It could ruin everything."

"It won't," Patsy insisted. "I promise. I'll wear a hat and—"

"No!" Betty shook her head. "No. Absolutely not."

"Why not?" Jane looked at Betty. "You weren't at the Rooster's Nest all of last night, and don't pretend that you were. I looked for you before I left. You were nowhere in sight. I thought you'd be waiting for us between the buildings, but you weren't."

Betty closed her eyes and pinched her lips together. "I was in the powder room."

"No, you weren't," Jane said.

They never argued, none of them, and worried it could prevent her from going tonight, Patsy stepped between them. Safeguarding their double lives was something they had agreed on since the beginning. "Let's not argue. Not among each other. Please."

Her sisters looked at her and then each other.

Afraid whatever was bothering them would ruin all that they had, she pleaded, "Please? Do either of you really want to go back to staying home every night? I don't."

"I don't," Jane said, looking at Betty.

"She's right," Betty said. "We can't let last night ruin anything. I'm sorry I was late. It won't happen again." Betty shook her head then. "But, Patsy, a date? Downtown? That's going against all of our rules."

"I know, but I'll be extra careful." Patsy used one finger to draw an imaginary X over her chest. "Cross my heart."

"Lane didn't question you meeting him at the Rooster's Nest?" Jane asked.

Patsy cringed slightly. "Yes, he wanted my address to pick me up. I didn't give it to him. Instead said I'd meet him at the Rooster's Nest, at eight forty-five. The party starts at seven, but I told him I had other commitments and he said that was fine because the party won't get into full swing until ten." She looked at Betty. "I have to go. This is my big chance. Lane is the best reporter in the city."

Betty closed her eyes for a moment, then asked, "Where at downtown?"

"An apartment," Patsy answered. "A friend of Lane's named Raymond Klein."

"Raymond Klein!" Jane slapped a hand over her mouth at her squeal. "Elephant eyebrows! The Raymond Klein? The screenwriter?"

Patsy nodded. Jane was as excited as she'd expected her to be.

"He and Ruby Lancaster are crushing." Jane's face was glowing. "I…uh…acquired another magazine the other day. He's in it. So is Ruby. Wouldn't it be something if you saw her there?"

"I will," Patsy said. "She and Raymond are getting married. This is their engagement party." She then added what Lane had told her about Raymond and Ruby going to New York to get married because that's where her family lived.

"How darb!" Jane looked at Betty. "We have to let her go to this party. It's sure to be the bee's knees, and it's not like she's going to be recognized. Not with the party full of famous people."

Betty sighed. "I agree. I'm just nervous. What if Lane questions you about where you live?"

Patsy clasped her hands over her chest. "I won't tell him. I won't. I promise."

Betty shook her head. Then nodded. Then shook her head again. "You need to have an answer for where you live, why you had to meet him at the Rooster's Nest. Something believable."

Patsy floundered a nod. Some sort of preplanned answer would be helpful, but she had no idea what it could be.

Jane snapped her fingers. "I know. You can tell him that the three of us live together, in an apartment that doesn't allow men. You know, like those ones near the secretarial school, and that the only way we can go out at night is to sneak out."

That was so true. There were apartments near the school, with caretakers who didn't let the girls go out, nor did they allow men to enter the buildings. Girls who attended the school from out of town lived in them. Patsy often wondered about the girls she'd befriended while at school and the secretarial classes, because once she'd graduated, she'd never had a chance to see any of them again.

"That could work," Betty said thoughtfully. "And explain why we'll be waiting for you at the trolley stop."

"Not could, it will work," Jane said. "We've all met some of the girls who live at those apartments at other speakeasies."

Patsy was as thrilled with the idea as she was with her sisters. This was how it had always been, the three of them working together. "The best part is, it's true," she said. "All of it." Glancing at her sisters, she admitted, "At times, it can be hard to remember things that aren't true."

"Isn't that the truth," Betty said with a sigh.

"So, we are in agreement?" Jane asked.

Patsy held out a hand, because that's what they always did, too. They made a pact on it by stacking their hands atop one another. "Agreed."

Jane slapped her hand on top of Patsy's. "Agreed."

Betty hesitated, but then slapped a hand atop of Jane's. "Agreed." She then glanced at Jane. "And I am sorry about last night."

Jane grinned and dropped the beater to slap her other hand over Betty's. "Forgiven."

Although Patsy had not been that upset over Betty being late, she slapped her other hand on top of Jane's. "Forgiven."

Betty smiled and dropped her rug beater before slapping her other hand on the top. "One for all and all for one."

They all three laughed, and hugged each other before they tugged the rug off the line, careful to not let it touch the ground. As they worked, they whispered about the fun Patsy would have that night, and how she had to tell them everything about it.

She readily agreed to tell them about any and all celebrities. However, she wasn't nearly as excited about who would be there as she was about being Lane's date. That was the thrilling part for her. Seeing him again. That sort of scared her, too. At how much she liked him. More and more each day.

Lane twisted to see the side of his head in the mirror as he drew the comb through his still-damp hair. He hadn't taken this amount of time on his appearance in years. His clothes were always clean, and his body, but he rarely used the mirror for anything more than the minutes it took to shave.

He took a step back from the sink to check his image, adjusting his tie and collar, and then checked his hair again. He smoothed back both sides at his temples with his fingers one last time. Satisfied, he spun about and left his bathroom, clicking off the light on his way out of the door.

The special attention he was paying to his appearance could be because Raymond's party would have a large number of celebrities in attendance, but he met stars and influential persons of all walks of life on a daily basis. It was because of Libby. He didn't want to admit that, even to himself, but it was, and the mystery behind her. Why she wouldn't tell him her address and why she couldn't be at the Rooster's Nest until almost nine added to his growing list of things he needed to find out about her. Simply wanting to be a reporter just didn't add up.

He walked through his sparsely furnished apartment that had suited him well the past few years. It shared the

same parking lot as the *Gazette* building, which made
the commute home after late nights at his office simple
and quick. Those nights were more often than not. However, the past year, they had slowed considerably because
he now had the perfect staff in place. From pressmen to
proofreaders, his staff were as dedicated to keeping the
Gazette the most read paper in the state as him.

His staff were also the reason he was able to focus on
prime stories, which was his passion.

At the door, he turned around and gave his apartment a
quick scan. The brown tweed couch, the spindle-leg side
table holding a single lamp, the short bookcase by the
door where he dropped his keys every night, the doorway that led to the kitchen, the one to the bathroom and
the one to the bedroom. The wood-paneled walls and the
wooden floors. There wasn't even a rug. For a moment,
he wondered what Naomi would think of it, of living
here, in this barren little apartment.

A hint of a smile tugged at his lips. She wouldn't have
lived here. They'd had dreams, big dreams of a house big
enough for four children. Two boys and two girls. That's
what she'd wanted. Keep everything even.

Naomi had been willing to do whatever it took to make
those dreams happen. Without complaint she'd found a
way to feed them both with little to nothing to spend on
groceries when he first bought the *Gazette*. That had
taken every penny he'd saved plus some, and he'd worked
night and day to make it pay off.

As he had a million times over the past few years, he
wished she could see how different things were now. He
could easily afford whatever house she may have wanted.
Except for one in Hollywoodland. He could afford it, but
he would never buy property from William Dryer. After
their last run-in, where he'd refused Dryer free adver-

tising and hadn't even acknowledged how the man had suggested that he had three eligible daughters, Dryer had tried to sully his name. He'd heard about it nearly everywhere he'd gone.

Which was precisely why Dryer was still working so hard to gain respect. He may have money, but his personality left little else but enemies in his wake.

His mind went to Libby then, wondering what she'd think of the modest and simple way he lived.

Flustered at himself for even wondering about that, he grabbed his keys, clicked off the light and left, locking the door behind him.

Once in his car, a red-and-black Chevrolet that, unlike his apartment, was brand new and one of the most expensive models on the market, he checked his watch. It was almost eight thirty. Perfect amount of time to drive to the Rooster's Nest.

He drove the Chevy out of the parking lot, and shifted into second as he rolled down Second Avenue. The two-door coupe purred like a kitten in a sunny window. The coupe, along with a few other models, was making automobile manufactures scratch their heads, trying to design something comparable. It hadn't happened yet, and the coupe was bypassing other models in sales nationwide.

Lane turned onto Broadway Boulevard. There was plenty of traffic, par for the course of downtown LA, but the smooth steering of the coupe had him swerving around cars two and three at a time. Traffic lessened the closer he got to the outskirts of town, and he shifted into third gear, rested his arm on the open window and pressed his foot on the pedal. The roar of the engine was music to his hears, and ate up the last couple of miles in no time.

He found a parking spot along the street near the corner where the streetcar would stop and got out of his car.

While walking around to the passenger side, he shined the chrome on the headlights with one hand, and then leaned against the front fender where he had a good view of the corner.

The streetcar should be along within a few minutes. The idea of checking for Libby inside the Rooster's Nest crossed his mind, but instincts said she wasn't there. She'd be getting off the streetcar. Along with the two other flappers he'd seen leave the Rooster's Nest last night, the same two who had jumped on the trolley from the alleyway along with her the other night.

He wondered what she'd be wearing tonight. Not that it mattered, she'd look cute no matter what, and chins were going to drop when he walked into Raymond's with her on his arm.

He clenched his jaw together at that thought. This was a job. Nothing more. He had to make sure she didn't write up what she knew about Gaynor and send it off to another paper. There was nothing more to this night than that.

Nothing.

The ring of the trolley sounded, and he rested an elbow on the hood of his car, waiting for the red-and-white streetcar to roll to a halt. A moment later, it stopped, and Libby stepped down the small set of stairs and onto the sidewalk.

Lane bit the inside of his lip to keep from reacting to the sight of her. She had on a black-and-white-striped dress, sleeveless, with a V neckline. A string of pearls made a choker around her neck and then hung down to the dropped waistline of her dress. The hem barely covered her knees, and a pair of rolled-down silk hose covered her ankles above a pair of shiny white shoes.

A smile built on her face with every step she took. By the time she arrived at his side, her teeth, as pearly white as the beads hanging around her neck, were showing behind her bright red lipstick.

"Well, hello, Oliver," she said. "Fancy meeting you here."

He glanced at the other two women who had gotten off the trolley after her. Neither of them cast so much of a glance his way, but he recognized they were the two he'd seen last night, and the night before. They were both blonde, petite like her, and trying too hard to not look their way.

Turning his attention back to Libby, he nodded. "Fancy that."

She laughed, and then reached out and straightened his tie. It was a simple action that felt far more intimate than it truly was.

"We match," she said. "We are both wearing black and white." She gave him an up-and-down appraisal. "You sure look spiffy, Oliver."

"You look very lovely," he said, surprised at how raspy his voice sounded. *Lovely* didn't even begin to describe her. The beaded hat covering her blond hair framed her face. Her bright blue eyes, creamy smooth complexion and, of course, those dual dimples in her cheeks were mesmerizing.

"Thank you." She did a perfect pirouette on the toe of one white shoe, giving him a glimpse of the back of the dress.

He sucked in a breath at how the dress left half of her upper back bare, and held it until the whistle itching to let loose dissolved. He knew actresses who were going to be green with envy tonight.

"Shall we?" he asked, stepping over to open the passenger door.

"Yes!" She pressed a hand to her mouth, stifling her giggle as she climbed in the coupe. "This is so exciting!"

"I hope you aren't disappointed."

"Disappointed in what?"

Needing to remind himself as much as her, he said, "Reporting isn't all fun and games. The party could be as flat as a tire on an old rust bucket." He closed the door and walked around the car. Raymond's party was sure to be a roaring time. It was him who would be the flat tire. He had to keep this all business.

"I promise I won't be disappointed, Oliver," she said as he climbed in.

He started the engine while asking, "Why do you want to be a reporter?"

She sighed and sat quiet for a moment, then said, "Because I want to learn all there is to learn about life, see all there is to see, and not from the sideline, not from just reading about it."

The hair on his arms quivered at her reply, because he knew exactly what she meant. He'd felt that exact same way while living on his family's farm, and while reading every newspaper he could get his hands on, he'd deduced that was the way he could learn and see everything firsthand, while getting paid to do it.

"I bet you think that sounds silly," she said quietly.

"No, no, I don't think it sounds weird." He pulled away from the curb and contemplated what he was about to say. "Being a reporter is a competitive field, and to be honest, there aren't a lot of women reporters."

"Only because people think women should be cleaning and cooking rather than having a real job."

The sarcasm in her voice was unmistakable, and he

could understand it. He'd embraced the new roles women had taken in life, in the workforce and at home. In society as a whole. He also understood the reality of making a house a home. "Not everyone thinks that. I don't. I think women should be able to pursue their interests, whatever they might be. I also know cooking and cleaning is hard work," he offered.

"Yeah, well, you're probably the only one who does think that." She huffed out a breath. "A person sure doesn't get to see much of the world cooking and cleaning all the time."

"I agree with you on that, too." He admired her honesty and could relate because he knew what it was like to be driven with one goal in sight.

"What made you want to be a reporter?" she asked.

He could lie, but there was no reason to. "For the same reason you just said. I wanted to learn about things, people, places, events, up close and in person, and then tell others about it." Oddly, she was the first person he'd ever told that to. The first person who'd ever asked him that question.

"Really?"

"Yes, really."

"Bee's knees," she whispered.

He grinned. "I tell you what, you write something about Raymond's party tonight, and if it's suitable, I'll see about printing it in the society section of the paper."

She gasped so hard she coughed. "You mean it, Lane?"

"Yes, I mean it." He was going to have to write something about Raymond's party. That was the main reason he'd been invited, the main reason he was invited to parties on a regular basis. He remembered what it was like striving to get his first article printed and figured it was only fair that he be the one to give her that shot.

"But be warned, some parts might change during the editing process."

"I don't care." She grabbed a hold of his arm. "Thank you. Thank you so much!"

Her excitement made him smile, which also made him warn, "Don't thank me yet. You haven't written anything and I haven't read it."

She giggled and released her hold on his arm. "You're right. But I will. I will."

He turned the corner, and shifted gears to speed up the boulevard, half wondering if he truly knew what he was doing. Giving a reporter a chance and taking her to Raymond's party weren't even close to going hand in hand, but, something inside him felt right. A part of him that had been empty, invisible, for a long time.

"I, uh, need to tell you something, Oliver, I mean, Lane."

His body tensed at how serious she sounded. "Oh?"

She sighed. "Yes."

She not only sounded somber, but also unsure. Maybe she was changing her mind about becoming a reporter. "What is it?"

"The reason I asked you to meet me at the Rooster's Nest."

He'd forgotten about that. She had a way of doing that to him. Made him forget certain aspects that should be filling his mind. "Why was that?"

"Because of where I live. No men are allowed there and I have to sneak out after others go to bed." She sighed. "You've heard of the secretarial school, haven't you?" Shaking her head, she continued, "Of course you have. Well, they have housing there for students and…"

Relief oozed out of him so completely he barely heard the rest of what she said. That made perfect sense. The headmistress of the school ruled with an iron ruler. One of the secretaries at the *Gazette* had gone to school there and had told him about the strict rules that all the girls attending had to adhere to or risk getting kicked out.

"...catch the red line by eleven forty-five."

The streetcars shut down at midnight, so that, too, made sense. "Those two girls that got off the trolley with you, are they students there, too?"

She grimaced while nodding.

He was glad that she'd admitted that, and that she'd told him about the school. "Don't worry, I'll have you back in time to catch the trolley."

"Thank you."

"Is that all?"

"Is that all what?"

"All that you had to tell me?"

"Yes."

They would arrive at Raymond's apartment building in a few minutes and her admission had made him remember a few other bits of information he still needed to know about her. "What about a last name?" he asked. "So I can introduce you to my friends."

"Oh."

He glanced her way, and saw how hard she swallowed. "Bell."

He refrained from letting his disbelief show. However, he couldn't help but ask, "Your name is Liberty Bell?"

She flinched and grimaced. "Yes, no. It's actually Bellamy."

No, it wasn't. He could call her out on that, but decided not to. Chasing a story was part of the fun, and finding the truth behind this one could be more fun than he'd had in a long time. "All right," he said. "Libby Bellamy it is."

"Yes, that's my name, Libby Bellamy."

Her shoulders rose as she drew in a deep breath.

He pulled into the parking lot of Raymond's complex, and had to circle the lines of cars in order to find a parking spot. The fact no one would know her real name was actually a good thing. There would be other reporters there, and a story about him would make headline news in some of the other papers.

She waited for him to climb out, and walk around to open her door. Stepping out, she smiled up at him. "You can just introduce me as Libby."

He shut the car door. "Why?"

She shrugged. "Why not?"

He held out his elbow for her to grasp. "Why not, indeed."

Giggling, she took a hold of his arm.

They crossed the parking lot and entered the building through a set of glass double doors held open by an aging doorman dressed in a red-and-gold suit.

"Mr. Cox," the man said. "Mr. Klein is expecting you." With a nod toward a young man wearing a matching uniform standing near an elevator cage, he added, "Jacob will show you the way."

"Thank you, Donald," Lane answered, having met the man on numerous occasions. As the doorman for the building, Donald Wallace knew more about the lives of popular stars and celebrities than anyone else in the city, and prided himself for never making a single comment about anyone.

With Libby still holding his arm, Lane proceeded to the elevator. "Good evening, Jacob."

The man slid back the iron cage door of the elevator. "Good evening, Mr. Cox. I hope all is well."

Jacob Wallace was Donald's son, and though his father had instructed him about keeping his lips closed, Jacob's eyes were another thing. They had settled on Libby the minute they'd walked through the door. Lane couldn't blame the young man. Libby was eye-catching, but it was more than that. She had a carefree air about her that was far more enticing than her beauty alone. Having her on his arm was even more enjoyable than he'd expected it to be, and they had yet to arrive at the party. It had been a long time, a very long time since he'd been excited to attend a party, yet he was now. Because of her.

"All is very well," Lane answered, guiding Libby into the elevator. "Thank you."

Chapter Six

Patsy had seen glamorous homes, including her own and many of those in Hollywoodland. When construction was completed on new homes, she and her sisters were given the tasks of making them sparkle and shine before the new owners moved in. However, she rarely saw those homes furnished. Not like this, anyway.

Everything in the apartment sparkled like jewels in the sunshine, from the highly polished wood to the gold-colored brocade curtains, draped across the span of windows that covered one entire wall, and the huge swan ice sculpture that sat in the center of a table full of food.

She tried to take it all in at once, and to lock it in her memory so she'd be able to write about it.

Write an article about it!

Although it had been her dream for years, she was still trying to grasp the idea of Lane actually printing one of her articles. It was surreal. So was the fact that he actually understood how she felt. No one understood that. Not even her sisters, who supported her idea of becoming a reporter. They merely understood what it felt like to be caged up like a bird. Lane understood how she wanted to experience life, and like he said, tell others about it.

The room was full of people, couples cozied together on the velvet-covered sofas and standing side by side, talking with others. The men were dressed in fancy suits and the women wore gowns so glamorous they took her breath away.

"Lane! You made it!" a tall man with curly blond hair shouted and waved from across the room.

Lane returned the man's wave and, as the man made his way toward them, whispered, "That's Raymond."

Patsy nodded, while whispering in return, "Why is everyone staring at us?"

Lane grinned. "Because you are the most beautiful woman in the room."

"Horsefeathers," she whispered. "It's because I'm with you."

"My guess is they are wondering who you are."

"Oh, dear."

He chuckled and settled a hand on her back. "It's part of being a reporter. You have something people want."

Excitement bubbled inside her at knowing what he meant. "An article about them."

He winked at her.

Biting her bottom lip, she drew in a deep breath. She did understand so much more about writing what people want, now, because of him, and thankfully, because of her nightly excursions as Libby, she knew how to work a crowd.

"So glad you made it, Lane," Raymond Klein said.

"I said I would," Lane answered, shaking Raymond's hand as he stopped directly in front of them.

"Ruby, you know Lane Cox," Raymond said, looking at the woman at his side.

Patsy couldn't believe she'd missed noticing Ruby Lancaster. She was as beautiful as her pictures.

"Yes." Ruby stepped forward and kissed Lane's cheek. "It's so nice of you to come." Ruby then cast a sweet smile at her. "And I'm assuming this is your date?"

Without an ounce of fear, Patsy held out her hand to shake Ruby's. "Yes, I'm Libby."

Lane's smile grew as he said, "Libby, this is Raymond Klein and Ruby Lancaster."

"It's so lovely to meet you," Ruby said, resting her hand on Raymond's chest. "We are honored to have both of you here."

Patsy couldn't help but notice the gorgeous engagement ring on Ruby's finger.

"We sure are," Raymond said, snapping his fingers in the air. A split second later, a waiter dressed in a tuxedo arrived with a tray of drinks. Taking two drinks off the tray, Raymond handed a stemmed glass to her. "Champagne for the women." Handing the other glass to Lane, he said, "And whiskey for the men."

"Thank you," she and Lane said at the same time.

Their eyes met then, and her stomach swooped at the shine in Lane's eyes.

Raymond handed a drink to Ruby and then took one for himself, and held it up.

"Allow me," Lane said. He held his glass in the air. "A toast to the happy couple!"

"Hear, hear!" filled the room as everyone held up their glasses.

"May they forever be as happy as they are at this moment!" Lane said.

Another round of "Hear, hear!" still echoed off the walls after Patsy had taken a sip of her champagne. She hoped the same for herself, that she could forever be as happy as she was at this moment.

Raymond waved a hand. "Let us show you around."

A sense of pride filled her as Lane kept his hand on her back as they walked from room to room. Each one was beautifully furnished and decorated with large ferns and vases filled with fresh flowers, gorgeous paintings and draped brocade curtains.

Every room was full of people she recognized from Jane's magazine that they'd scoured through after returning the rug to the living room this afternoon.

Lane never left her side and drew her into conversations as if her opinion was as important as his on many different subjects. It was quite uplifting, to be at the side of someone who was sought out by so many. Lane's laughter and quick wit made it fun, and soon she was so caught up in the liveliness of the party, she was chatting with celebrities like she'd known them forever.

She discovered one thing for certain. Lane was the most handsome man in the room. Not even the famous actors looked as debonair as he did. He was also more popular. Everyone in every room made it a point of saying hello to him.

Being his date was amazing. The entire party was amazing. Including the champagne. It was delicious and she savored each sip. Because it was for the most part imported, Betty claimed it was the only alcoholic beverage that could safely be consumed.

They eventually ended up in a room where the furniture and rugs had been removed, exposing the thickly varnished floor for dancing. A man played the piano, and another the saxophone, and couples whirled around the dance floor.

A tall man with black hair winked at her as he sashayed another woman past where she and Lane stood. Unimpressed, she turned away.

"Do you know who that is?" Lane asked.

"Who?"

"The guy on the dance floor."

She shook her head. "No. Should I?"

"You don't go to many movies, do you?"

"No." She and her sisters had gone to a movie one night, instead of a speakeasy, and though it had been enjoyable, the speakeasies were much more exciting. They snuck out to be with people, not sit in a dark room.

"That's Karl VanBuren, a very famous actor," Lane said.

Karl VanBuren had been in the magazine Jane had, which made her frown. "He doesn't look like the picture I saw of him."

Lane chuckled and whispered, "That's because he had his nose broke a while ago for sticking it in a place it didn't belong."

She giggled at the amusement in Lane's eyes. "I hope he learned a lesson."

"Probably not."

She truly didn't care about the actor. "Lots of people at this party are famous," she said. "Including you."

He leaned closer. "You've heard the old saying keep your friends close, and your enemies closer?"

Curious as to what he meant, she nodded. "Yes."

"That's what I am. An enemy. People want to keep me close, thinking that will keep me from writing anything bad about them."

"You are not. Furthermore, you only print the truth," she said.

"Not everyone sees it that way. You'll learn that quick enough."

His words, the way he talked as if she truly was an up-and-coming reporter, filled her with joy. Much like the joyous clapping that filled the room as the music ended. A moment later, someone tapped her shoulder.

She turned, found herself face-to-face with Karl Van-Buren, and bit her lips together at how crooked his nose was up close.

"I'm going to steal your date, Cox," Karl said, winking at her again.

"No, you're not," Lane replied.

"Just one dance," Karl said. "Didn't your mother teach you to share?"

"Some things." Lane took her glass and handed it to the man. "Have some champagne, Karl." He then took her hand and led her onto the dance floor.

The shocked look on the actor's face made her laugh. So did the way Lane twirled her beneath his arm before pulling her up next to him.

"I'll get you another glass of champagne," he said.

"I'd rather dance than drink champagne any day," she replied.

Lane then waltzed her around the dance floor, making her feel as if she was floating on air most of the time. Dancing with him was so dreamlike, all other thoughts escaped her.

Until the song ended and the next one started. It was the shimmy. The beat of the music immediately filled her, and she crouched down.

Lane laughed, threw his arms in the air and stepped backward, giving her room to shimmy upward. Then he grasped her hands, and shimmied along with her. Her laughter joined the shouts of glee that echoed off the walls as dancers shook and shimmied across the dance floor.

Breathless by the time the song ended, Patsy leaned against Lane's shoulder while waiting for others to move so they could leave the dance floor.

They were still waiting when someone shouted, "We can't let Ray and Ruby have all the fun tonight!"

Lane's arm was around her and she kept her hand on his chest as they both twisted toward the shout.

It was Karl VanBuren. Standing on top of a table, he reached down and plucked a long-stemmed red rose out of the vase by his feet. "The woman lucky enough to catch this flower will become my next wife!" he shouted, and then threw the flower into the air.

Hoots and hollers filled the room.

Looking up at Lane, Patsy said, "He can't be serious."

The words had no sooner left her mouth than the flower came tumbling down, and landed on the crook of her arm that was up against Lane's chest.

"There she is, folks, my next wife!" VanBuren shouted.

The room grew eerily silent as Lane seized the flower stem with his free hand. Patsy's heart thudded so hard it echoed in her ears.

With a snap of his wrist, Lane shot the flower across the room like an arrow. "Try again, Karl. This one's taken." Lane then twisted them both about and placed his hand on the small of her back to guide her forward.

Laughter and clapping followed them as they crossed the room, along with shouts of congratulations to Lane.

"Why are they congratulating you?" she asked.

He shook his head. "For getting one over on Van-Buren."

She smiled and nodded at a few people still shouting congratulations as they walked out of the room, and down the hallway.

Then, as they entered the big front room, an older woman approached them and very purposefully elbowed Patsy aside.

"Lane, darling," the woman said, kissing the air beside both of Lane's cheeks.

A blaze ignited inside Patsy and she elbowed her way back to Lane's side, and flashed a grin at the older woman as his hand settled on the small of her back again.

The woman cast her a look of scorn, but instantly smiled at Lane again. "I haven't seen you in ages, darling."

"Hello, Victoria," Lane said. "This is my date. Libby, this is Victoria Lloyd."

Prideful at the way Lane smiled down at her, Patsy kept her chin high as she gave the woman a slight nod. "Hello."

The woman didn't even acknowledge her before saying to Lane, "Darling, I'm having a party tomorrow night, and I insist you be there."

Patsy was irritated by the woman in several ways. The pink-and-yellow feather in her hat did not match her dark purple and black dress at all. She also had on way too much makeup. The bright red lipstick was running into the wrinkles around her lips. Most of all, she did not like the way she kept calling Lane *darling*. "Of course we'll be there," she said. "Won't we, Lane?"

The smile never left his face, but Patsy swallowed at the way Lane stiffened and he lifted a brow at her.

"Of course," he said. "Tomorrow night."

"Lovely!" The woman kissed the air next to his cheek again. "See you then, darling."

"Sorry," Patsy said once the woman was out of hearing distance.

"You don't know who that is, do you?" he asked.

"Victoria someone. Lloyd, maybe." Shrugging, she added, "I don't recall." She did recall. The woman's name would be forever in her mind. Pushing her aside like she had and calling him *darling* over and over.

"Yes," he said. "Victoria Lloyd. I worked for her husband, and bought the *Gazette* from him shortly before he died."

"Oh." Sensing from the way he'd stiffened and looked at her earlier, she said, "And you don't want to go to her party, do you?"

"No."

She shrugged. "Then we won't go."

"Yes, we will." He gestured toward the doorway with his chin. "Let's go."

"Where?"

He held up his other hand, exposing the watch on his wrist. "It's after eleven. We have just enough time to say goodbye to Raymond and Ruby and then get to the red line in time."

She had no idea it was already that late, and was glad to see the host and hostess standing near the front door.

Smiling brightly as they approached, Raymond said, "Did I just hear correctly? That you're engaged?"

Patsy's entire being went ice cold.

"Why didn't you tell me that the other night?" Raymond asked.

"Nothing is official," Lane said, and made a hasty goodbye while nearly shoving her out the door.

Shoving because her legs were frozen stiff. Once they were in the elevator, she whispered, "Why did he think we are engaged?"

Lane shot a glance toward the elevator man, and reading the look on his face, she pinched her lips together, holding in her questions until they were outside. "Why—"

"Because I threw Karl back his flower," Lane said.

"But that wouldn't—"

"That is exactly how rumors get started," Lane said, walking faster. "We have to hurry to catch the red line."

Once they were in the car, heading toward the boulevard, she asked, "What are we going to do about it?"

"About what?"

"That rumor!" She couldn't be engaged. Not even to him. She wasn't going to get married. Not ever. An odd inkling made that thought shift slightly. Well, maybe someday, but not until after she became a reporter.

Lane shifted into another gear. "Rumors are like cars. If they aren't fed, filled with gas, they won't go anywhere."

She felt a small sense of relief, but was still chilled by the idea of even a rumor of being engaged. That was not what she wanted.

"Don't worry about it," Lane said as he swung the car around the corner near the Rooster's Nest and pulled it up along the curb. "VanBuren's already been married five times, so he's never taken seriously."

Patsy's heart skipped a beat. The trolley was rolling to a stop and her sisters were already waiting to board. Without waiting for him to climb out and open her door, she threw it open and quickly jumped out of the car.

"I'll be here at the same time tomorrow night," Lane said, standing near the driver's door.

"So will I," she shouted, running toward the trolley.

He was there the next night, leaning against his car, looking as handsome as he had the night before. This time, he wore a gray suit, with silver pinstripes, a shimmering silver shirt and red tie.

Once again, she giggled because they matched. Her dress was gray with layers upon layers of silver fringes.

Her floppy-brimmed hat was gray with silver stitching, and hosted a bright red feather. Her shoes and gloves were red, as well.

"Hello." He pushed off the side of his car to open the door for her.

"Hello." Excitement at seeing him filled her, but there was also a layer of guilt swishing around. "We could just go to the Rooster's Nest tonight."

He waved a hand for her to climb in the car. "No, we can't."

She climbed in, smoothed the hem of her dress over her knees and then squeezed her trembling hands together. She was more nervous than she may ever have been. The article in her pocket was the reason. She truly, truly hoped he'd like it.

Jane had sat on the edge of her bed for hours last night, asking about every person at the party. Patsy had told her everything about the party, except the flower and possible rumor about her and Lane being engaged, and then about the article she needed to write for him. Jane had been excited about that, and had even read the article earlier today, saying it was as good as many of the ones in the magazines she snuck into the house.

Patsy was nervous because she'd taken to heart what he'd said about people wanting to read about themselves and others, and had used as many names as she could remember, including his. He was more popular and interesting than many of the others at the party. There wasn't a subject he couldn't carry on a conversation about, and he was nice, genuinely nice, to everyone. And so very handsome.

"You look lovely tonight," he said while climbing in the car.

She was so nervous, it was as if a flock of butterflies

had taken up residence in her stomach tonight. "Thank you. You look extremely handsome."

He pulled away from the curb. "Extremely?"

Her cheeks flushed with heat, yet she didn't change her mind. "Yes. Extremely."

He chuckled. "Then, allow me to say that you look extravagantly lovely."

They both laughed, and then he asked, "So, did you write an article about last night?"

Holding her breath, she nodded.

He held out his hand.

She slid her hand in her pocket. "It's too dark for you to read it, and you're driving."

"I'll pull over once we get downtown, under a streetlight." He wiggled his fingers. "Hand it over."

She was nervous, but not afraid. Even if he didn't like it, he would be nice about it. He was always nice. Pulling out the paper, she laid it in his hand.

He pulled over shortly afterward, beneath a glowing light.

Patsy held her breath as he unfolded the paper and began to read.

"This is good, Libby. Really good."

A quiver tickled her spine as he called her Libby. "If you decide to print it I... I..."

"You what?"

"Would prefer that you don't use my name."

He frowned. "I thought you wanted to be a reporter."

"I do, but..." She couldn't use her real name, and using Libby seemed to be too large of a lie. No name was better.

"But not in the society page," he said. "You want to wait for a headline."

That was a reason she could live with. "Yes."

"All right, I won't use your name." He folded the paper

and put it in his pocket. "I'll let you know the payment after it's edited."

"Payment?"

"Yes. The *Gazette* pays per word."

"No, I mean, you are going to print it? Really print it?"

"Yes, it's good. Raymond and Ruby's engagement is definitely something people want to read about, and you really put your heart in this. Gave it feeling. Excitement. People like that."

Full of excitement herself, she squealed and then spun in her seat so she could hug him. "Thank you, Lane. Thank you so much!"

She pulled back to look at him, and say thank you again, but something in his eyes made her heart stop. Or beat faster. She wasn't exactly sure. Wasn't exactly sure what was happening inside her at all because the craziest thought ever had crossed her mind. That of kissing him.

Releasing his shoulders, she sat back in her seat, wiggled a little closer to the door even. This was strange. It was as if every part of her body that had touched his was on fire. She'd touched him before. Danced with him more times than she could count, but hugging him just now had been very, very different.

Too very, very different.

She was still contemplating that when, after driving for some distance, he asked if she went to the ocean very often.

"No, why?"

"Victoria lives in a house that overlooks the ocean," he answered.

"I haven't been there in years," she said, not able to remember the last time she'd gone to the ocean. Her mind was still trying to figure out what was happening inside her.

"Why not?"

"No reason to go," she said.

"You don't swim?"

"Never learned how."

"Everyone should know how to swim." He turned off the highway onto a gravel road that went up a hill.

"Why?"

"Because. What if you fell in?"

Considering she rarely went near any water, she shook her head. "That's not likely."

He topped the hill, and the golden glow of electric lights shone from every window of a large brownstone house set amid a grove of trees.

"We're here," he said.

"It's hard to tell in the dark, but it looks like a lovely home," Patsy said, peering through the windshield to make out as much as she could between the moonlight and the car's headlights.

He parked the car behind several others. "It is a nice place."

"We don't have to stay long," she said, worried because she couldn't get the idea of kissing him out of her mind.

Lane climbed out and walked around the car. It wasn't leaving he was worried about, it was entering the party. His phone hadn't stopped ringing all day. Everyone wanted to know who the cute blonde was whom he was engaged to. He should have known how fast a rumor like that would spread, and grow. He opened her car door and held out a hand for her to climb out, and made the mistake of looking directly into her eyes.

It was as if she cast a spell on him whenever she looked at him through those long lashes. The desire to kiss her struck so hard it was nearly impossible to contain it. That had happened a short time ago, when she'd hugged him, and it had taken thirty minutes of driving before he could even speak.

Stepping back, needing the distance, he closed the car door. "We won't be able to stay long. We have to catch the red line again, remember?"

She nodded. "Yes, I remember."

Damn. He was half-afraid to even touch her, but mustered up and laid a hand on her back to guide her around the car and up the walkway.

A flapper, young, with dyed red chin-length hair, greeted them at the door. The party was in peak performance. The crowd wasn't the same as last night, and there wasn't any champagne, but the drinks were flowing. Music, piercing rumbles from a trumpet combined with the higher blare of a saxophone and the twinkling of piano notes, filled the air, along with gleeful shouts, the clinking of glasses and boisterous laughter.

"There will be a dance-off in five minutes." The redheaded flapper pointed toward a set of French doors that a line of people was entering. "In that room over there."

He wasn't in the mood for a dance-off, but if they were on the dance floor, no one would be able to question them about being engaged.

He grabbed Libby's hand. "Looks like we've arrived just in time."

"I do believe we have." She giggled. "Oliver."

The way she said that nickname tripled his heartbeat. He'd forgotten so many things about what it felt like to be attracted to someone, but was readily recognizing each and every one of them.

"Lane, darling, you're here."

His spine stiffened at Victoria Lloyd's high-pitched

voice. More than a couple of decades older than him, Victoria had made it plain that everything her husband had had could be his. He'd made it clear that he wasn't interested, but she continued.

He placed a hand on Libby's back, to guide her toward the French doors, and twisted to glance over his shoulder. "We are here, Victoria. Just in time to win a dance contest."

There were no numbers pinned to their backs this time. As the band struck the first note, dozens of couples ran to the center of the room, and began dancing everything from the Charleston to the foxtrot. It was a free-for-all, and knowing they needed to reserve their energies, Lane started out slow, gracefully leading Libby around the parquet floor.

Dual chandeliers hung overhead, making the silver thread in her hat sparkle and shine as she twirled beneath their clutched hands and then slid back up against his chest again. Her features were so delicate—she was so delicate looking—yet she was more full of life than anyone he'd known.

"It's a lovely party," she said.

He couldn't comment on the party. They hadn't been there long enough, and he hadn't paid enough attention to comment.

"Are you invited to a party every night?" she asked.

"Practically," he admitted. "But I spend a lot of evenings working."

"Doing what?"

"Investigating, writing, editing." He twirled her beneath his arm. "Not all stories happen during the day."

The song ended and the next one started with little more than a pause. It had a faster beat, and other couples sped around the dance floor like roadsters racing to the finish line. Keeping their pace slow and even, he said, "We'll let them wear themselves out, save our energy for the last song."

Without missing a step, she exclaimed, "And win!" Then performed a double graceful twirl, which had the bystanders clapping with enthusiasm.

"You have an audience," he said.

"We have an audience." With her face aglow, she added, "You sure are a good dancer, Oliver."

"So are you, Libby." His remark was rewarded by her delightful laugh that truly floated on the air and kept echoing in his ears over and over.

Four songs later, he was winded, but wasn't about to slow down. There were only four couples left on the dance floor, and he was committed to them winning this dance contest, hands down.

One couple was barely staying upright, but the other two were still going strong. He and Libby were going to have to step it up in order to win.

As if she read his mind, Libby danced out of his arms, and crouched down, until her knees almost touched the floor. He knew what was coming, and couldn't hold back a whistle as she started dancing the shimmy. Arms out at her sides, the sparkling silver fringes on her dress flipped and flapped and the bystanders went wild, cheering as she shook her torso, shimmying her way up again.

He followed suit, crouching down and shimmying his way up, then dancing toward her. Right before connecting, they'd separate, leap backward and crouch down again.

Her laughter was the main sound he heard.

She could dance the shimmy like no one he'd seen, and though others on the dance floor tried, they didn't hold a candle to her. The roar of the crowd said they agreed with him.

Without a pause this time, the musicians ended one song and started another with a beat just as fast.

The one couple stumbled, then, with arms and legs flaying, they hit the floor. Recalling how that had taken them out of the last contest, Lane shouted to her, "Let's move to the other side."

She nodded, shimmying toward him. He spun around, and with his back to her, shimmied his way toward an open area where no one would stumble into them.

The crowd became louder than the music when, out of the blue, she jumped on his back. Laughing at her ingenuity, he hooked her behind the knees with his elbows and, with her riding piggyback style, he glided across the room like an ice skater.

She was still shaking her torso. He could see her arms out of his peripheral vision, feel her body moving and the fringes of her dress flipping in his hair.

Another couple attempted to copy them, but it didn't work out. The minute the woman jumped on the man's back, they somersaulted. All the way across the floor and into the crowd.

"We are going to win this, Oliver!" she shouted over his head.

"Yes, we are!"

Either the other couple had heard them, or simply decided they didn't have a chance at winning because they stopped dancing, and after a bow, held their arms out toward him and Libby.

As the band played the final bars of the song with a grand finesse, Lane glided a full circle around the floor. The crowd's cheering said they expected a grand finale from him and Libby, too.

He moved to the center of the floor, and then released his hold on her knees. As soon as she slid off his back, he spun around, wrapped an arm around her waist and another around her shoulders.

The crowd cheered and clapped as she hooked her arms around his neck and he dipped her low.

Her hat fell off, releasing blond tresses that brushed the floor. That, along with her sparkling eyes, deeply indented dimples and smiling lips, was more than he could resist.

Any final bits of control he may have had were gone.

He leaned over her and did exactly what he'd been fighting against doing.

Kissed her.

Chapter Seven

It may have been his own senses returning, or the thunder of the crowd that finally penetrated through the echoing of his own heart in his ears that forced Lane to end the sweetest kiss he'd ever experienced.

Regrettably.

He could have gone on kissing her for hours.

Days.

"Ladies and gents! We have the winners!" someone shouted.

She pressed a hand to her lips as he lifted her upright, and kept it there, with her eyes closed. Not sure if she'd heard the announcement, he whispered, "We won."

Her eyelids flew open. "We won?"

He nodded.

Her smile lit up her face as she exclaimed, "We won! We won, Oliver!"

He made sure she was steady on her feet before releasing her. "Yes, we did."

"Hallelujah and jubilee!" she shouted. "We won!"

Laughing, he bent down and picked up her hat. That, too, held regret. She was adorable with her hats on, but that long blond hair hanging loose and carefree around her face was enough to take his breath away.

Her eyes went wide and the smile left her lips as her mouth gaped open at the sight of her hat in his hand.

"Oh!" She grabbed it and quickly slapped it on her head.

With shouts of congratulations, the crowd rushed them. Lane wrapped an arm around her shoulders to keep from becoming separated as they accepted numerous compliments about their dancing.

Then, as soon as the crowd began to disperse, he steered her across the dance floor, toward the makeshift bar that had been set up along one wall.

"Let's get a drink."

"I need to find a powder room first," she replied.

"You have to be dying of thirst. I know I am."

She stopped at the edge of the dance floor. "I am, but have to put my hat back on properly."

Her shoulders were up and she was looking down as if cowering. He lifted her chin, looked her in the eyes. "No, you don't," he insisted. "You look fine without it."

Biting her bottom lip, she shook her head. "No, I don't. I—I didn't wash my hair this morning."

That's what she'd said the other night, too. He ran his fingers through the hair tumbling over her shoulder. "It doesn't look dirty to me."

"Well, it is. Do you know where the powder room is?"

Using his chin, he nodded toward the doorway. "Out the door and down the hall on the left."

"Thank you. I'll be right back."

She hurried toward the doorway and he weaved his way through the crowd to the bar. After selecting a beer for himself and a cocktail for her, he worked his way toward the hallway to meet her when she emerged from the powder room, only to be stopped by Victoria as soon as he walked through the doorway.

"Lane, darling," she drawled. "I never imagined you'd be one to take up with a deb."

Momentarily confused, because his eyes were down the hall, on the powder room door, bemoaning that Libby was in there hiding the tresses that had felt like pure silk between his fingers, he frowned. "What?"

"A debutante doesn't seem like your style." Victoria lifted her chin "Being your age, I assumed you'd prefer a more mature and experienced woman."

Lane shook his head, not in the mood for Victoria's innuendoes. She was an attractive woman, just not to him. And most certainly not compared with Libby.

"I am a bit surprised that William let any of his daughters out from under his thumb," Victoria continued. "He's kept them under lock and key since they left grammar school. And now you are engaged to one."

The hair on Lane's neck quivered. Slowly, he shifted to get a better look at Victoria. "What are you talking about? Who are you talking about?"

"Your fiancée. William Dryer's daughter."

A roar rumbled in his ears. He twisted, peering again past the crowd lining the hallway and at the powder room door. It couldn't be. Libby couldn't be William Dryer's daughter. That was absurd.

"Patsy, isn't that her name? Or is it Jane? I know the oldest is Betty, but always got the younger two confused."

He turned his gaze back to Victoria as his entire body went cold.

A wicked gleam of amusement flashed in her eyes. "I can see why you've kept it a secret, but not William. Marrying them off to the rich and famous is his goal. He hopes that will finally get him accepted into the upper class."

He'd been duped. This whole time. Libby. He knew that wasn't her name. Dryer had to be behind all this. The man had been furious when he'd left his office last month. "When have you seen Dryer's daughters?" he asked.

"Church," Victoria said. "That's the only place William lets them go." She shrugged. "He was so worried men would snatch them up. Men after his money." She laughed. "I swear, that man squeaks when he walks he's so tight. His wealth is the only thing he guards more closely than his daughters."

Satisfied every last lock of her hair was tightly tucked beneath her hat, Patsy turned away from the mirror. If she wasn't so light-headed from Lane kissing her, truly kissing her, she might take a moment to admire the fine furnishings of the powder room. Everything in the room glittered like gold beneath the glow of the overhead light.

Or maybe she was still seeing stars. Kissing Lane had been like something out of this world. She was still breathless over it. She'd been kissed before, since she'd started living two lives, but none of those other pecks could even compare to Lane's kiss.

Couldn't even come close.

No, siree.

Lord, but that had been amazing!

His kiss had lit up her insides like fireworks. Her heart was still beating ten times faster than it should, and just thinking about it had her insides humming and tingling, and…crazy. Pure crazy.

She couldn't wait to get to his side. Stand next to him. Smell his cologne. Feel the heat of his body. Have him lay a hand on the small of her back.

She wouldn't have left his side if her hat had stayed in place. It wasn't likely anyone had recognized her, but if anyone was to ever recognize her or her sisters, it would be because of their hair. Everyone else in the entire world had fashionable short hair, except for her and her sisters. And Mother. Father refused to let any of them do more than trim the ends of their long tresses. That's why they always wore hats or full headdresses that they could securely tuck their hair beneath, when they went out at night.

She pulled open the door and stepped into the crowded hallway. The butterflies took flight in her stomach all over again. Lane was near the doorway to the room they'd danced in. He was so darb. So handsome. And could cut a rug like no other.

She started making her way down the hallway, smiling, until someone behind him caught her attention. Her smile fell as recognition hit.

Charlie! Could it be him? The same man who'd told her about the money.

The money. Rex Gaynor. How had all that slipped her mind? Now that she knew more about writing, she had to…

Her thoughts slipped back to kissing Lane. Why had he kissed her?

Because he liked her?

That couldn't happen.

She couldn't like him, either.

Not to the point they kissed each other.

That would ruin everything.

Shouldering her way along the hall, squeezing up against the wall at times to make it past neatly dressed men and women taking up more space than necessary, she kept an eye on Charlie. It was him. She was sure of it. And he was walking toward the stairs leading to the second floor behind Lane.

Her stomach clenched. Lane was waiting for her. He had a cocktail in one hand, but she had to ask Charlie where he'd learned about the money and might not get another chance.

She hurried past Lane and had one foot on the stairway, when a hand grabbed her arm.

"Where are you going?" Lane asked.

"That's him," she whispered, nodding toward Charlie, who was at the top of the landing talking to another man. "The man with the mustache."

"Him who?"

"The man who told me about the money Rex Gaynor had stolen," she answered quietly. "I have to ask him how he knows about it."

Lane's hold on her arm tightened.

She glanced toward him, wondering why he wouldn't let her go, and froze at the frown on his face, the angry glare in his eyes. "What's wrong?"

He shook his head and looked away. "It's time for us to leave."

"It can't be," she said. "Not yet. I need to talk to that man. I may not get another chance."

"No."

She twisted her arm but couldn't break his hold. "He's right there on the landing. The one with the mustache."

Still frowning, Lane looked up the staircase, at the men still standing there, talking. He squinted, and was still squinting when he looked back at her. "This game you're playing is over. We're leaving."

"Game? What game?"

He didn't answer, just pulled her to the door, and out it, and then toward the car without saying a word.

What had happened while she was in the powder room to make him so angry? She hadn't been gone that long.

Her stomach suddenly sank. Was he angry about kissing her? About how she'd kissed him back? Nothing else had happened.

Or had it? Had he seen that Charlie, and knew that's who she'd gotten the information about the money from and wanted to get the scoop on her? He must have.

He'd read her writing and was now trying to get the scoop on her!

They'd arrived at the car and he'd opened her door. Shooting him a glare as nasty as the one on his face, she climbed in and grabbed the door, slamming it shut.

She'd thought he was different, was someone she could trust, but he wasn't. He'd probably made up all that stuff about why he'd wanted to become a reporter just to get her to trust him, and now that he knew who her informant was…

She squeezed her eyes shut at how they suddenly burned and breathed through her nose at the pain clenching her chest. Maybe Father was right when he said that she and her sister weren't allowed to date because they had no idea how to spot a good man. An honest one who wouldn't just be nice to them only because they wanted their father's money.

He may not know about her father's money, but he had wanted to know where she'd gotten her information about the stolen money.

Her insides flinched when Lane climbed in and shut his door.

As he started the car and steered around the parked cars in front of them, she continued to breathe through her nose, promising herself that she wasn't going to say a word. Not a single word. In fact, she was never going to talk to him again.

Ever.

"It's time you told me what's really going on here."

"Why don't you tell me?" she snapped, then clamped her teeth together at having already broken the oath she'd made to herself.

"No, Patsy, I think you have more to say than I do."

She kept her chin up and stared out the passenger window.

"That is your name, isn't it? Patsy Dryer?"

Her stomach dropped, and her hands started to shake. He had called her Patsy. Twice. No. No. No! This couldn't be happening!

"How long did you think you were going to get away using a name like Liberty Bell?"

A knot formed in her stomach. That had been foolish, but he'd caught her off guard by asking about her last name yesterday. They'd been driving by a church, with a bell tower, and Bell had just shot out of her mouth. Swallowing against a fat lump filling her throat, she asked, "Who told you?"

"Does it matter?" He huffed out a breath. "No, it doesn't. What matters is that I won't be duped, Patsy. Not by you or your father."

She went cold. "My father?"

"No more games, Patsy."

"Wh—what does my father have to do with anything?"

"He's the one who put you up to this, pretending to want to become a reporter."

"No, he's not. He doesn't—" She pressed her lips shut. She couldn't tell him the truth, rat out her sisters.

"Doesn't what?"

She folded her arms across her chest, tucked her trembling hands beneath her arms and stared straight ahead, willing her tongue to not defy her again.

After a short time, he said, "I'll be talking to him tomorrow. Put an end to this whole sham."

Her heart leaped into her throat. "No! You can't talk to my father. Please, Lane, please, please, please. He doesn't know anything about anything."

"I don't believe that for a minute. Your father has been searching for husbands for his daughters, and set you on me. I'm not one of them. Won't be one of them. I'm not marrying anyone."

"I'm not, either! I don't want to get married. Not ever."

He shook his head.

Tears pouring down her face burned her cheeks. "I'm telling the truth, Lane. That's why I want to be a reporter, so I don't have to get married. It's the truth, I swear!"

He turned a corner, and cold dread filled her as they rolled past the Rooster's Nest. Her sisters were going to be so mad at her. This truly would ruin everything.

The car rolled to a stop near the street corner. She grabbed a hold of the door handle.

He reached over and grasped her wrist. "The streetcar won't be here for at least half an hour."

She closed her eyes against the tears that continued to flow. "My father doesn't know about us going out at night," she said, hoping the truth would help. "We don't want to marry the men he's chosen for us."

"Chosen?"

She nodded, although Father had mentioned only whom Betty would marry, she was certain the others would be like James Bauer. "You aren't one of them. I swear." Her sisters were going to be so angry. "Wh— who told you my name?"

He released her wrist and she flinched slightly because for a moment, she thought he was going to touch her face, but then he put his hand on the car shifter. "Victoria Lloyd. She recognized you from church."

Patsy closed her eyes. She wouldn't recall having seen Victoria at church, because like everywhere else, Father didn't allow them to interact with very many people. "I'm telling the truth, Lane, I swear. My father knows nothing about this." She pulled open the door handle. "Please believe me."

She leaped out of the car, shut the door and ran to the space between the buildings to wait for her sisters. Tears still ran down her cheeks. Once between the buildings, she leaned against the solid bricks as sobs shook her entire body. Her life was over.

Over.

What was she going to do?

How could everything go from wonderful to awful in the blink of an eye?

She had to think. Think of something she could do.

Pushing off the wall, she paced between the two buildings. It hadn't gone to disastrous yet. Her father didn't know. Or her sisters.

But even if Lane didn't tell her father, Victoria Lloyd might.

Oh, this was awful. Completely awful.

There had to be something she could do.

By the time Jane appeared in the opening between the buildings, Patsy had concluded that she wouldn't tell them what had happened.

Not yet.

"Come on," Jane whispered. "The trolley's coming. Betty's right behind me."

Patsy hurried out from between the buildings, and her

didn't own that property, mainly because it was too hilly to be developed.

Air stuck in his lungs as Libby—no Patsy—entered his mind. He still wasn't sure if she was serious about becoming a reporter, or if that truly had been a ruse put in place by her father, hoping to find her a rich husband. A completely sleepless night hadn't given him any insight, either.

He'd done some researching on the guy, Charlie, she'd pointed out last night. Turns out the man's name was Vincent Burrows. He was fairly new to the bootlegging scene, but not to the mob. He had connections that went back to this house, and the original owners. The house was only a mile down the road from the Dryer home and that made him wonder if there was more of a connection that she hadn't told him about.

Lane knelt down and ran a hand over the trampled grass. Then glanced at the length of the trail again. From the gravel road, to the paved street. This wasn't a game trail. It was a people trail.

Odd place for one.

He stood and walked toward the large pillared porch on the front of the boarded-up house.

Odd, too, was the fact the front door was unlocked.

Boards had been nailed over the windows from the outside, and it took his eyes a moment to adjust to the darkness after stepping inside.

Dust motes floated in the light coming in from the open door behind him, and busy spiders had spun webs between the spindles of the curved staircase leading to the second floor.

But what he noticed most was the floor, and how the dust had been disturbed. He couldn't make out actual feet stumbled over themselves at the sight of Lane's car still parked at the curb. He was still in it, too.

She caught her footing and ran past it, following Jane to the corner, where they climbed onto the trolley, along with Betty, who arrived right behind them.

They took separate seats, and remained silent until after stepping off the streetcar again.

Then Jane wanted to know about the party. Patsy tried to sound normal, happy, and told them she and Lane won the dance-off, which almost caused her to start crying again. For the first time ever, she was glad to see the tree line of their property, and the silence that came as they entered it.

Once inside, she went straight to her room, and locked the door so Jane wouldn't be able to come in and ask any more questions.

She lay down on her bed, and let the tears flow. The sorrow filling her was so great, her entire being hurt, and a large part of that hurt was due to Lane, of how angry he'd been. How he'd thought she'd been lying to him.

The kiss they'd shared had been so amazing, everything about him had been so amazing, and now all of that, all of her memories, were tarnished.

She was still sick to her stomach and worried about what to do when it was time to get out of bed. After getting dressed in an ankle-length dull blue dress, she brushed her hair and made sure there were no traces of makeup on her face before going downstairs.

Where things got worse when a row at breakfast, over whose turn it was to drive Mother downtown shopping, made Betty so angry she left the table without eating, and slammed her bedroom door. Betty never slammed doors, never argued with Father. He'd stormed out shortly afterward complaining about how ungrateful they all were.

Patsy had sat silent, trembling, through the entire row, knowing if he ever learned about their flapper lives, he'd be furious. It had been Betty's turn to drive Mother, something they usually each looked forward to. Mother had agreed that Jane could drive her, but Father had said no, that it was Betty's turn, and Betty would be the one to go, insisting that Jane had other chores to complete.

They always had other chores to complete. It was Father's way of keeping them home, keeping them busy.

Betty's eyes were puffy and rimmed red when she left with Mother, and Jane instantly started rolling up the rugs downstairs because it was mopping day.

Patsy went upstairs to do the same, but the minute she noticed the bathroom window was open, she knew what she had to do. She had to go see Lane.

Chapter Eight

Lane surveyed the property as he walked toward the house. He'd parked down the road and would keep on walking past if he saw any movement.

The house wasn't old, or in bad shape, except for the fact it had sat empty for almost three years. A mob boss had built it, and used it to house the operation of his liquor distribution. The bust of this place had been one of the biggest in LA by federal prohibition agents. One of the few, too. Without the support from local police, who despised having to cooperate with the agents, busts had dwindled down to nothing more than clearing out a speakeasy for a night every now and again to merely make it look like the federal law was being enforced.

There was no real sign that anyone had been to the house on a regular basis, other than what looked like a trail that led through the side of the yard near a row of trees. It went from the gravel road behind the house all the way to the paved street in front of it.

He left the street to take a closer look at how the grass had been trampled. At first, he'd wondered if it had been some sort of wild game, coming down from the Santa Monica Mountains across the gravel road. William Dryer

footprints, but someone had been here recently. There was a clear dust-free path.

He eased the door closed and waited another moment for his eyes to adjust to the almost complete darkness and then walked past the staircase toward the hallway and the other rooms it led to.

The area was completely void of furniture, and even his soft footsteps echoed off the walls and high ceiling.

Following the pathway on the floor, he made his way down the hallway and into a kitchen, again void of furniture and appliances, but hosting built-in cupboards, counters, and a sink. The only light was from small cracks between the boards nailed outside the window. Not enough light to see where the path in the dust on the floor went, but it had definitely led to this room.

There were three doors. One obviously went outside, and was nailed shut by boards that covered the window from the outside. Of the other two, one wasn't shut tight. He'd guess that's where whoever had been here had gone.

A basement.

He stepped carefully, quietly. Someone could be down there.

"Is anyone here?"

His heart slammed against his rib cage and he momentarily froze, until he realized the sound of a woman's voice had come from the front door.

"Lane?"

Recognizing the voice, he ground his back teeth together. He spun on one heel, rushed out of the room and into the hallway. Where he ran directly into her.

Libby. No. Patsy.

"What the hell—"

"What are you doing here?" she continued.

She'd spoken at the same time as him, only louder.

He pressed a hand to her lips and rather than answering, whispered, "What are you doing here?" He already knew. "Looking for Burrows?"

She pushed his hand aside to whisper, "Who?"

"Vincent Burrows, the Charlie you pointed out last night."

"That's his name?"

"Yes." Flustered, he ran a hand through his hair. It was dark in the hallway, but not that dark. He could make out her features perfectly, as well as the blond waves of hair cascading over her shoulders. "What are you doing here?"

"I saw you walk inside." She glanced up at the cobwebs hanging down from the ceiling. "No one's lived here for a long time."

He took a hold of her arm, spun her around and held his breath as her perfume wafted in the air. "Let's go."

She took a step, but then stopped. "What are you doing here?"

Not willing to go into his reasons behind anything right now, he asked, "Do your parents know you're here?"

"Of course not." She twisted her arm, trying to break his hold. "I snuck out to go to the *Gazette*, to see you."

"Why?"

"Because you have to believe I'm telling the truth. That my father doesn't know anything about me knowing you, about me wanting to become a reporter."

The pleading in her eyes was enough to gut him.

"The only thing I lied to you about is my name, and now... Now, I've ruined everything."

Frustration burned his chest. "What's *everything*?"

She sighed and leaned back against the wall. "My father is very strict. Very, very strict, and now that we've all grown up, it's become worse. He's already found a man for Betty to marry, but she doesn't want to marry James.

None of us want to marry the men Father will choose because he's only worried about them having enough money so they won't want any of his."

He'd witnessed that, so had to believe that much.

"None of us really even want to get married," she continued. "We want to live. See things. Do things. We've had someone telling us what to do our entire lives, and once Father finds out…" She shook her head.

He didn't want to tell her father anything, but would have to soon, with the way the rumor of their engagement was spreading. Two of his own reporters had asked him about it this morning.

"I won't bother you anymore," she said. "I won't send you any more articles or—"

They both froze at the sound of thudding footsteps. The light in the hallway had already told him she'd left the front door open, partially at least. He pressed a finger to his lips and pulled her backward, into the kitchen. Convinced whoever had just arrived on the front porch would be heading toward the basement door that had been left open a crack, he opened the other door and pulled her inside.

It was a broom closet.

A small one that had them pressed together, chest to chest. It was dark too, but, because they were so close, his eyes adjusted enough to see her clearly.

"Who—?"

"Shh!" he whispered. Their lips were but inches apart, and he instantly thought of last night, when they'd kissed. The very thing he'd tried not to think about since the moment it happened. She'd responded to that kiss with the same enthusiasm she displayed while dancing the shimmy. Unabashed exuberance.

Her eyes grew wide at the sound of approaching footsteps. Hurried ones.

He wrapped his arms around her waist and pulled her tighter against him, and hoped she knew, believed, that he'd protect her from whatever, whoever, was out there. He would. He just couldn't protect her from her father. That was none of his business and he couldn't get involved in that.

The footsteps went past the closet door, and a moment later, they echoed off the basement steps, and faded.

Patsy looked up at him.

He gave her a reassuring smile.

"Who would be in this house?" she asked, barely making a sound.

"Burrows," he answered, just as quietly.

"Why?" Her eyes grew wide. "The money."

"Shh!"

She nodded, and then closed her eyes and leaned her forehead against his chest. He gave her a reassuring hug. He would protect her from Burrows. Fully. Completely. No one would blame him that a story got in the way of that this time. That's what had happened with Naomi. Her parents had blamed him for her and Sarah's deaths. Had said if he had been more committed to his family than his newspaper, he would have been on the train with them, could have protected them.

The silence burned his ears, and memories burned his stomach, his chest. The newspaper hadn't meant more to him. He'd been working day and night back then, for his family, so that he would have the money to properly take care of them. Feed them. Clothe them. House them. Her parents hadn't seen it that way.

Naomi had. She'd known how hard he was working, and that's why she'd gone to her mother's, to have help with Sarah until she was feeling better. She'd been distraught over not being able to keep up with cooking, cleaning and taking care of Sarah. He hadn't minded helping out with those things, and truly had just wanted her to feel better. When she'd suggested going to San Diego, he'd struggled with agreeing and vowed to help her more, until he'd come home and found her slumped over the kitchen table, asleep, and a pot of potatoes almost boiled dry on the stove.

It had been seven years ago, and they'd had some wonderful times during their short two years together, yet, that was the image he recalled every time he thought of her. Pale. Lifeless. A ghost of the sweet, gentle woman he'd married.

Patsy lifted her head and stretched on her toes to whisper next to his ear, "Do we dare make a run for it? I can run fast. Really fast."

Despite hiding in a closet of an abandoned house, a chuckle formed in the back of his throat. She was spirited and daring and believed she could do anything she set her mind to. Why couldn't her father see that?

"No," he answered. "We are not going to make a run for it."

"Then what are we going to do? We can't stay here forever."

"Don't worry. We won't stay here forever."

She dropped back down on her heels and looked up at him while nibbling on her bottom lip. He'd seen her do that often, and knew she was thinking about something. Making a run for it, no doubt. Probably how to convince him that's what they should do. The thought of kissing her, just to get the idea of making a run for it of out her mind, crossed his.

Actually, it hadn't just crossed his mind. He'd been

thinking about it the entire time they've been in the closet. Even while other thoughts and memories had floated by.

"I'm not worried," she said. "I—"

"Shh!" he interrupted and pressed her against his chest.

And held her there for two reasons.

One to keep her quiet.

Two, to keep him from kissing her.

The thudding of footsteps sounded again, and grew closer. Coming up the steps. They stopped momentarily, then started again as a door shut. The steps weren't as fast this time. They were slow, almost purposeful.

She trembled. He rested his chin atop her head and tightened his hold on her even more.

The footsteps went past the closet door, and continued.

Lane held his breath, hoping that would allow him to hear better. Still, the footsteps faded beyond hearing distance, but a moment later, the front door closed.

Releasing the air in his lungs, he also lessened his hold on Patsy. Finding the doorknob was easy. It had been jabbing into his hip the entire time. He shifted enough to grasp a hold of it. "Wait here."

She clutched onto his suit coat with both hands. "Where are you going?"

"To see if the coast is clear."

"Oh." She let go of his coat and smoothed the material flat again. "Be careful."

He turned the knob and pushed open the door enough to peer out. Sensing the space was empty more than seeing due to the darkness, he eased out and glanced around. Nothing.

Quietly, he stepped out of the closet, and keeping his heels off the floor, he walked on the balls of his feet across the kitchen, then down the hall, and then through the front room. Arriving at the door, he carefully pushed aside the stiff-with-dust curtain covering the round window in the door.

A man was walking away, toward the corner of the house, and every muscle in Lane's body tensed at the man's build. His broad shoulders, lean hips, long and lanky legs, and at his coal-black hair. "Rex Gaynor."

"Where?"

Lane spun around.

Patsy shot past him and pulled back the curtain to peer out. "That's Rex Gaynor? How do you know?"

"I told you to stay in the closet."

"I wasn't staying in there by myself." She pulled open the door. "We have to see where he's going."

She was out the door before he could stop her.

"Shh!" he hissed while closing the door behind him.

She slowed, and shot him a grimace over her shoulder as she rose onto her tiptoes and stepped down the porch steps. He crossed the porch in one leap and took the stairs in another one, grabbing her around the waist with one hand on his way. Crouched low, they snuck past the porch and to the side of the house.

The man, Gaynor, was walking toward the gravel road.

"Where is he going?" she asked.

"I don't know," he answered.

Gaynor was zigzagging between the trees and bushes in the yard as he walked, to stay as hidden as possible. He was also carrying something that he kept glancing at.

"What's in his hand?" Patsy asked.

"I don't know. I think it's a piece of paper."

Patsy's heart was beating so fast and furiously she could barely breathe. She bit her lip but couldn't keep silent. "It's a map," she whispered. "Of where he hid the money!" She shot upright. "We have to follow him."

Lane tightened his hold on her waist. "You aren't going anywhere."

"He's crossing the road. There's nothing up there but woods and foothills of the Santa Monica Mountains." Urgency filled her. "We'll lose him if we don't hurry."

"There is no *we* in this." Lane twisted her around. "You are going home. Now."

"No, I'm not." She leaned back to glance around the corner of the house. Gaynor had crossed the road and would soon disappear in the thick bushes and then heavy woods. Lane had released her waist and taken a step back. She had to act fast. "You can go home if you want to, but I'm following him."

Spinning around, she ran to a big tree, and then peered around the side, making sure that Gaynor hadn't noticed anything.

It appeared he hadn't because he kept walking, straight into the bushes.

She was about to run to the next tree when Lane grabbed her waist again and spun her around to face him. Pinching her lips together, she closed her eyes. Being stuck in the closet with him had done something to her. She'd felt dizzy and couldn't stop thinking about kissing him again. That feeling was still there, making thinking straight difficult. She'd dreamed about him last night, during the few minutes she'd slept. About kissing him.

She'd been shocked to see him enter the abandoned house while walking down the road, but was overly glad that she didn't have to venture all the way downtown in order to talk to him.

"You are not following him."

She snapped open her eyes. "Yes, I am." He wasn't

the only one she had to worry about telling their father about her escapade. Victoria Lloyd might. But this. This could be her answer. If she could catch Gaynor, turn him over to the police. She could tell her father that's why she'd snuck out last night, to find out where he was hiding. It was everyone's civic duty to assist the police whenever possible.

"What are you going to do when he sees you? Knows you're following him? He's much bigger and stronger than you."

He would have to point that out. She glanced over her shoulder, around the tree. Gaynor was no longer in sight. Her chance was slipping away.

Knowing Lane would stop her if he could, she slumped against the tree and pulled his hands off her waist. "Fine."

He released her. "Fine, you'll go home?"

She nodded.

He let out a long sigh and stepped back. "I know—"

"I'll go home later." She spun around and shot out from behind the tree, and didn't stop running until she'd crossed the gravel road and entered the brush. That's when Lane grabbed a hold of her waist again and lifted her right off the ground.

Twisting to look at him over her shoulder, she saw a car instead, coming up the road. "Duck! Someone's coming up the road."

Lane put her down, and they both crouched down behind the bushes. The car, a big black one, rolled past and continued up the road.

"We can't let him get away, Lane," she whispered. "Just can't."

He huffed out a breath. "I know."

"The longer we waste arguing, the farther away he gets."

"I know that, too."

Hoping that he'd finally stop arguing with her, she added, "We'll just follow him, see where he goes. Then we can tell the police and they can arrest him."

He shook his head.

She clasped her hands together and held them against her chest. "Please, Lane. Please. I have to do this."

"You're wearing a dress."

"So?" She pointed to his clothes, a brown suit and white shirt, which made him look as handsome as ever. "You're wearing a suit and tie."

He glanced around and then shook his head as his gaze landed on her again. "You'll come back, won't you? If I make you leave, you'll come back."

"Yes."

Huffing out a breath, he stood and helped her upright. "Let's go, then, but stay behind me, and obey everything I say."

Excitement flared inside her. "I will. I promise."

He turned around and led the way deeper into the brush.

She stayed right on his heels. "How do you know which way to go?" she asked when he'd veered left.

"The broken branches." He pointed toward the bushes. "See how the leaves have been knocked off?"

"Yes. How did you know to look for that?"

"From being a kid, roaming in the woods."

This was so thrilling, sneaking through the woods with him, whispering. "Really? That must have been fun."

"It was." He held a branch so it wouldn't hit her. "I used to camp out in the woods, too, with my father and grandfather."

"Did you live around here?"

"No, we'd lived up north when I was younger. They are both gone now. My father died in the war, my grandfather had died before then."

She had to wait until he walked through a narrow space between the thick bushes before she could ask, "What about your mother?"

"She died a few years after my dad did."

"I'm sorry." She was. The odd tightening in her chest said so. Her parents may have rules that drove her crazy, but she did love them, and couldn't imagine how awful it would be if one of them were to die.

"Thank you."

The brush was giving way to tall trees and more open ground. He paused, scanning the ground carefully, and then started walking again.

"Stay close," he whispered, "and be careful where you step."

"Why?"

His expression was completely serious. "Snakes."

They'd had plenty of snakes in their yard, and though they startled her, they didn't frighten her. "Too bad we don't have a shovel." She glanced around and saw a long stick. Walking over, she picked it up. "Here's the next best thing."

Frowning, he asked, "What are you going to do with that?"

"Kill a snake if I see one." Shrugging, she walked back to his side. "Most likely we won't see one. They'll probably feel us coming and slither away."

He started walking. "Who taught you that?"

"My father. Snakes come down the hills all the time."

He nodded and then weaved left. "This way."

Though trees surrounded them, there was an opening

near their peaks, where she could see the side of a big hill. And movement. "Look. Is that him?"

Lane peered in the direction she pointed. "Yes," he whispered. "Sound carries out here." He pressed a finger to his lips.

That was exactly why she and her sisters never spoke upon entering their own yard each night. Clamping her lips together, she nodded.

He grinned and shook his head as if amused.

Happiness welled up inside her as they continued forward, through tall grass, over fallen logs and around massive trees, moving as fast as possible. Lane seemed to know exactly where to step, where to weave left and right. Without him, Patsy was sure she'd have lost Rex Gaynor's trail long ago. Not Lane. One more thing he was amazing at. He kept weaving around or through whatever was in front of them, finding the right path to keep them going forward, and up the side of the foothills.

She was thankful for the stick she'd picked up. Not because of snakes. Because it gave her something to hold onto as the trek became steeper. Lane gave her his hand, and helped her over some of the steeper rocks.

As she made it to the top of a flat formation, Lane pressed a finger to his lips. "There's a cabin," he said so softly she barely heard.

"Where?" she mouthed.

He pointed down the other side. She scanned the area, not seeing anything except trees.

"Look right between those two big ponderosa pine trees," he whispered.

She saw it then, a small wooden structure. "What do we do now?"

Chapter Nine

Lane stared down the hill, to the shack that Gaynor had entered. The smart thing to do would be to head back down the hill and call the police, tell them where the convict was hiding out. That would take time and there was no telling how long Gaynor would be here. Maybe that had been a map in Gaynor's hand, and this was where the money was hidden. Cross country, it wasn't that far from where the train robbery had taken place. Seven years ago, the city wasn't as big, and getting here would have been a cinch.

Or, Gaynor could have left the money someplace, had someone else hide it, and this was where they did just that.

Hard telling.

The money was of no consequence to him. Getting Gaynor back behind bars was what he wanted to see. He'd forgotten that the last couple days. Had been too interested in other things. Mainly the flapper beside him. That had never happened before. In fact, she had been the reason he'd gone to the abandoned house this morning. "I'm going down there," he whispered. "You wait here."

"I'm not waiting here." She planted her walking stick in the ground. "This stick is for snakes, not bears."

For someone he'd sworn whom he was never going to see again, he'd spent the last two hours, or more, with her, and enjoyed it. She'd just trekked over a mile without a single complaint. In a dress. She wasn't wearing heels, but the flat shoes she was wearing didn't have very good soles. Watching her climb the rocks had made him nervous that she might fall, get hurt.

He was nervous about leaving her here alone, too, and about having her follow him down the hill. Of the two, keeping her close was the best choice, so he nodded. "All right, but you are not going in the cabin."

"Deal," she whispered, gesturing with her chin. "That's not a cabin. It's a dilapidated shack."

He didn't bother agreeing, already convinced the shack was going to look worse the closer they got.

It did.

If not for the solid and chinked-together logs, the old hut would have fallen down years ago.

Keeping her close to his side, Lane had worked their way down the hill and around to the front of the windowless shack. There was only the one door, and Gaynor had left it partially open. Not enough to see if anyone was inside. He couldn't hear anything, either, but was convinced Gaynor was in there.

He'd chosen a spot with plenty of cover for Patsy to watch the front door while he made his way around to the other, and then, inside.

Huffing out a breath, he whispered, "Watch the front door." That would keep her in place better than telling her to stay put.

He hoped.

"You have to keep an eye on the door for me," he repeated, reinforcing his hope that she would stay hidden.

She nodded and handed him her walking stick. He took it. Figuring it was better than nothing. The idea of kissing her, just a quick one, made him spin around and take off. That couldn't happen again. He was already going to pay hell for being anywhere near her.

That was a given, and there wasn't anything he could do about it right now, except to keep her safe.

Staying low to the ground, he made his way through the shrub and pines to the side of the shack, and then quietly crept along the outside wall, mentally preparing himself to rush the door. He had no experience on such things, definitely not in his normal line of work, and was going strictly on instinct.

Once at the corner, and not sure what else to do, he counted to three, then jumped around the corner and kicked the door wide open. Holding the stick with both hands, and angled across the front of him, he shouted, "Gaynor!"

"Lane? I wasn't sure if that was you following me or not. It's not Gaynor, it's Henry Randall."

The words shocked Lane. So did the man who stepped out from behind the door. "Henry?"

"Yeah, it's me," Henry said, holding out a hand. "I've been hoping to talk to you."

Lane leaned Patsy's walking stick against the outside wall and pumped the man's hand. Henry was an FBI agent, and had worked on the train robbery. The two of them had gotten to know each other during that time, but last he'd heard, Henry had gone back east, to Washington, DC. "What are you doing here?"

"Off the record?" Henry asked.

"Of course."

"Pretending to be Rex Gaynor."

"Why?"

"Because Gaynor's dead."

"Dead?"

Henry nodded.

Lane hadn't seen Gaynor in years, but would never forget what he looked like. Henry's height, broad build and black hair were similar enough to Rex's that some could believe he was Gaynor, from the back, like he had, but from the front, Henry's facial features weren't chiseled enough. Gaynor's face had looked like it had been carved out of stone, with deep-set dark eyes that had shimmered with evil. Henry's eyes weren't deep set, or evil, and even when he was serious, they looked like he was hiding a smile.

Lane had been prepared to come face-to-face with Gaynor, face the revenge the man had instilled in him years ago, and hearing the man was dead left him in a quandary. He held no remorse, but Gaynor's death meant there was no one to avenge for Naomi's and Sarah's deaths. He was contemplating that when Patsy arrived at his side.

"Why did you shake his hand?" she asked, flipping her long hair away from her face.

"Because I know him." Lane stopped before saying more. The heavy rise and fall of her chest said she'd ran down the hill, and the way she held another stick in her hand said she was ready to use it. He grasped the stick and lowered it to the ground.

She glanced at Henry. "Who is he?"

Lane looked toward Henry, offering an apology because Patsy had already figured out he wasn't Rex Gaynor. She knew he wouldn't have shaken hands with

Gaynor. Henry was undercover, and the answer to that question was up to him.

Henry's return gaze was full of questions as he glanced between him and Patsy.

"She's trustworthy," Lane said.

Henry gave her a quick nod. "Henry Randall, ma'am."

The frown between her eyes grew. "Where's Rex Gaynor?"

"He's not here," Lane said.

"It's not much, but come in." Henry, dressed in a pair of gray trousers, white shirt and suspenders, stepped aside and waved them to enter the cabin.

Lane rested a hand on Patsy's back, encouraging her to step in first. He followed.

"I'll leave the door open so we have some light," Henry said.

Lane nodded as he and Patsy entered the small cabin. The inside was in better shape than the outside. They sat down on the two chairs at a small table in the center of the room that Henry gestured toward.

"Does she work for you?" Henry asked while he took a seat on a cot covered with a blanket.

There was also a small coal cookstove, cabinet and a suitcase in the corner. Lane completed his scan of the room by returning his gaze to Henry. Having contemplated how to answer, he gave a nod. "Yes, she's working with me." He had to bite back a smile at the way Patsy's neck snapped around. The shocked look on her face quickly disappeared and a smile formed. That was partially true, and Lane needed to know what was going on with Henry and Gaynor.

"So, what did she find out from Vincent Burrows?" Henry asked.

The hair on Lane's arms stood.

"What's going on here?" Patsy asked. "Who are you?" She looked at Lane. "Who is he? How do you know him?"

Henry shrugged, letting Lane know it was up to him to answer.

Careful, knowing she'd soak up everything he said, Lane gestured toward Henry. "This is Henry Russell, an FBI agent who worked on the Rex Gaynor case when the train was robbed."

"I would have contacted you, Lane, if I'd been able to." Henry shook his head. "I knew the news of Gaynor's escape would be distressing for you."

"More like unbelievable," Lane admitted. Henry knew about Naomi and Sarah, and how Lane had not only reported about it, he'd helped see that Gaynor was put behind bars for the rest of his life. "Gaynor's dead?" Lane asked, solidifying the fact in his mind.

Henry nodded.

"Dead?" Patsy asked. "The newspaper said he escaped."

"That's what I was told," Lane replied. It didn't make sense for officials to make up a story that he'd escaped. "He was in a maximum security prison," Lane added. "What happened?"

Henry lifted a brow. "Someone killed him."

"Who? How?"

"Moonshine," Henry answered. "The first cup."

Generally, the first drops out of a still were pure poison. Widow-maker juice. Not only did it smell like rubbing alcohol, it tasted awful. Moonshiners commonly discarded the first cup out of every batch because the shine produced before optimal temperature was reached was pure methanol. Even a small amount could cause blindness or death. "How did he acquire moonshine in prison?"

"Don't know." Henry flashed a brief glance toward Patsy. "The man who presumably gave it to him was found dead, too. With an empty flask."

"When?" Lane asked.

"A week ago," Henry answered as his gaze shifted to Patsy again. "We believe Vincent Burrows was behind it. The man who presumably gave Gaynor the moonshine used to work for Burrows, one of his torpedoes, and had recently received a visit from a petite blonde woman."

Lane didn't like the way Henry was looking at Patsy. "It wasn't her."

The shiver that rippled up Patsy's spine made her gasp. "Me? You think it was me?" Her insides started trembling.

Lane reached over and took a hold of her hand. "No."

"He does." She leveled a glare at Henry. If he really worked for the FBI, why was he holed up in the woods, pretending to be an escaped convict? She'd find out, right after finding out why he would think she had anything to do with it. "Why would you think it was me?"

Henry leaned back and folded his arms over his chest. "You appeared to know Burrows well the other night at the Rooster's Nest."

Her entire body went stiff. Lane squeezed her hand, but it didn't ease the way her insides quivered due to the distrust shimmering in the other man's eyes.

"The way the two of you talked and danced," Henry continued.

"I was trying to find out more information about Rex Gaynor." Determined to prove her innocence, she added, "And I did. He told me about the money."

Her heart skipped a beat at the way Henry looked at Lane. As if he was now questioning him.

Lane shook his head. "I've never told anyone about the money." He glanced at her, and nodded. "Burrows told her. Proving he knows about it. Question is, who told him?"

"That's why I'm undercover," Henry said. "We figure that's why Gaynor was offed. Someone knows about the unrecovered money, and is now looking to recover it." He stood and the look in his eyes was somewhat sympathetic. "It's been years, Lane, and considering all you lost in that accident—"

Lane released her hand and stood. "Hold on, Henry. You can't possibly believe that I have anything to do behind this."

Confusion filled Patsy.

"I hope not, Lane, but we have to look at every avenue. You lost your wife and daughter in that train robbery, a man doesn't get over that easily, and—"

"No, they don't. But do you honestly think that now, after all these years, I'd decide to partner up with the mob and off a prisoner?"

Patsy swallowed the lump in her throat. Wife and daughter? Lane had a wife and daughter who died during the train robbery? She looked up at Lane, wondering why he'd never mentioned that. Why he hadn't told her this was more than a story, that he was seeking justice for himself, his family. A knot formed in her stomach. No wonder he'd said he wasn't interested in marrying anyone.

Henry let out a long sigh and ran a hand through his hair. "No, Lane, I don't." He sat down on the cot again. "But I, we, had expected Burrows to take the bait, think I was Gaynor, but so far, that hasn't happened. I've given him chances, too. At the docks and at speakeasies. Either Burrows knows I'm not him, or he knows Gaynor died."

Patsy glanced between Henry and Lane, who both appeared to be deep in thought. She bit down on her bottom lip, and tried to stop herself from thinking about the other questions hopping about in her head, like why he'd kissed her, when he was still in love with his wife, but truly couldn't hold her silence any longer. She had to help. That would prove to him that she'd been telling the truth. That she was doing this because she wanted to be a reporter. "I could find out."

Both men turned to her. Lane was frowning and shaking his head, but Henry appeared to like the idea.

"I know I could make him tell me," she said. Burrows had told her about the money and would surely tell her more.

"No," Lane said. "It's too dangerous."

"Not with you, and me, nearby," Henry said.

"No," Lane repeated. "It won't work." Pointing at her, he continued, "She sneaks out at night, to go to speakeasies. If her father finds out, even the FBI will be in trouble."

Frowning, Henry stood, and looked at her for so long she was sure he was boring a hole smack into the center of her forehead. Finally, with an odd gleam in his eyes, he asked, "You're one of William Dryer's daughters, aren't you?"

Frustration and a hint of fear had her holding her breath.

"Yes, she is," Lane said.

Henry muttered a curse under his breath. She didn't hear the exact word, but knew it was a curse.

Huffing out the hot air burning her lungs, she said, "That doesn't matter. I'm careful. My father won't know anything about it. No one will." Certain that wasn't changing their minds, she continued, "Vincent Burrows was at a party Lane and I were at last night. I'm sure he'll be at another one. I'll ask him to dance, and question him, and—"

"No," both men said at the same time.

Flustered, she jumped to her feet. "What else are you going to do? Everyone knows who Lane is, so Burrows will never talk to him, and you said you already tried, that he must not believe you are Gaynor." She could help him. Had to help him. It would prove that their kiss meant nothing to her, too. That she didn't want to get married, either. This was all about solving the case. Getting the scoop on the story. The idea of truly helping Lane, not only on a story, but in assisting the authorities capture a criminal, filled her with excitement. "I can do this. I know I can."

"No," Lane said. "It's too dangerous."

"Lane's right," Henry said. "I have other agents working with me. We'll get Burrows."

"How?" Patsy asked, convinced she could get the information they needed, if they'd give her the chance.

"Do you think he's already found the money?" Lane asked.

"I don't know," Henry said. "We know Gaynor is a killer, but he maintained his claim that he wasn't the one who had blown up the train until the day he died. He insisted he didn't know where the dynamite came from or who lit it. He and his partner, Billy Phillips, were in the baggage car, stealing the money, when the dynamite exploded. Their plan had been to ride off in separate ways, and meet up later. That's what Gaynor did, ride off, but someone killed Billy at the robbery site, took his horse and his share of the money. That person was never found. Rex was captured that night, because his horse had gone lame. He said it was dark, and that he didn't know where he buried his share of the money. Authorities searched the entire area between the robbery site and where they captured Gaynor numerous times, but nothing was ever recovered."

Patsy's heart was thudding at learning so much about the train robbery. She looked at Lane. "None of that was in the newspaper."

"No, it wasn't," Lane said. "Billy Phillips was Gaynor's partner, but Gaynor swore he hadn't killed him, that he knew nothing about a third person, and the authorities never released that any money had been stolen off the train, because they couldn't."

"Why?" She sat down, completely committed to hearing all they'd tell her.

"Because the government didn't want anyone to know that the Federal Reserve was shipping old money to LA to be destroyed," Lane answered. "If word had gotten out, every train on the rails would have been robbed for months on end."

Patsy didn't understand one thing. "What do you mean, old money?"

"Bills wear out, and are replaced, but until they are destroyed, they spend as well as any others," Lane answered.

She was listening to everything he said, but still confused. "So you mean it wasn't any good? The money."

"No, the money was still good," Lane said. "Every dollar printed is backed by gold held by the government. As the paper wears out, the bills are collected, destroyed and replaced with new ones. However, in this instance, those old bills had already been replaced with new ones, ultimately, meaning the government had bills out there without the Federal Reserve having enough gold to back them, which is illegal."

"Even for the government?" she asked.

Henry let out a grunt. "Especially for the government. Not all Americans trust the government. A large percentage don't agree with the politicians and their laws. The shipments of old bills were to be kept quiet because the politicians weren't following their own law. The railroad didn't even know they were carrying them."

Lane laid a hand on her shoulder. "It's a bit confusing. A lot of people didn't even know the changes that were happening. The war had ended, the economy was building again and the newly appointed members of the Federal Reserve Board were focused on implementing a system where a specific amount of every bank's assets was on deposit as Federal Reserve funds. Part of that included replacing all old currency with Federal Reserve notes."

Finding this all very interesting, Patsy added, "And destroying all the old bills."

Lane nodded. "Yes, but they'd failed to destroy the old bills before printing the new ones. Banks had been required to destroy the old bills as they received them, but that wasn't happening. Ultimately, Federal agents were sent out to collect the old bills, deliver them to central locations and oversee their destruction."

"Somehow Rex Gaynor, or Billy Phillips, found out that an agent was on that train, with a shipment of money for destruction," Henry said. "And robbed the train."

While absorbing everything, she asked, "Was the agent killed?"

Henry glanced at Lane. "No one in the passenger car survived."

Her stomach clenched as Lane nodded. Thinking again about his wife and daughter, how tragic that had to have been for him, she quietly acknowledged, "How terrible." There was pain in his eyes, even after all this time. That could be why he hadn't told her. It still hurt him too much to talk about it. That made her want to help capture whoever was responsible even more. She stood up and wrapped a hand around his arm. "Who was the man who blew up the train and killed Billy Phillips?"

"The authorities thought Gaynor was lying. That he'd killed Phillips and taken all the money," Lane said.

"Up until Gaynor was killed," Henry said. "I wouldn't tell this to just anyone, but the case was opened back up when Gaynor was killed. Because I'd been on the case years ago, I was assigned to it again. I'd just finished up a case in Arizona, so wasn't far away, and while reviewing the old file, I found an interesting piece of information that another agent had collected, but no one had followed up on."

"What is that?" Lane asked.

"A ticket agent in San Diego who had provided a roster of the passengers, and assisted with identifying the bodies, stated back then that one passenger on his roster hadn't been accounted for. The ticket agent said he'd sold the man a ticket, and that he'd been a big guy, with black hair and a black mustache."

Patsy's heart skipped a beat and she tightened her hold on Lane's arm. "Vincent Burrows."

"Possibly," Henry said.

"That description could fit a lot of men," Lane said. "Burrows is new around here. The only connection I could find on him was to the abandoned house we followed you from."

Henry nodded. "His uncle is who built that house, right after moving out here from New Jersey. The family had a bootlegging business in Jersey and the uncle was sent out here to start a new branch. The house was to be the headquarters, but agents were one up on him and the bust happened before things got too big. The house has quite an ingenious design, which is why the government had federal agents board it up, and still owns it."

Not following what he meant, Patsy asked, "What's ingenious about the design?"

"The tunnel," Henry answered.

"What tunnel?" she asked, looking at Lane.

Lane was frowning, too.

Henry looked a bit skeptical. "You didn't know about the tunnel?"

"No," Lane answered.

"I figured you did for sure." Henry shrugged. "Seems like that is one secret that never got out. The house has a tunnel that goes from the basement to downtown, to the laundromat. That had been their distribution center."

"The Rooster's Nest," Patsy said.

"It was known as the Closet back then," Lane said. "Until new owners bought the laundromat and reopened the speakeasy, as well."

She was learning so much, and it was so thrilling to be in on so many secrets. "That's where you saw me dancing with Vincent Burrows."

"Yes, it was." Henry rubbed his chin. "You didn't know him before then?"

"No. I'd asked some dockworkers what the news on the dock was, and one pointed at Vincent Burrows and told me to ask him. The dockworker didn't say his name, just said that guy knew everything going on at the docks. So I asked him to dance, and because I was interested in learning more about Rex Gaynor, I mentioned that the chin music was that people should stay home and keep their doors locked. He said that I shouldn't worry. That

Rex Gaynor had broken out in order to recover the stash of cash he'd stolen from the train."

"He said that?" Henry asked.

"Yes, that's exactly what he said." Still hoping they'd let her help, she added, "I'm sure he'd tell me more."

Henry shook his head, but asked, "He was at a party last night? Where?"

"Victoria Lloyd's house," Patsy said. "But I didn't talk to him."

"And you aren't going to talk to him again," Lane said. Looking at Henry, he continued, "Burrows wasn't here seven years ago."

Henry nodded. "Yes, he was. For a short time, with his uncle, but, coincidentally , Burrows went back to New Jersey right after the train robbery. Where he worked in the family bootlegging business, until he was ousted earlier this year."

"If he's a bootlegger, why hasn't he been arrested?" Patsy asked. "Bootlegging is illegal."

Henry shrugged. "Yes, it is, but state laws aren't as strict as the Volstead Act, which is what the prohibition agents enforce. And, there are a lot of bootleggers out there. Agents have to focus on the big dogs and refer to local law enforcement to do what they can about the smaller operations."

"Ousted," Lane said. "And needed money to start over. Here."

Henry nodded.

Chapter Ten

Patsy wanted to say that she would talk to Burrows again, because neither Lane nor Henry could. Burrows was sure to know who they were, or weren't in Henry's case, but she held her silence. They'd see that they needed her. The thrill of that had her curling her toes inside her shoes. This was exactly what she'd wanted, getting to the nitty-gritty of things. Her life was no longer boring, that was for sure. Hadn't been since she'd met Lane.

"I bet Burrows supplied the whiskey for Victoria's party last night," Lane said to Henry. "And that's why he was at the Rooster's Nest, trying to market his supply. I'll do some investigating, find out how to get in contact with him, and anything else that could be helpful."

"Appreciate it, Lane. Our plan was to draw him out, attempt to capture me, but, as I said, so far, he hasn't taken the bait. I'm starting to think he's not worried about Gaynor because he knows for sure he's dead." Henry slid his hands in his pockets and rocked on his heels. "I need to get this case wrapped up because I have some personal business to take care of, but can't until after this case is solved."

It was darker than night, except for the flashes of lightning that were so close the hair on her arms was standing on end.

He wrapped an arm around her. "We're safe here. We'll just wait it out."

Storms had never bothered her before. Then again, it didn't rain that often, most certainly not during the summer months, and she'd never been outside during thunder and lightning.

He leaned back against the wall and she rested her neck on his arm. It made a good pillow. The storm wasn't so bad, now that they were no longer getting soaked.

"How long do you think it will rain?"

"It never lasts long," he said.

She hadn't considered the time before, but did now. "What time do you think it is?"

He held up his other hand and stared at his wrist. "Looks like it's a little after two."

Nodding, she bit her lip. Mother's shopping trips always lasted until four, so as long as she was home before then, all would be fine. She could trust Jane to not say anything—as long as she told her sister exactly where she'd been.

She would do that. Jane was sure to be as excited about all this as she was, and would most likely agree with her that she had to speak to Vincent Burrows again. Get the information that Lane, and Henry, needed.

A shiver rippled over her.

"Cold?"

"Wet," she answered, then nodded. "And cold." Rubbing her arms, she added, "Because I'm wet."

"Take the jacket off. That should help."

She shrugged off his suit coat, and instantly missed

"Knew," Patsy said aloud, thinking about exactly what Burrows had said.

"Knew what?" Lane asked.

"Burrows, when we danced that night, he said only Gaynor knew where the money was. Not *knows*. *Knew*, as if he was sure he was dead."

"You're sure?" Henry asked.

"Positive," she replied, her heart beat increasing.

"I'll get on it right away." Lane rested a hand on her back as he twisted them both toward the door. "Let's meet up tomorrow night, at the Rooster's Nest."

"I'll be there." Henry followed them to the door, and once they'd all stepped outside, he let out a low whistle. "Look at those clouds. You two better hurry. There's a storm on the horizon."

The sky that earlier had been bright blue was now coated with gray-streaked clouds. Patsy turned toward the direction the clouds were rolling in from. The clouds farther west, over the ocean, where most summer storms rolled in from, were tinted an odd shade of green.

"Let's go," Lane said, and then bid a hasty farewell to Henry while rushing her toward the trail they'd followed earlier.

"You're sure Burrows said *knew*?" Lane asked as they hurried along the trail.

"Yes. It's right there in my head," she answered. "I can remember it clearly."

"I believe you. The details in the articles you wrote about the dance-off and Raymond's party were precise. You have a good memory." He grinned at her. "Reporters need good memories."

Happiness bubbled inside her. "Thank you."

"You still want to be a reporter?" he asked.

"Yes," she instantly replied.

"Even after this? Trekking through the woods?"

The wind had picked up, too, and she had to hold the hair whipping in her face aside before she could say, "Even more now." Not just for herself. Knowing what he'd gone through, the loss of his wife and child, made her more determined than ever. He was kind and caring and deserved justice. "This is living, Lane. It's exciting. Fun."

They topped the hill and started their way down the other side. "It's not going to be fun in a few minutes, when that rain hits."

"I won't mind," she said. And didn't, even when the rain hit with huge, cold drops that the wind blew straight into their faces, making it nearly impossible to see.

Lane stopped and removed his suit jacket. "Here, put this on."

"I'm already wet," she said.

He draped it over her shoulders. "It will keep you from getting soaked."

She stuck her arms in the jacket, and had to push up the sleeve in order to grasp his hand again. The warmth did feel good. "Thank you."

"We'll go as fast as we can," Lane said, tugging her forward, "but watch your step. The ground's already turning to mud."

Before they were halfway down the other side, the rumbles of thunder that had come along with the rain grew closer, and flashes of lightning could be seen in the clouds.

"This way!" Lane shouted over the wind. "We have to find shelter, get away from these trees until the lightning passes."

Clutching his hand tightly, she followed him blindly. Not only was the rain making it impossible to see, the

wind whipped branches around, slapping her from tip to toe with wet leaves from all directions. She was dually thankful for the extra layer of protection his jacket provided and tucked her chin down into the folded-up lapels.

Lane stopped at her side and said something, but she couldn't hear what. The storm was too loud. He wrapped a hand around her waist and pushed her head down with his other hand, then shoved her forward, into a bush.

She squealed as water gushed over her.

"Keep going," Lane shouted.

He was behind her, pushing her to continue onward. It took her a moment and a flash of lightning to realize he'd found a cave for them to hide in. A small one, more of a recessed cliff overhang, but shelter nonetheless.

Dropping onto her knees, she crawled up against the back wall and sat down. She wiped the water off her face and squeezed it out of her hair while glancing around. Due to the downward curvature of the overhang, which had water pouring off it like a waterfall, the space was dry.

"How did you see this?" she asked as Lane sat down beside her.

"I'm not sure." He ran both hands through his wet hair. "It just all of a sudden was there."

A crack of thunder and flash of lightning so close the little cave lit up and the ground shook had her jolting backward. The back of her head hit the rock wall. "Ouch." She rubbed the back of her head, feeling for a lump.

"Are you all right?" he asked.

"I'm fine. Was just startled."

"Let me see."

She twisted so the back of her head was toward him, but said, "It's too dark for you to see anything. There's not even a lump."

its warmth, yet knew her dress would dry faster without being covered.

"That rain sure hit fast," he said as she leaned back again.

"And hard."

"The farmers will be happy."

"We won't have to water the garden tomorrow," she said. "Or the flowers." As her mind started to think about that, home, family, she thought about his wife and daughter. "I'm sorry about your wife and daughter, Lane."

"Thank you."

Once again, her tongue acted before she could stop it. "What were their names?"

"My wife's name was Naomi and our daughter's name was Sarah."

Glad he didn't seem upset by her questions, she continued, "Those are nice names. How old was Sarah?"

"Just a few months. Still a baby."

Her heart clenched in her chest. "I truly am sorry."

"I can tell," he said. "Naomi had taken Sarah down to San Diego, to spend a few weeks with her family. They were on their way home when the robbery occurred."

She waited for another rumble of thunder to fade before asking, "How long had you been married?"

"A year and a half."

Patsy closed her eyes at the way her heart constricted, as if feeling his pain. "Do you still miss them?"

"Yes," he answered quietly. "Mostly I miss the life I believe we could have had together, as a family."

For all the complaining she did about her family, she was sincerely grateful for them being in her life. All of them.

"Was Naomi a reporter, too?"

"No, she…"

Patsy lifted her head to look him in the face.

A half smile appeared. "She loved being at home, taking care of things there. That worked for us because I was working all the time. Had just bought the *Gazette* from Victoria's husband because he was too sick to run it. It had taken all the money we had, but Naomi wasn't fazed. She could make a meal out of nothing."

"I can't." Patsy's insides cringed. She hadn't meant to compare herself with Naomi, but it was the truth. She was allowed only to mix things together, not do the actual cooking. Too many burnt things in the past. Mother said it was because her mind was always on something else, instead of what she was doing. That could be true.

He chuckled. "There's nothing wrong with that."

No, there wasn't because it proved she would not make a good wife. To anyone, but especially him. Someone who was used to those things. "But I know I could get Vincent Burrows to tell me more."

Lane shook his head, yet there was still a hint of a smile on his lips. "You probably could, but you heard Henry. Burrows is a dangerous man. One you need to stay away from."

"Yes, but he knows who you are, so, he won't talk to you."

"I don't need him to talk to me."

"But you told Henry you'd find out how to get in contact with Burrows."

"And I will, but that doesn't mean I'll talk to him."

Arguing with him truly got her nowhere. She needed to take a different route. Leaning her head back against his arm again, she asked, "Do you think he was behind Rex Gaynor's death?"

"Henry is one of the best agents out there. If he believes Burrows was behind it, then I do, too."

"What about the train? Do you think he was on it?"

"Yes, I do now, having heard what Henry said."

She sighed. "I do, too, and I wish you'd let me help you catch him."

He put a knuckle under her chin and turned her face toward him. "I don't need help catching him. That's Henry's job."

"Yes, you do. He blew up the train. He's the reason your wife and daughter di—"

Lane pressed a finger against her lips and shook his head.

Then, leaning so close their noses almost touched, he continued, "It's your safety I'm worried about right now."

Lightning lit up the small cave, and for a flash of a moment, she could see her reflection in his eyes. And more. She could see the sincerity in his.

Despite the turmoil, the anguish over his loss, a warmth filled her and the butterflies took flight as Lane leaned even closer.

"I don't want anything to happen to you, Patsy."

An unexplainable magic happened then. It made her entire being tingle, especially her lips. She should move, but she couldn't. Couldn't pull her eyes off his, either.

She wanted him to kiss her, like he had last night.

She shouldn't want that. Knowing all that she did. But she did, and that want grew stronger. So strong, she arched upward, so their lips could meet.

Her eyes closed of their own accord as his lips pressed more firmly against hers, and she moved closer, wanting to keep her lips against his. The connection, the magic, was so amazing, she felt an ecstasy she'd never known existed.

Lost in the kiss, she wasn't sure how long it lasted, but Lane ended the kiss as softly as he'd started it, and then pulled her up against his chest, holding her there. She could hear his heart, feel it beating beneath her cheek.

Blissful, that's what it was. Even though the storm continued to rage on, the thunder and lightning no longer startled her. She was surrounded by Lane's arms. By his strength and warmth. The wonderful smell of his after-shave. Of him.

Fully content, she snuggled in closer.

"The article you wrote about Raymond's party is in today's paper," he said.

"It is?" she asked, even though at this moment her mind couldn't focus on anything but him.

"Yes, it is," he said. "Congratulations."

"Thank you." She closed her eyes, but she was past being able to concentrate.

Lane leaned back against the cave wall, berating himself for being so weak. He'd blurted that out about her article because he was trying to get his mind off what he'd done. What he shouldn't have done. He shouldn't have kissed her. Nothing could take his mind off that, or how it had done exactly what he'd known it would—made him want more.

He had to get control over himself, over the feelings encompassing him. She'd stirred up his insides since the first moment he'd seen her, in ways he'd never have believed possible. Not even talking about Naomi and Sarah had lessened the magnetism he felt toward Patsy.

Yes, Patsy. He no longer thought of her as Libby. The name was of no consequence. She had a charm, an alluring charm, that sucked him in, and the mere idea of her being anywhere near Burrows made him shudder.

She shifted slightly, and her slow, even breathing said she'd fallen asleep. He flattened his back against the wall and tightened his arms around her. That was the best thing that could happen. Her falling asleep. The rain didn't show any sign of letting up, and stuck here, alone, was more of a temptation than he needed right now.

He closed his eyes, tried to focus on what Henry had said about Gaynor, and Burrows. Tried to lay out a plan of where he'd go first to gather information that would help Henry bring a case against Burrows, but his body wouldn't let his mind have control.

Patsy's warmth had his body fully aware and throbbing with needs he'd ignored for years. The thought of ever marrying again had never crossed his mind. If it had, in some odd and inconceivable way, he'd stifled it and buried it so deep it couldn't dig its way out.

He focused on doing that again, burying any thoughts of caring enough about someone he was willing to change his life. Marriage did that. Changed a person's life. He didn't need that again. Didn't need change. He liked his life just as it was.

But it wasn't going to stay the way it was. As soon as the rain let up, he'd have to take her home, and tell Dryer about the rumor of their engagement.

His heart clenched in his chest at that thought. He didn't know how Dryer would respond, but knew how the man treated others, including people who worked for him. Very few contractors built a second house for Dryer. Most bought the land outright and then built their own houses to sell.

City council members didn't care for Dryer, either. He'd been removed and subsequently banned from attending meetings in the past.

In fact, Lane couldn't think of a single person who did like William Dryer.

He couldn't imagine having a man like that as a father. His father had been tough when he'd needed to be, but also caring. The exact kind of father Lane had hoped to be to Sarah.

He rarely compared himself or his life with others, but at the moment, he had to wonder about justice. How Dryer had three daughters, whom he'd had since the day they were born, and how his own daughter, his own sweet baby, died long before her first birthday. It didn't seem fair, but it was what it was, and all he could hope, was that deep down Dryer appreciated his good fortune when it came to his daughters.

A soft moan had him looking down. The smile that appeared as she opened her eyes had to have been the sweetest one he'd ever seen.

She covered a yawn with one hand and then shook her head. "Goodness, I think I dozed off."

"You did." He released his hold on her. "The trek through the woods must have worn you out."

She sat up and smoothed her hair away from her face. "No. I didn't sleep well last night." Stretching her arms out in front of her, she said, "Looks like the rain is letting up."

Lane hadn't noticed that, not until now. The dark clouds had moved on, giving way for the sun to peek through, and the rain was now simply falling straight down rather than being blown in all directions. "It is. It's no longer thundering and lightning, either."

She rubbed her eyes and stifled another yawn. "Goodness. What time is it?"

He glanced at his watch, and did a double take. Had they truly been here that long? "It's four thirty."

Fear flashed in her eyes. "Four thirty? We have to go! Now!"

He grasped her arm as she flipped onto her hands and knees to crawl to the opening. "It's still raining."

"That doesn't matter. We have to go."

"We can't. We still have the rockiest part to climb down. It's too dangerous in the rain. Those rocks will be slicker than grease."

"We'll be careful, but we have to leave, Lane. We have to."

"Why are you suddenly in such a hurry?"

"It's getting late."

"Not that late. It won't be dark for hours." He wasn't game on sitting here for all evening, but he didn't want to see her slide to the bottom of the rocks, either. She could easily break an ankle, or worse.

She sat back on her heels. "Dark isn't the issue."

"Then what is?"

"Everyone will be home by five, and if I'm not there..." She shook her head. "We have to leave. Now."

"Even if we left right now, we wouldn't make it to your house by five."

She started to tremble, and rubbed her arms. "We wouldn't?"

"No, we wouldn't."

All color drained from her face.

He brushed a handful of damp tendrils away from her face. "We'll leave as soon as the rain stops. You won't be that late."

"You don't understand." Her voice was barely a whisper. "I can't be late at all."

Her demeanor was so downtrodden, he had to know what that meant. "Why? What will happen if you're late?"

Her hair flipped as she shook her head. "I just can't be late. Just can't. Please, can we leave now? We'll just have to be careful on the rocks."

The rain had let up, a waterfall no longer cascaded over the outcropping's opening, and although he still worried about the slickness of the rocks, it was apparent waiting any longer would only add to her distress.

He picked up his suit coat. It was still wet, but would provide her protection from the elements. "Here, put this back on before we leave."

"Thank you, Lane," she said, putting on the jacket. "Thank you."

He wasn't nearly as eager to leave while it was still raining, and felt compelled to warn, "There could be mudslides. We have to be extra careful."

She nodded, then flipped on her hands and knees again.

He grasped her wrist. "I'll go first. You wait here until I say."

"Just hurry, please." Impatient, she added, "We have to hurry."

On his hands and knees, he crawled past her. "We will, but we will also be careful." Once he made it through the brush, he stood, and tested the solidity of the ground before he pushed the branches aside to make an opening for her to crawl through. "It's really muddy, so be careful."

She scrambled through the brush like a cat on a hot tin roof.

He grasped her waist as she shot to her feet and nearly tumbled over. "I said be careful."

Holding onto his arms, she stabilized her footing. "Oh, my, the ground is slick."

"Yes, it is."

Blinking at the rain hitting her face, she said, "It's still raining."

"Yes, it is." He could have easily said *I told you so* both times, but there was no sense in that. Her mind was made up to go home. So, home they would go. And hopefully not break a leg along the way.

Holding her around the waist with one hand, he carefully picked their way downhill. The grassy spots were just as slick as the muddier sections. One misstep and they'd end up tumbling ass over teakettle all the way to the bottom of the hill.

He usually wasn't an overly sympathetic man, but her concern over getting home had softened something inside him. That was disturbing. So was the way he'd already started to care too much about her.

He wouldn't want any woman to take a tumble and get hurt, but there was more to it when it came to her. The fact she was so headstrong could be part of it. Left on her own, she was sure to end up injured in some way.

"That stick I had earlier would come in handy right about now," she said, using the branches on bushes to aid her as the slope grew steeper.

He stopped shy of explaining how dangerous a stick like that could be if she stumbled in this rain, but he was nobody's fool. She'd take it as an insult, and that would get him nowhere. Furthermore, she was wet, and cold. He simply needed to get her home and then run as far away from her as he could possibly get. Worrying about her, protecting her, kissing her were all things he didn't need to be thinking about right now. Or ever.

"You can stay here," she said. "I can make it down by myself."

Lane huffed out a laugh. "I don't think so."

She pinched her lips together and kept trudging along beside him.

He should have kept his mouth shut and not responded to that comment, either. They both needed to concentrate on their steps.

"I could make it down the hill alone," she finally said, although there was a hint of sorrow in her voice rather than determination.

"I'm sure you could, but I'm the reason you're out here, and I'll see you get down safely."

"You aren't the reason."

He wasn't going to argue the point.

Thankfully, a few steps later, they were off the steepest section. Now it was just thick brush to get through before they'd finally arrive at the road. Then he would walk her home, and explain why she was late for supper.

That had to be the reason she needed to be home, for supper. And her father was the reason she'd looked so scared. It didn't take a genius to figure that out. Dryer couldn't be that different when it came to his family. People didn't refer to him as "the Land Baron" for no reason. He was as haughty and coldhearted as they came. A baron was the lowest ranking in the line of nobility, yet, often, thought of themselves as the highest. That description fit Dryer to the core. His land wasn't worth any more than other acreage in the area, except for the fact that Dryer had advertised it as the closest thing to paradise in the state. That had worked for him. It stroked the already high egos of many, and continued to do so. Hollywoodland was already known as a neighborhood for the elite—because those were the only people Dryer would sell to.

Lane wasn't looking forward to seeing Dryer. He'd had to defend himself, his actions, to a woman's family before. Naomi's. And had sworn to never put himself in that position again.

Chapter Eleven

The rain was little more than a drizzle, besides the droplets falling off the branches overhead when they left the taller trees and began walking through the brush lining the roadway. Patsy had barely said a word the last half hour or more. Lane knew why. They were getting closer to her home, and he could tell her fears were mounting with every step.

He waited until they were on the road before he turned to look at her. The droplets on her cheeks were not rain. They were tears.

His throat thickened at the compassion filling him. How? Why had he let her touch him so deeply? In a place that hadn't been touched in a very long time. He liked his solitary life, had found peace in it and didn't want that to change.

"Goodbye, Lane." In a flash, she was running up the road.

He had only a split second to decide if he was going to accept the changes that had happened in his life or not.

Accept them?

He didn't have a choice. She'd already changed his life. Whether he liked that or not, he was the reason she'd trekked up the hill today, and he had to take responsibility for that.

He ran, caught up to her in no time and snagged her around the waist with one arm, knowing that was the only way to slow her down.

Her legs flayed near his ankles as she pleaded, "Put me down! I have to get home!"

He set her feet down on the ground, but kept a hold of her waist. "I know, and I'm going with you."

Patsy had been scared, worried and frightened about going home. Now, in this very instant, she was petrified. "You can't!"

"Yes, I can, and I am."

She dug her heels into the gravel as he tried to urge her forward. "No. No. No!"

"I'll explain why you were late for supper."

The tears that had been slipping out of her eyes fell faster. "It's not that." She pressed the back of one hand against her nose as she sniffled. Anyone else, she might be able to lie to, and they'd believe her, but not him. He sought the truth. Not just for his stories, for his newspaper, but in life. It was imbedded in him. A part of who he was. She had no choice but to provide it, and hope that would make him leave. "You can't walk me home. Can't explain where we've been."

"Yes, I can. I won't let out the details of our meeting with Henry, but—"

"No!" Patsy swallowed against the fire in her throat. "We—my sisters and I—aren't allowed to be in the company of men, at anytime, anywhere. Not until we're engaged. You'll ruin everything if you walk me home."

Lane frowned slightly while keeping his gaze on her,

as if reading her mind, getting to the very bottom of her words.

"By *ruin everything* you mean the fact you and your sisters dress up as flappers and sneak out to go to speak-easies every night."

He'd read her mind all right, and got to the very bottom of things. She didn't nod, or shake her head. There was no point. He knew. The air in her lungs was so heavy it hurt as she huffed it out.

"How long did you think you could get away with it?"

She and her sisters hadn't set a timeline. They just loved the freedom, and didn't want it to change. It had been the only time in their lives that they'd had any amount of control, of liberty. She didn't want to be the catalyst that changed it all, either. "It's more than that, Lane." Her voice was little more than a whisper. It was all she could muster. The implication of what had happened today was why. If her father ever learned that she and Lane had kissed. More than once.

He averted his gaze and shook his head. "I know there's more to it, Patsy."

He was thinking about the kiss, too. She was sure of it. And regretting it. Rightfully so.

Putting pressure on her back, he coaxed her forward, one step at a time. Her legs felt as if they weighed a hundred pounds each. The dread inside her weighed even more. Her father was going to be furious, but it was her sisters she was thinking about. She'd let them down. She'd promised that she wouldn't let her dates with Lane ruin everything, yet that's exactly what had happened.

By the time her house came into sight, she was trembling from head to toe and her stomach was churning so hard and fast bile burned the back of her throat. If it had just been her, she'd have snuck in through the backyard, but it wasn't just her. Or even her and her sisters. Lane was with her, and he was marching them straight to the front door framed with the big white pillars that stretched to the second floor.

The floor that she'd be locked in the rest of her life.

No. She wouldn't be locked up there.

She'd be sent away.

Trepidation sent shivers through her entire system. Her father had made grown men cry before with his yelling and berating, and threats of ruining their lives. Unable to go any farther, she stopped and willed her shaking legs to keep her upright.

Holding back renewed tears with all she had, she whispered, "Leave now, please, Lane. Don't come any farther."

"I can't leave, Patsy." He tightened the hold around her waist. "Let's go."

"You have to leave. The only men allowed—" Her protest was interrupted by a familiar booming voice that split the air.

"What the hell is going on here?"

Patsy nearly slumped to the ground at the sound of her father's voice, would have if Lane hadn't been holding her up, and she may have ran in the opposite direction at the sight of her father storming his way out the front door and down the steps if Lane hadn't forced her to move forward.

He legs weighed a thousand pounds now, and her mouth was dry. Her thoughts a jumbled mess of regrets and fear.

"Hello, William," Lane said.

Even filled with desperation, Patsy was shocked by how calm and casual Lane sounded, as if he and her father were merely running into one another on a busy street corner.

"Who the—" Her father paused in his steps and speech. Leveling a glowering frown, he shook his head as if seeing things. "Lane Cox? What are you doing here?" Father's gaze turned to her.

She shivered from head to toe.

Father was a tall man, with wide shoulders and snow-white hair that he had shaved short each month at the barbershop on Fifth Avenue, and right now his face was fire red. All in all, he looked taller, and madder than she'd ever seen.

Lane's hand tightened on her waist. "I took your advice, but unfortunately, Patsy and I got caught in the storm this afternoon," Lane said.

"My advice... Caught in the storm?" Father's brows knit tighter together.

"Yes, your advice to consider dating one of your daughters," Lane said.

Patsy's insides shivered as she turned to look at him.

He grinned at her, and her father. "You remember, William, when you asked if I'd be interested in one of your daughters?"

Father's jaw dropped.

"I am," Lane said. "Patsy."

Patsy nearly jolted out of her shoes. This was all her fault, and she had to do something about it. But what? Lane was making things worse.

Wide-eyed, she looked at him. Half sick and half scared to death at the same time.

"An engagement." Once again, Lane turned to her father. "With your permission, of course."

Permission? The weight on her shoulders pressed down harder. Father would never give his permission.

"My permission." Father shook his head and then, grinning, nodded. "Yes, yes, I remember. Come in. Come in." Father waved a hand. "You will join us for supper."

"I'd be honored," Lane said.

No! Patsy wanted to shout, but couldn't. Her throat was locked up. Father may have appeared approachable then, but that wouldn't last long.

"But first," he continued, "Patsy needs a bath and a change of clothing."

Patsy was too dumbfounded to reply. It was almost as if she was dreaming—actually having a nightmare—where things were happening and she couldn't stop them or even react to them.

No, it wasn't a dream, it was just her life.

A life that would soon be over.

Lane aided her forward, all the way to the house, up the steps and through the front door. As they stepped into the foyer, Father instructed her to go change her clothing. She wasn't trying to disobey, but her feet wouldn't move. Some form of invisible glue had her stuck to the floor.

Or it may have been pure fear. Fear of what would happen, would be said, once she was out of hearing distance.

"Go," Lane said quietly. "I'll be here when you come down."

Patsy shook her head.

"Marlys!" Father barked mother's name. "Set another plate at the table. Mr. Cox will be joining us."

"You can do this, Libby," Lane whispered, and gave her a tiny shove toward the wide, curved staircase that led to the second floor.

Her feet seemed to come unglued from the floor and a strange reverie overcame her. In a trance, with one focus, she grabbed a hold of the banister post, and with a sense of panic, knowing she didn't have much time, she shot up the stairs. Still sick to her stomach and worried over what was being said, she ran to the bathroom, pulled off her wet clothing, washed quickly and then ran to her bedroom, where she threw on clean clothes and shoes, and combed her hair.

Her heart was racing and her breathing quick, having performed every task in record time all the while thinking about how Lane didn't know any of Father's rules. Whatever had possessed him to say an engagement ? Did he think that would help? There was no hope in this situation.

No hope for any of them.

She didn't want to be engaged.

Didn't want to be married.

Especially to one of the men Father chose.

Which was Lane!

She liked him, but she didn't want to be engaged to him. Married to him.

She had to explain that they weren't engaged, and get him out of the house immediately.

With no time to lose, she ran down the stairs, swung around the molded banister post and shot down the hallway to her father's office.

The door was open. The room empty.

She could hear her heart pounding, her breath gasping. Spinning around, she flew back to the foyer and through the living room, toward the dining room, and skidded to a halt just outside the doorway.

Her entire family sat there. Father. Mother. Betty. Jane. And Lane.

Her heart sank.

He lifted a brow and then gave a very subtle nod toward the empty chair next to him.

She swallowed so hard she almost choked, and then

forced her feet to move. One in front of the other until arriving at the table.

"Mother kept supper warm," Father said gruffly.

The trance was still there, surrounding her, making everything foggy, yet, knowing and following the rules, Patsy acknowledged his statement. "Thank you, Mother." She then sat down, in the chair next to Lane, and folded her quivering hands in her lap.

Father said grace, which was a hypocrisy because there wasn't a single person in the room who was thankful to be where they were at this precise moment. Her sisters were shooting questioning looks her way under their lashes. She could imagine what they were thinking.

It's over.

That's what they were thinking, and they were right.

It's over.

Mother was frowning terribly. Father was breathing through his nose, which echoed off the walls, and Lane— she felt the sorriest for him—was sitting upright and pretending the silence was normal, that all was fine.

Another hypocrisy.

Nothing would ever be fine again. Not for any of them.

She and her sisters would be sent to the convent, like Father had warned them for years, where they would live the rest of their lives in prayer, silence, penance and sacrifice. Just like Aunt Joan.

Platters were passed with little more than *please* and *thank you*, which were the rules, and forks clanked against plates as everyone ate.

Patsy was already sick to her stomach, and each swallow threatened to come right back up.

It was the longest meal since the beginning of time.

What felt like hours later, Father's nod, signaling that

the meal had ended, had both Betty and Jane gathering and stacking the plates and platters in front of them.

Rising to his feet, Father said, "Mr. Cox, you and I shall retire to my office."

Lane stood and Patsy shot to her feet beside him.

"I'll—"

"You will help your mother and sisters in the kitchen," Father interrupted. "I will talk to you later."

Patsy gritted her back teeth together, trying to gather the gumption to say more. She had to say more, but was afraid. So afraid.

Lane gave her arm a gentle squeeze as he followed her father out of the room.

Turning to her mother, she pleaded, "Mother, please, I must—"

"You must do as your father says, Patsy," Mother said sternly. "He was very upset when you weren't home. We were all worried something had happened to you."

"Yes, we were," Jane added, eyes wide with questions and vexation.

Patsy grimaced. "I just went—"

"We won't speak of this now." Mother picked up the platter still holding several pieces of fried chicken. "There's work to be done."

The trance around her shattered. Patsy threw her napkin on the table. "There's always work to be done. And always will be. I have to go explain—"

"Patsy Loraine Dryer, you will do as I say," Mother snapped.

"No, I can't, I have to explain what happened, and—"

"You can't," Betty said quietly. "It'll only make things worse." She held out several stacked plates. "Take these to the kitchen."

"Do as your sister says, Patsy." Mother said. "Your

father will have plenty to say to you when he's finished with Mr. Cox."

With dread filling her, Patsy glanced over her shoulder, at the doorway toward the living room. That's what she was afraid of, Father finishing with Lane.

Lane leaned back in the leather chair and took a sip of the glass in his hand. Top-shelf, the whiskey slid over his palate and down his throat as smooth as nectar. Dryer was smooth, too. For all the gruffness and silence at the table, once they'd entered his office, he'd acted as if the two of them were old friends.

They weren't.

Lane wasn't about to pretend they were, either. The small amount of time he'd spent in this household would have anyone climbing out the windows at night, and he could understand Patsy's desperation to be out from under her father's hand. Anger filled him at the thought of her practically being kept under lock and key. She was too full of curiosity for that, and the way she was being treated here was starving her of the life she craved.

His hands balled into fists. Dryer had no concern for his daughter in this, no worries over what she wanted, including marriage. Dryer was thinking only of himself, and how he could come out the winner in this.

Which irritated Lane to no end. He had been biting his tongue for over two hours, throughout the longest meal known to man, and then listening to Dryer speak of his daughters like they were stray dogs that had wandered into his yard and he was looking for someone to take them before he was forced to take them out in the woods and leave them for the coyotes. He'd acted as if he should receive sympathy for having daughters instead of sons, and how hard he'd looked to find suitable arrangements for each of them, while becoming one of the richest men in the state.

Dryer had been sure to point that out several times. He'd claimed to have settled on a man for the oldest, Betty, and a possible one for Jane to marry, but hadn't yet found one to take on Patsy, and was glad his search was over because finding men who had their own money— and were not after his—was an extremely difficult task for a man of his wealth and status.

Thoughts of Sarah had entered Lane's mind several times since being sequestered in Dryer's office. He wondered how he'd have reacted if she'd have lived, grown into a young woman and brought a man home who wanted to court her. Try as he might, Lane couldn't make a comparison. Not because Sarah hadn't lived beyond infanthood, but because he knew he'd never have been the kind of father William Dryer was.

Memories of his own childhood had entered his mind several times, too. Of dinners around the table with his parents and grandparents. It had been nothing like the family dinner he'd sat through earlier. His mother's kitchen had been small and cramped compared with the Dryers' dining room. There had been red gingham curtains on the windows, not velvet draperies, and the plates had been hardy stoneware, not fine china, but his mother's kitchen had been booming with conversation and laughter. Not only during mealtime. The house he'd grown up in had been a happy place, full of people who truly cared about and truly loved each other.

That was lacking in the Dryer house.

He'd bet the walls of this place rarely heard laughter. The house was sparkling clean. The wood floors and furnishing gleamed with new polish and the rugs and upholstered furniture didn't show a speck of wear. It was like the place wasn't, nor ever had been, lived in.

Which made him understand Patsy even more why she wanted to live, because she sure wasn't given the opportunity to do so here.

Lane finished his drink, emptying the glass completely, and then leaned forward to set it on the corner of Dryer's huge mahogany desk. "Aren't you curious as to how I met Patsy?"

Dryer tossed back the last of his drink. "I'm assuming that once you came to your senses about marrying one of my daughters, you came to the house." He leaned back in his chair. "Something I will talk to her about since she shouldn't have left without permission."

Lane's plan was to stick as close to the truth as possible. The truth had always been his motto, but right now, he was thinking about Patsy, and Henry. William Dryer did not need to know anything about Henry or Vincent Burrows, or Rex Gaynor. A man who was willing to trade his daughter off for weekly advertisements—Dryer had referenced free advertisements for family near the onset of their conversation—was thinking only about what he had to gain, not about anyone else.

Lane was. He was thinking about several people. He'd sworn the man who had killed Naomi and Sarah would pay. Up until today, he'd thought that man was Rex Gaynor. Now he knew differently, and knowing differently added several other people into the mix. This was no longer about only the train robbery. Henry's secret location was at risk, which could put his ability to find Burrows at risk. Burrows needed to be caught, but there was more to it than that. Patsy was at risk, too. Of never having a chance to pursue her dream. If that meant going along with a false engagement for a week, so be it.

He'd discovered more about William Dryer this evening than he'd ever expected to know. In fact, Dryer was the epitome of expectations. He was used to getting what he wanted because it was exactly what he expected, and used his size and gruffness to coerce, even terrorize, people at times, break them down until he got exactly that.

That wouldn't work on him. As a reporter, he was used to people attempting to intimidate him, to give them what they expected. He had expectations, too, for himself and others, and had learned years ago how to not give people like Dryer any control over the situation. In truth, he'd used coercion himself on a regular basis when digging for the truth behind deceptions and closed doors.

The difference between him and Dryer was the reason behind it all. Lane fought for justice for all. Dryer fought only for himself.

"You'll find out soon enough, Patsy is a bit strong-willed," Dryer said. "It takes a heavy hand to keep her in line."

A rush of annoyance washed over Lane. Keeping his temper in check because he didn't want to make things worse for Patsy, he gave the older man a condescending look. "I do know she's strong-willed, and admire that. As well as many other things about her."

"Her mother and I have made sure she knows all there is to know about being a wife. Cooking and cleaning. Knowing her place," Dryer said with pride.

Dryer had the right to be proud of his daughters, but Lane couldn't find any pride in keeping them locked up the way he had. "If I was to marry Patsy—"

"If? There's no *if*."

"Yes, there is. The right wife is as important to a man as the right husband is to a woman," Lane said. This was one time Dryer wasn't going to be in charge. "If I was to marry Patsy, her 'knowing her place,' as you say, would be different from what she's had here at home. My position, and therefore that of my wife, includes a lot of social affairs, and I need to know that Patsy is capable of that. Therefore I suggest a trial period of—"

"Trial period! Now, see here!" Dryer shouted.

"Of seeing if Patsy would make a suitable wife," Lane continued. He figured the Burrows case would be all wrapped up within the week, then life could get back to normal. "Surely you can understand that, William, a man of your standing?"

William blustered, but eventually nodded. "How long?"

Lane didn't want to push things too far, nor want to drag this out longer than necessary, either. "A week, and I give you my solemn oath that her virtue will never be compromised in any way."

William regarded him with a long thoughtful gaze before he nodded. "I appreciate that you understand my concerns, and I can understand yours. I will agree to one week, on the condition that your outings with my daughter will be in public places."

Lane nodded, and hoped Patsy would agree to it, too. She didn't want to get married any more than he did, and this was a solution that would work for both of them. Being seen in public would quell the rumors of their engagement, and by this time next week, the gossipmongers would have new targets.

"As you can see, Lane, I'm a reasonable man," Dryer said, standing up.

Chapter Twelve

A sense of dread washed over Lane when he thought of how William was going to act when it came time to call this whole charade off, and his mind floundered on if he'd made the right decisions as he watched Dryer walk toward the door to call in Patsy. She'd been scared out of her wits when they'd arrived at the house. If she walked into the room and told the truth.... "Wait," Lane said.

Dryer stopped short of pulling the door open.

"I would like a moment alone with Patsy," Lane said.

Frowning, Dryer lifted his chin, as if considering the idea for a moment. A brief moment because the next minute, he shook his head. "I believe you've had enough time alone with my daughter today."

Lane had to give the man that one.

"Pour yourself another drink, Lane, while I find Patsy and her mother." William opened the door. "You may need it."

Lane glanced at his empty glass, and seriously considered refilling it. William Dryer was a solid adversary. Marrying his daughters off to well-to-do men was a goal Dryer wasn't going to give up on.

Lane didn't pour another drink because he needed his

mind to be as clear and sharp as possible to make sure that Patsy didn't let anything slip about Henry or Vincent Burrows. Squeezing his temples with one hand, he admitted this had been one hell of a day.

It was also far from over, and by the end of today, no one may come out of this a winner. Unless he came up with a plan, quick.

It didn't make sense that he cared so much about her. That he was going to this level, but he was. Why? A story. He'd written thousands of stories and never pretended to be engaged before. Yes, Burrows needed to be caught. But even that oath didn't hold enough weight for this. Putting Burrows behind bars wouldn't bring his family back to life any more than putting Gaynor behind bars seven years ago had. He knew that, and could no longer claim that was his motive. He'd been given a chance once, and he wanted Patsy to have that. What could happen in a week? He could pretend to be engaged to her for that long. It wouldn't be that hard. He just wouldn't kiss her again. Which shouldn't be hard, either. He'd kept his emotions sealed for years.

The door opened and he stood, then walked over to greet Patsy as she stepped over the threshold.

The eyes that glanced up at him were red rimmed and puffy, and the shameful way she bowed her head made his stomach clench. She was the reason he was doing all this, because he'd seen the Libby she kept locked up inside her. He'd been like that once. His father hadn't been like William, but his father had expected him to take over the farm, and he hadn't wanted to be a farmer. Like her, he'd wanted to get out and live, see things, experience things and report his findings to others. His chance to do so had happened when the war broke out. His father went to serve, and had died overseas. His mother had then sold the farm, and the two of them had moved to Los Angeles, where he met Charles Lloyd, who had believed in him enough to print his first article.

Patsy deserved to have someone believe in her that much, too. Her writing was rough, but showed potential. She not only had an eye for detail, she could put it on paper, and that was a unique talent. He gave her arm a gentle squeeze as her father directed everyone to sit down.

Lane led her to a long sofa along one wall, but didn't sit down beside her. Instead, he stood next to the arm of the sofa and kept one hand on her shoulder.

"Disobedience has never been allowed in this house, Patsy," Dryer started, sounding as stern as a judge laying out a life sentence to a criminal. "Your behavior today is far from acceptable and we are faced with the need to rectify the situation as soon as possible."

Her eyes fluttered shut and she nodded. "Yes, Father."

Lane increased the pressure of his hand on her shoulder. Her demeanor, that of a disgraced child, was nothing like the young woman he knew, and that goaded him. He also now understood why William had told him he might need another drink. His demeanor had gone back to how he'd been at the supper table. In full control. The ruler of his domain.

Straightening his stance, Lane let his disdain show. "Patsy has not done anything to be ashamed of. In fact, sir—" he paused so the significant use of the word could settle "—you and your wife should be proud of the young woman you raised. Did you know that Patsy has aspirations of becoming a writer?"

Patsy snapped her head up. Her eyes were full of surprise, and laced with what he had to admit was horror.

Her mother, from whom Patsy got her petite structure, blond hair and delicate features, gasped. Pressing a hand to her chest, she asked, "A writer? Patsy, you never mentioned that."

Dryer's frown overtook his entire face. He clearly didn't appreciate that Lane had just thrown a curveball and significantly shifted control of the game. He instantly tried to get it back. "That has nothing to do with what happened today."

Lane drew in a breath. While jumping to her defense, he'd let the cat out of the bag, and now had to make sure it didn't escape completely. "I believe it does. It shows she is committed to the future, and someone committed to the future is not interested in making mistakes that will hamper their abilities to obtain their goal."

Both William and his wife were frowning. So was Patsy. Lane knew he was playing with words, and was also buying time. Dryer was obviously ready to jump right into the subject of marriage, and Lane couldn't have Patsy telling them the truth. Not until he talked to her about it.

Yet, he also knew, the subject had to be brought up. Smiling down at her, he said, "Your father has agreed to give us a week to decide if we would be compatible for an engagement."

Her jaw dropped as she turned her gaze to her father.

"A marriage," William said. "You have a week to prove you'll make Lane a good wife. Which shouldn't be hard. Your mother has taught you everything you need to know."

Patsy's heart was pounding so hard, it echoed in her ears. A marriage? No. No. No. That couldn't happen. This couldn't be happening.

"I understand that isn't much time," Lane said.

"If you were anyone else, you two would be getting married tonight," Father said. "The only reason I've agreed to wait is because I'd already considered you as a viable option for Patsy to marry. However, this family will not host a scandal."

She pressed a hand to her temple, at the pounding that was happening inside her head.

"There will be no scandal," Lane said.

Patsy shook her head because this already was a scandal. They'd kissed. More than once, but she couldn't pretend to be engaged to him. Not Lane. He still missed his wife and daughter. He couldn't have agreed to this.

"A wedding date can be decided after the official announcement of our engagement," Lane said.

This couldn't be happening. It truly couldn't be.

"No, the date can be decided here, now," Father replied.

Patsy closed her eyes as the two men went back and forth as if bidding against one another for something on an auction block. A sense of panic built inside her as the voices grew in velocity. The enormity of the situation, of what she'd caused, grew overwhelming. "Stop!" She leaped to her feet. "Please, just stop!" Anything she said would only make matters worse, so she spun around and ran for the door, despite both her father and Lane shouting her name.

Lane caught up with her as she grabbed the banister on her way around the edge of the stairs leading to the second floor. "Come outside with me," he said next to her ear. "I'll explain."

"I can't!"

"Yes, you can." He placed his hand over hers. "Everything's all right, I promise."

Patsy let him lead her out the door because she had

no idea what else to do. All she'd wanted was to get out of her father's office, away from the arguing. But that, running away, wouldn't solve anything. She'd created this problem and needed to figure out what to do now.

The cool evening air may have been what cleared her mind, or it may have just happened. Either way, as soon as she and Lane were outside, with the door closed behind them, she said, "I'm sorry, Lane, so sorry."

"You don't have anything to be sorry about."

She huffed out a breath and walked down the porch steps. "Yes, I do. For my father, for him saying you have to marry me."

He took her elbow and led her across the front lawn, to where a cluster of three palm trees stood prominently in the front yard.

There, he cupped her cheek with one hand. "You don't have to be sorry, or afraid on my behalf. Not ever." He glanced at the house. "I could have said no."

Confused, Patsy asked, "Why didn't you?"

The corner of Lane's mouth curled into the tiniest grin. "Because this is your chance, Patsy."

She still didn't understand. "My chance at what?"

"To become a reporter."

Her heart thudded and she wasn't sure if it was due to his smile, or to his words. "How?"

"I told your father I need a week to decide if you would make an appropriate wife for me. During that time, he's agreed to let you attend functions with me. You'll be able to go places, experience things and write about them."

That all sounded wonderful, but a chill inside had her asking, "Why?"

He grimaced slightly. "For several reasons. Once people see us out together, the rumors of our engagement will stop and—"

"No, they won't," she interrupted. "It'll make it worse."

"You'd think so, but actually, that's not the way it works. Once a rumor is confirmed, people forget about it, move on to the next. A week will also give Henry time to catch Vincent Burrows." The pressure of his hand still on her cheek increased. "No one can know where Henry is staying. You can't tell anyone."

She'd never intended to tell anyone. "Of course I won't, but what happens when the week is up?"

He shrugged. "That we aren't compatible."

Her heart leaped into her throat, and stuck there. Wouldn't budge even when she tried coughing to dislodge it. "F-Father won't like that."

"By then, you'll be a reporter. Burrows will be caught, and you'll have helped write the headline story about his capture. Your father will like the publicity that'll bring to your family."

He could be right about that, but there was so much more to it than that. "I don't know, Lane. This could be more dangerous than chasing down Vincent Burrows ever could be." He said he didn't want to be married and neither did she, but what if something happened? What if they kissed again? She couldn't stop it before. Hadn't wanted to stop it. What was she going to do?

Glancing toward the house, he said, "Well, if you're that afraid, I can go talk to your father right now. Call it all off."

She bit her lips together, wondering if that would be the best choice. It would be awful, but it would be awful a week from now, too.

"I know one thing," Lane said. "Liberty Bellamy wouldn't be afraid. She'd be excited to get this chance."

She had to keep biting her lips together. This time it wasn't to stay quiet. It was to keep from smiling. Libby would jump at this chance. She wouldn't be afraid at all. He knew that. His smile said so. She released hers, and the air in her lungs. "Yes, she would. She is."

"Good." He grasped her hand. "We'll have to stick together on this. Let your family believe that we'll announce our engagement in a week. Even your sisters."

She nodded, even though she knew that would be the hardest part, not telling her sisters the truth. They'd never kept secrets from each other.

No, that wasn't true. She had already been keeping secrets from them. About Lane kissing her, and how Victoria Lloyd knew— She grabbed a hold of his arm. "Victoria Lloyd, Lane. She might still tell my father about me being at her party."

"I'll talk to her."

That might have satisfied Patsy, but the Libby in her said, "We'll talk to her."

Later that night, as Patsy lay in bed, she wondered what had happened in the house while she'd been outside with Lane because when he'd walked her back inside, her father agreed that they could announce their engagement in a week.

Engagement.

The word scared the dickens out of her. So did marriage. She didn't want to get married. Didn't want a life like her mother had, leaving the house only to go shopping once a week. She'd never realized just how boring that life was until she'd graduated school and completed the secretarial course. Because that's when that became her life, too.

Even a week of freedom felt like a dream.

Her stomach gurgled at that thought, too.

She had one week to become a reporter. A real reporter.

Flipping back the pink brocade bedspread and white sheet, she reached over and clicked on her lamp. There was still a copy of the article she'd written about the dance-off in her suitcase. Now that she knew how people wanted to read about real people, she decided to rewrite it. She couldn't use Betty's name, and didn't know the man's name whom Betty had danced with, so that was a dilemma. Betty wasn't home. She and Jane had snuck out. They'd been gone when she came up to bed.

Funny, she didn't miss going out with them tonight. Her day had been full of adventure. Trekking into the woods, meeting an FBI agent, taking shelter in the cave and then all that had happened once Lane had walked her home—how he'd given her the chance to truly be liberated for a week.

And they'd kissed, but she was trying hard to not think about that. Had to. If she let herself remember that, she wouldn't be able to think about anything else.

She glanced back down at the pad of paper. She had to write. Had to become a reporter within the week. Lane had said Libby would be... That's it! She could use Oliver and Libby and combine the dance-off at the Rooster's Nest with the one at Victoria's.

She closed her eyes, recalling how Lane had spun her around, and dipped her at the end of the dance contest. And the exact moment he had kissed her. How the pressure of his lips had awakened things inside her. How her body had tingled, and how a temptation had arisen, a need that was hard to describe, but one that had made her body come to life in a very womanly way.

Lane had kissed Libby, not Patsy. Either way, she wouldn't put how she felt in the article, but she wouldn't ever forget it, that was for sure, but she could write it as Libby.

Lane was right. Libby could do it. She'd prove it.

With newfound determination, she picked up the pen and started to write, and write, and write.

The article was finished and she was reading through it, making small changes, when she heard a muffled thud from the bathroom next door. She shot off the bed, ran to the door and pulled it open. Betty was already entering her bedroom and she shut her door without a backward glance.

Patsy glanced into the bathroom, where Jane shrugged.

"She's been grumpy all day," Jane whispered. "Going out only made it worse."

"Because of me?" Patsy asked.

"Who knows? She was adamant that we go out tonight, even though Mother and Father were still awake. They didn't realize we were gone, did they?" Jane asked.

"No. They never came upstairs or asked about either of you."

Jane pulled the beaded hat off her head and shook out her long hair. "Are you okay? What happened to you today? Where were you?"

Patsy grabbed her hand and dragged her into her bedroom. "I was helping Lane on the Rex Gaynor story."

"Hot socks!" Jane jumped onto the bed and folded her legs. "Spill the beans!"

Careful to not mention Henry, which became difficult when she told Jane about the cabin in the woods, Patsy gave a step-by-step, minus the kiss—she couldn't tell anyone about that, not even Jane—account of the day, including the cave and ultimately the engagement.

"Engaged?" Jane eyed her closely. "Baloney!"

Patsy felt the excitement swirl in her stomach. The engagement was baloney, but at the moment, it made her happy. She wasn't totally sure why, but nodded. "Yes. To Lane."

"Bee's knees!" Jane leaped off the bed and grabbed Patsy's shoulders. "Do you know what this means? It means we do have a choice! Father won't force us to marry only who he deems appropriate!"

Patsy froze momentarily and swallowed against the wave of guilt at not being able to tell her sister the engagement was pretend, and that Lane had actually been one of the men Father had considered as a viable option— that was what he'd said. *Viable option.*

"This is beyond bee's knees!" Jane jumped up and down and muffled a giggle with both hands. "Oh, Patsy, I could kiss you! I am going to kiss you!" Clasping Patsy's head with both hands, her sister planted a kiss on her forehead. "This is copacetic! Copacetic!" Grabbing her hand, Jane added, "We have to tell Betty!"

They hurried out of the room and down the hall. Betty's door was locked. They knocked as loud as they dared, but Betty didn't respond.

"She must be asleep," Patsy whispered.

"We'll have to tell her in the morning." Jane clapped her hands silently and then blew a kiss at Patsy. "Night!"

"Night," she responded quietly as Jane entered her bedroom, leaving Patsy alone in the hallway. Alone with a mixture of sentiments filling her. A week from now, when they discovered this was all a hoax, her sisters were not going to be happy.

No one was going to be happy.

Including her father.

He'd chosen Lane as a viable option for her. When? Why? Was this whole thing a setup between Lane and her father?

Patsy trudged her way back into her bedroom and crawled into bed, trembling from head to toe.

Her sleepless night left her with one option.

To go talk to Lane.

She was greeted with smiling faces at the breakfast table, which made her so nervous she knew she wouldn't be able to eat.

Taking her seat, she glanced at the empty one beside her. The one where Lane had sat last night. He certainly had agreed to all this quickly. So had Father.

The food was passed about and the meal consumed in silence, as usual, but rather than merely nodding and raising from his chair when he'd finished eating, Father set down his napkin and folded his hands together, elbows on the table.

Patsy held her breath with impending dread.

Nodding at her, Father said, "It appears that Patsy's hobby of sending letters to the newspaper has provided a suitable match for her."

The hair on her arms stood at the realization that he knew about her writing articles and mailing them to the newspapers. She'd been certain neither he nor Mother knew about that. Unless Lane had told him. Which made her wonder what else he'd told them, as well as what he hadn't told her.

"Mr. Cox is a prominent member of society," Father said. "A man with the ways and means to provide for a family, a man of wealth and status, which has been my concern when it comes to finding suitable husbands for each of you. Their wedding date will be set next week upon the announcement of Patsy's engagement to Lane Cox and today you will all go shopping with your mother. She has a list of things that will be needed in the near future."

As if that had been a speech to the masses, he then nodded, stood and left the room.

Patsy squeezed her eyes shut, trying to come up with something to say in the silence that was sure to remain in his wake.

To her surprise, that wasn't the case.

"Let's hurry," Mother said excitedly. "We have a wedding to plan, and your father has insisted that we spare no expense. After all, Patsy will be marrying a wealthy man."

Patsy shuddered. She was being duped. Duped into marrying exactly whom her father wanted her to marry. Someone Father had chosen because he had money. Someone who didn't want to marry her any more than she wanted to marry him. Even though she couldn't forget kissing him. That wasn't enough to want to marry someone. Which she didn't want.

Within record time, the dishes were done, the women dressed for shopping and they were in the car, with Betty driving them downtown. Patsy was sick to her stomach and couldn't figure out why Lane would do this. He'd said he didn't want to get married again, but had that been a lie, too?

Mother was busy talking, telling them the shops they would visit, when Patsy caught sight of the *Gazette* building. With several rows of paned windows, it was one of the tallest buildings downtown. Lane's car was in the parking lot next to it.

She bit her tongue to keep from shouting for Betty to stop and let her out. That would never do. Ultimately, she was going to have to do what she did best, sneak away.

Her opportunity arose when Mother instructed Betty to park the car only two blocks away from Lane's newspaper office. Upon entering Wickerman's, a store they'd all dreamed of shopping at, Patsy told her mother, "I'm going to find the powder room."

Not even the displays of shimmering, gorgeous gowns distracted her from finding the back of the store and, eventually, the backdoor that led into an alleyway.

She'd barely taken a step out the door when a hand caught her arm.

"Where are you going?"

Twisting, she was thankful it was Jane. "I'm going to see Lane. I have to."

Jane released her arm. "Are you trying to ruin everything?"

That was exactly what she was trying not to do. "No. I just need to talk to him about—about the story I'm working on with him." She pulled the article out of her purse and waved it in front of Jane. "I'll be back as soon as I can."

"What if we go to another store?"

She didn't have this all planned out. "I don't know. I'll find you, or take the A-line home."

Jane huffed out a sigh and reentered the store.

Patsy started down the alley, truly having no idea what she was going to do, other than to find out the truth. After all, that's what reporters did.

Real reporters.

The overhead sun was warm, and sweat was beading on the nape of her neck by the time she reached the *Gazette* building. Lane's car was still in the parking lot, and trepidation bubbled in her stomach as she pushed open the wide glass door.

Having never stepped inside the building before, the noise surprised her, as did the number of people. Behind a tall counter that ran the width of the room were rows and rows of desks. Men and women were seated at each one.

Something about the steady click of typewriters and the jangle of telephones echoing off the bronze ceiling tiles overhead was thrilling. She'd imagined this. Somehow, in some way, she'd imagined this was exactly what a newspaper office would be like. Massive filing cabinets lined one wall, and open shelves, stacked high with boxes and piles of papers, lined the other wall. The rows of desks continued to the very back of the room. She could almost see herself sitting at one of those desks one day.

Being a reporter.

That's how all this had started, but now she wondered if that dream was worth what she was going through right now. If she ended up married to Lane, would he even let her be a reporter? Or would he expect her to stay home, like her mother, like his first wife, Naomi. He'd said it didn't matter that she didn't know how to cook, but... She stopped her thought right there. He didn't want to get married, and she didn't, either. And he knew she wanted to be a reporter, more than anything.

So why was he doing this?

"Papers are two cents. You can drop the money in the dish."

Patsy glanced to the right, where a woman had stepped up behind the long counter. Petite, with her black hair cut in a bob and wearing a plaid brown-and-tan dress, the woman looked as if she truly belonged here. The pencil stuck in one ear completed the look.

"They are right there," the woman said, pointing toward a stack of daily papers on the counter.

Patsy had to shake her head to get her mind back in order. She had to get something else in order, too. She wasn't Patsy. She was Libby. Lifting her chin, she said, "I'm not here to buy a paper. I'd like to see Mr. Cox, please."

The woman frowned. "Do you have an appointment?"

"No, but I'm sure he'll see me."

Shaking her head, the woman smiled. "Sorry, Mr. Cox is a busy man. I can't let you see him without an appointment."

Scanning the desks, searching to see if Lane sat at one of them, she nodded. "I know how busy he is, but could you just tell him that Patsy is here and needs to talk to him? I know he'll see me." She didn't know that, but had to act as if she did and kept a level gaze on the other woman.

Although she appeared doubtful, the woman said, "Wait here, I'll go ask him."

"Thank you."

The woman walked only a short distance, and then stepped into an opening between two of the large wooden file cabinets lining the one wall. Realizing that had to be the door to Lane's office, and not totally convinced that he would see her, Patsy shot around the long counter. She arrived at the exact same time the black-haired woman opened the door with Lane's name painted across it in big white letters.

"Sorry to disturb you, but there is a woman named Patsy here…" The black-haired woman's words faded as she realized Lane was looking over her shoulder.

Patsy waved at him, and then smiled at the woman as she turned around.

"I told you to wait—"

"It's all right, Nancy," Lane said, standing up behind his paper-covered desk. "I'll see her."

Patsy held the smile on her face even as the woman frowned.

"Thank you," she said, skirting around the woman and into Lane's office.

Lane walked around his desk as the other woman stepped out and closed the door behind her.

The butterflies in her stomach hit with a vengeance at the way he leaned one hip against the corner of his desk. He had a pencil stuck behind one ear, too, and was wearing a pair of glasses that made him look extremely intelligent, besides overly handsome.

Briefly, she imagined just how amazing it would be to work here, with him, every day.

"What are you doing here?" he asked. "How did you get here?"

Working with him every day, seeing him every day, would almost be like being his wife.

Oh, dear.

Patsy was brought back to reality as if a bird had just dropped her out of the sky. She wanted to slump against the tall filing cabinet beside her, but Libby wouldn't do that, so she didn't, either. Being Libby, she pulled the article she'd written out of her purse. "I brought this over for you to read."

Chapter Thirteen

Lane crossed his legs at the ankles to keep from walking across the room. His heart had kicked into fourth gear at the sight of her smiling face peeking through his doorway. He truly had no idea seeing her would affect him so strongly, but it had. Wearing a white dress covered with big yellow flowers and carrying a matching yellow purse, she had looked like a burst of sunlight when she'd stepped out from behind Nancy Wells.

This, seeing her every day, was going to be harder than he'd told himself it would be. The emotions he'd kept in check for years weren't collaborating with him. It was as if he had no control over them anymore. She'd awakened them, and they leaped to life again at the sight of her. Made him remember kissing her. How soft her lips were, how welcoming.

He diverted his gaze long enough to tell himself he wouldn't react to anything happening inside him, before he asked, "What is it?"

"I rewrote my article about the dance-offs."

He had to grin, if only to himself. Right now, she was a mixture of Patsy and Libby. He could tell. She was trying to be Libby, but some of Patsy's insecurities were showing.

Giving her the opportunity to decide who she wanted to be, he held out his hand. Libby would cross the room without delay. Patsy would bite her lip and think about what she was doing.

She crossed the room and handed it to him.

He was amazed by how well he knew her. Glancing down, he read the first few lines, and grinned at her use of the names *Libby* and *Oliver*. Reading farther, he was again impressed by how the article came to life. "This is really good. Really good." He read all the way to the end, and considered running out the door, shouting "Stop the presses"! He might have if it had been a headline story. This wasn't. But it was an article that he'd print in tomorrow's edition, and told her so. "This will be in the society column tomorrow."

"Why?"

Surprised by her response, he set the article on his desk. "Because it's that good."

"Is it, or are you just pretending because you are a viable option?"

Lost by her question, he asked, "A viable option for what?"

"To marry me." She paced the floor. "You said you didn't want to get married, yet you complied awfully quick. Why is that?"

"So you could have a real chance to become a reporter."

"And why would you do that?" She planted both hands on her hips. "When did you know you were someone my father had selected as a possible husband for me?"

Her questioning all fell into place, like bricks stacking up to form a wall.

"If you knew that, why would you agree to this? A fake engagement? Especially after...already being married once."

He couldn't blame her for being skeptical. He had been skeptical of her, too, after Victoria had revealed she was one of William's daughters. He'd thought she was duping him that evening. That her father had put her up to it. Pointing to a picture hanging on the wall, one that had been there for years, he used the same reasoning he'd given himself. "That's why. That is Naomi, Sarah and me, shortly after Sarah was born. And shortly before they died in the train robbery."

Prior to the train robbery, he'd only reported on the news, but needing justice for his family, he'd dug in his heels and become an integral part of the investigation. That had changed many things for him. Law enforcement had accepted him as an ally, a source they could trust, and that had changed him as a reporter. He'd no longer just wanted the story, he'd wanted the truth, and printing the truth, no matter what the subject, had bolstered his business.

Oddly, he'd never acknowledged that until this very moment. But it was true. Naomi and Sarah's deaths had greatly contributed to the success of the *Gazette*. To his success, and understanding that gave him a knot in his stomach.

"I'm sorry I doubted you," Patsy said, standing near the picture. "She was very pretty."

"Yes, she was, and she was a wonderful person. They both had their entire lives ahead of them." He didn't feel the anger he used to when thinking about Naomi's and Sarah's deaths, but he still felt the loss. It wasn't as strong, as overwhelming, but they had been a part of his life, as was losing them. "I swore I'd see Gaynor behind bars for their deaths."

"You must have been very upset when you heard he'd escaped," she said solemnly.

"I was mad," he admitted. "And shocked that it had happened."

"And now you want to see Burrows arrested because of them."

He did want to see Burrows arrested, but strangely enough, it wasn't because of the train robbery. She was more of the reason. That realization didn't settle well inside him, either.

"I want justice to be served." Not willing to look into things any deeper inside him than that right now, he continued, "To answer your other question, your father was in to see me a few weeks ago, about advertising, and suggested that he had eligible daughters." He tried to make that sound less inappropriate than William had at the time. "I told him I wasn't interested in marriage, and I'm still not, but I am interested in helping you become a reporter."

"Why?"

He leaned back against his desk, "Because Charles Lloyd gave me the break I needed, and I would like to do that for you." He didn't want to sound arrogant, but she did need to know what she was up against. "I know the newspaper business well, including most of the people in it. I told you before that there are very few women reporters, and that could be a hindrance for you, one that others may not look beyond."

She looked at him thoughtfully. "Why are you willing to?"

He picked up the article she'd given him. "Because I've read your work. It's not perfect, but it shows potential. More potential than I've seen from a newbie ever before. You could become a reporter, Patsy. A good one. You have the drive and the potential. All you need is the opportunity." He wasn't exactly sure why he was so driven to give her that chance. The articles the *Gazette* received from newbies was never-ending, and he could easily choose one of those writers, but he didn't want to choose someone else. He wanted to help her. She had talent and he wanted to see her succeed, excel.

She plopped down in one of the chairs in front of his desk as if the wind had just left her sails. "But what if I can't do it, Lane? My sisters. They think this is real, our engagement, and that is giving them hope that things could be different for them."

"Maybe this can make things different for them," he said honestly.

She shook her head. "My mother took us shopping this morning, for a wedding dress, and trying to pretend, while knowing it's all a lie…" She sighed. "I just don't think I can do it."

He heard the authenticity in her voice. She may have lived two lives, an isolated heiress by day and an outgoing flapper by night, but she'd been honest in both lives.

Snagged by one thing she'd said, he glanced at his watch. "That had to have been a quick shopping trip. It's only ten o'clock."

She leaned her head back and stared up at the ceiling. "I snuck out of the first store we entered."

He had to grin at his own thoughts of her being as honest as possible, while continually sneaking out. "You really need to stop doing that."

"Doing what?"

"Sneaking out."

She covered her face with both hands. "I know, but

they are going to hate me when they learn the truth. Hate me for ruining everything."

Last night, after leaving her house, his focus had been on finding out all he could about Burrows, and he had. Trouble was that his informant would only talk if it was tit for tat. In other words, Victoria Lloyd now knew that their engagement was a fraud. Ironically, Victoria had laughed at the idea that Patsy was finding a way to pursue her dreams despite her father's heavy hand, and had agreed to help them in any way she could. Which had included information on Burrows, and his new distillery business.

He walked over, knelt down in front of Patsy and wrapped his hands around her wrists. "Hey," he said, pulling her hands away from her face. There it was again, the warmth she instilled inside him. It welled, filling up his chest. He didn't want to see her hurt, or to see her eyes so full of sadness.

She attempted to pull up a smile, but couldn't quite muster it. It was so cute. She was so adorable. He glanced away, hoping that would help the feelings inside him. His gaze landed on the picture of him, Naomi and Sarah. How could he be so drawn to her when she was so different from Naomi? Night and day in appearance and personality. He'd planned on spending the rest of his life with Naomi, would still be married if she hadn't died.

His gaze had returned to Patsy, and the temptation of touching his lips to hers was still there. Stronger than ever despite all he knew. All he'd told himself. Maintaining a modicum of control, he only allowed his lips to barely brush the tip of her nose before pulling back.

He would never do that with another woman, especially a potential employee, so why couldn't he control himself when it came to her? It was as if he was playing with fire. Enticed by it, even while knowing the dangers. "You can do this," he said, both for her and himself. Then, wondering if that was part of the problem, that he'd wanted this more than her, he added, "Become a reporter, make things different for you and your sisters, but it is up to you. You either want it badly enough to go against all the odds, all the doubts inside you, or you don't. You are the only one who can make that choice."

"I do want it, Lane. I want things to be different, but I'm scared that when the truth comes out…" She shrugged and shook her head.

"More scared than sneaking out to visit speakeasies every night?"

"That was different. It was all three of us."

"You aren't alone this time, either. I'm with you."

She grinned and nodded, then frowned. "For now."

Remembering the envelope he'd put in his pocket this morning, he pulled it out and handed it to her. "Here."

"What's this?"

"Your first payment. For the article about Raymond's party. You'll have another one once I've edited the article you just gave me. It's not much, not enough to live on, but it's a start."

A shine entered her eyes. "I've never earned any money before."

"Then you've already taken the first step."

"I have, haven't I?"

"You have." The desire to kiss her struck, and he stood, took a step back. "I went to see Victoria Lloyd last night. She agreed to not tell your father about you being at her house, and she told me that Burrows had supplied the alcohol for her party."

"She did?"

Although Lane normally kept information to himself,

until his story went to print, this case was different. He wasn't certain how much would go to print. That could very well depend upon Henry. The FBI was stingy with what they allowed to be released as public information.

"Yes." He sat in the chair next to hers. After a moment of pondering as to where to start explaining all Victoria had told him, Lane let out a sigh. It truly didn't matter where he started. He knew Patsy, and she was going to ask questions until all the holes were filled in.

"The timing of my visit couldn't have been better because Victoria was mad at him because several people, including herself, had gotten sick."

"From drinking too much?" Patsy asked.

"That may have been the case for a few people, but Victoria claimed differently," he answered. Victoria had looked like death warmed over last night, and it hadn't all been because she hadn't been wearing any makeup. "She thinks Burrows tried to poison her."

"Really? Like Rex Gaynor?"

"Possibly." Lane nodded. "Victoria explained that Burrows had come to her a couple of months ago, looking for investment money for his distillery. She's known for doing that, investing in new ventures, but she wasn't aware of his connection to the mob, not his uncle who had lived here, or his family in New Jersey. She said he'd convinced her he already had distribution lined up and promised her a big return, but she hasn't seen anything yet, and is now wondering if she will."

"So he needs the money that Rex Gaynor hid," Patsy said.

Lane wasn't convinced that was the case, not after all he'd learned. "Victoria claimed the whiskey at her party wasn't the same as what he'd given her while convincing her to invest in his company." Lane had figured if

Burrows had done that to her, he'd done it to others, and though bar owners were tight-lipped about where they got their booze, he'd still be able to verify that had happened to nearly every speakeasy Burrows had convinced to buy his product. The samples had been good, the actual product not.

"Why would he do that?" Patsy asked.

"I don't know, it doesn't make sense, unless his distillery is a cover-up for something else."

"Like what?"

"I don't know. Maybe Henry will have more answers when we meet him tonight."

Lifting a hand, with one finger up, she said, "We have to tell Henry. Now, that Burrows is manufacturing booze, the FBI can bust him."

He had to grin at her insight, and how she'd retained everything Henry had said. "That's true."

"Did Victoria tell you where the distillery is?"

"No. She doesn't know. But the first night I met you, someone told me about a new distillery that had started up…"

She snapped her fingers. "The docks. It has to be. That one dockworker told me that Burrows had been cruising the docks for weeks."

"Do you know how big the dock area is?"

She shook her head.

"It's huge. Miles and miles long, and it's the most dangerous place in LA."

"But that's where it is, isn't it?"

He wasn't surprised that she had worked it out. "Probably."

She sat quietly, deep in thought, before looking up at him. "There's more than one story here, Lane. There's the Rex Gaynor story, how someone offed him, which can't be written until Vincent Burrows is caught and the FBI releases the information about Rex being dead. Then, there's the story about whiskey being switched, that people and speakeasies need to be warned about, which can be written now, just not the part about who's possibly behind it. And then there's the Vincent Burrows story, how he's involved in both and what he's truly up to."

He couldn't stop a grin from forming. A sense of pride filled him, too. "You are going to make a good reporter, Patsy. You have the insight."

She sat straighter in her chair. "Thank you." Then, with determination sparkling in her eyes, she asked, "What time are you picking me up tonight?"

"So, you want to continue, go ahead with—"

"Yes," she said before he could finish. "We have to. We have to write these stories so people know the truth. We have to."

He nodded, yet had an inkling he should now be telling her they should call it off. It was as if he was on a tightrope, and didn't know which way to go to get off safely.

"Six o'clock?" she asked. "Unless you want to have supper with us," she said, "then you should arrive by five thirty. Father always has a predinner drink at five thirty."

He wasn't going through that torture again. "I'll be there at six. I've been invited to the grand opening of a new restaurant downtown. We'll go there before going to the Rooster's Nest."

"Invited so you'll write an article about them?"

"Yes."

"Ducky, I can help you with that." She stood and spun on one white-heeled shoe, toward the door.

Standing, he caught her arm. "Where are you going now?" Although he had numerous employees, he'd continued to work alone for years, both in researching and writing his own articles, yet, he was enthused to have her working with him. Like a partner.

"Back to Wickerman's," she said. "That's where my mother took us shopping."

The name of the high-end clothing store didn't surprise him. "How do you know your mother will still be there?"

She shrugged. "I don't, but I'm betting that they still are. Jane and Betty aren't going to pass up the chance of getting a dress from Wickerman's."

But she had, to come see him. "I'll drive you."

"It's only a block and a half away, through the alley and the back door."

What was it with her and alleys? "I'll still drive you, in case your mother is no longer there." He kept one hand on her elbow and walked her out of his office.

"This place is amazing," she said. "I didn't expect it to be so big, or have so many people working here. Are they all reporters?"

Pride filled him. More than usual at her appreciation of the business he'd built. "No," he replied. "When I bought the paper, there were six full-time employees. Now there are over twenty and a wide variety of positions besides reporters. I'll show you around someday."

"I'd like that." Scanning the room as they walked, she asked, "Where do you print the newspapers?"

He nodded toward the far end. "Through those doors."

"The pressroom?"

"Yes." He paused at Nancy's desk. "I'll be back in a little while."

She smiled, but he also saw the questions in her eyes as she glanced at Patsy. "Yes, sir."

Nancy was sure to be curious. She'd been with the

Gazette for five years and was a very integral part of keeping the place running smoothly, but she'd just have to remain curious when it came to Patsy. For now.

He opened the door and held it for Patsy to step out into the bright sunlight. "My car is over there, in the parking lot."

"I know," she said. "I saw it when we drove past." Looking up at him, she then asked, "Where do you live?"

He gestured toward the building across the parking lot.

She frowned. "You don't have a house?"

"No. Just an apartment." He wondered how she felt about that, couldn't tell by the way she smiled, yet chose not to ask because it shouldn't matter to him. This was about her becoming a reporter. Business, and he couldn't let it become personal.

He huffed out a breath. Not any more personal than he'd already let it become.

"Wickerman's is just around that corner," Patsy said as Lane drove out of the parking lot. She was amazed by how different she felt now than when she'd arrived. Lane was right. This could make things very different for her sisters. Once she became a reporter, with her name in the paper, Father would have to let her keep writing. People would expect it. He'd have to recognize how she had to be allowed to go out, see things, experience things in order to write about them. And if it was all right for her to do that, it would have to be all right for her sisters, too.

Her sisters would be so thankful to her for that. Thankful to Lane, too. She certainly was. So very thankful. He was so smart, and kind, and handsome, and wonderful.

Her stomach flipped at just how much she liked him. So very much. What would her sisters think when she didn't marry Lane?

She was just beginning to contemplate what that meant, how that made her stomach flip again, when she spotted her mother's green Buick. Pointing it out, she hopped out of Lane's car as soon as he stopped, refusing his offer to walk her inside.

Oh, dear, what would people say about him when their engagement, their pretend engagement, was called off? That could hurt his reputation, if people started gossiping that he'd done something wrong. What would she do about that?

She didn't have time to contemplate that any further, either, because Jane saw her walking through the front door of the store.

Her sister grabbed her arm and pulled her forward. "Mother has three dresses for you to try on."

Surprised, Patsy asked, "She doesn't know I was gone?"

"She didn't ask, so I didn't say a word. She's looking for you right now. I guess she thought you've been in the powder room or looking at dresses this entire time."

Patsy tried on the three dresses, which turned out to be very fashionable and of her liking. Mother insisted that she buy all three.

Holding up the dark blue one that had an overlay of delicate silver lace, Patsy said, "Lane is taking me to a restaurant tonight. I think I'll wear this one." She bit the tip of her tongue then, waiting for her mother's reaction, half expecting her to say they'd have to talk to her father about going out with Lane tonight.

Looking at the dress, Mother tapped the side of her cheek with the tip of one finger. "Do you have a gray purse?"

"No," Patsy answered.

"Then we'll get you one."

Patsy ended up with gray shoes to match the purse, and had asked the sales clerk several questions about the store, wondering if she should write an article about them, and ultimately decided to ask Lane about that.

He arrived promptly at six o'clock that evening, and after a cordial exchange with her parents, he led her out to his car. Her heart had never raced so fast. She was going out, at night, and there was no sneaking involved.

All thanks to him.

He wore his gray suit, and looked so very handsome, with his hair combed to one side and his crisp black bow tie beneath his chin.

"The restaurant is called Dominica's," he said while starting his car. "They opened last week, but tonight is by invitation only."

"Will there be other reporters there?"

"Yes, I'm sure they've invited all of the newspapers."

"But your article is the one that could make or break them."

"I wouldn't say that," he said.

"I would." It was the truth. His paper was known for just that. The truth. Integrity. Just like him. Determination rose inside her. She would not be the one to sully his reputation. Would not. She'd become the best reporter ever.

Dominica's was down by the bay, and she'd never seen anything quite like the huge wooden building built next to the shoreline with one wall that was nothing but windows that overlooked the ocean. The table they'd been seated at by a man who had a white cloth draped over one of his arms and wearing a black-and-red suit was right beside that wall of windows. Patsy was in awe at watching the sun fall lower and lower in the sky while listening to soft music playing and eating a meal consisting of salad, soup, iced shrimp and rockfish and rice. Looking at Lane over the delicate flicker of the single candle on the table was just as splendid as the setting sun.

He was as popular here as he had been at the parties they'd attended. Nearly every person who walked past their table stopped to say hello to him. It had seemed strange at first, for him to introduce her as Patsy rather than Libby.

"What are you smiling about?" he asked.

Too full to take another bite, she set down her fork and dabbed her mouth with her napkin. "Just thinking about something."

"Whatever it was, it made you smile."

Glancing to make sure no one was approaching their table, she leaned forward. "Liberty Bellamy."

"Your alias."

"Yes."

"Why? Do you miss her?"

She had to think about that for a moment, just to make sure. "No."

"Are you sure?"

His skeptical frown made her giggle. Being Libby had been fun, but right now, being Patsy was far better. "Yes, very." She turned to the window. The sky was now a mixture of oranges and reds beaming down and reflecting off the ocean. "Look, Lane. Look at that sunset. Have you ever seen anything so beautiful?"

"Yes, I have."

The tenderness of his voice had her slowly turning to look at him. He wasn't looking out the window, but directly at her with such intensity her cheeks grew warm. Instantly, she was remembering yesterday, in the cave when he'd kissed her. A warm wave spread through her system and settled low in her stomach, leaving an odd ache in her very core.

"We better make our way over to the Rooster's Nest," he said, pushing away from the table.

Within a few minutes, they were in the car and driving across town. Once again, she thought about being Libby and the fast-paced atmospheres of the speakeasies and the parties she'd attended with Lane. That had all been fun, there was no denying that, but this, riding in the car with him, was rather amazing in itself. She liked being alone with him and how they could talk about things, all sorts of things.

He found a parking spot near the Rooster's Nest, and held her hand as they walked along the sidewalk and down the steps, into the speakeasy.

The place was hopping. People were dancing to the music the piano player was providing, while others mingled about, adding boisterous laughter to the music in the air, while others were seated at tables, smoking cigarettes and downing drinks, while carrying on more hushed conversations.

Of habit, Patsy reached up to check her hat. A brief second of panic hit her as she felt nothing but hair, until she remembered she wasn't wearing a hat. Didn't need to. She was no longer Libby. No longer hiding.

"Let's sit over there," Lane said, pointing toward a table near the wall.

Patsy nodded, but said, "I'm going to visit the powder room."

"I'll get us some drinks," Lane said, releasing her hand.

She visited the powder room, and as she exited, a man approached her.

"Hey, doll, wanna dance?"

She glanced at the table where Lane was sitting, and shook her head. "No, thank you, I'm with my fiancé."

"Just my luck," the man said, turning away.

"Who was that?" Lane asked as she sat down.

She shrugged. "I don't know. He asked me to dance."

"You don't want to dance?" Lane asked.

"No," she said. Amazingly, she didn't. "I'd much rather sit here with you."

"Your sister is staring at you."

"What sister?"

"Jane."

She didn't scan the room. Didn't look anywhere but directly at him. "I don't have any sisters here."

"Oh, are you Libby again?"

"No, I'm Patsy, but Patsy doesn't have sisters who would be at a speakeasy. They aren't allowed."

"How do they feel about that?" he asked.

"That I'm doing the right thing," she answered. "Father has to understand that there are other choices besides marriage or the convent."

He frowned. "The convent?"

"That's what would happen if we broke one of Father's rules. We'd be sent to the convent."

"Seriously?"

"Yes. We've all had appointments with Sister Martha Margaret to learn what would be expected of us, if we entered the convent."

"You aren't serious."

"Yes, I am. Why would I joke about that?"

He lifted his glass and took a swallow. "Why indeed."

Patsy questioned what he meant. There was no reason for her to joke about something so serious.

Lane set his glass down and held his hand out to her. "Do you want to dance?"

She did, with him, and reached out, took a hold of his hand, but then recalled she wasn't here to dance. "What if Henry arrives while we're dancing?"

"We can see just as much from the dance floor as we can from here," Lane said. "We'll keep an eye out for him."

She didn't need to be coaxed, yet the way Lane laced his fingers between hers did just that. Coaxed her into standing up and following him onto the floor. The song being played was a slow, wistful tune, and the way Lane's arms folded around her, pulling her flush against him, filled her with a dreamy sensation.

Eyes closed, she rested her cheek on his shoulder as he swept her around the dance floor. Being in his arms was so magical it made her light-headed.

By the time the song ended, she was nearly dizzy.

He laughed as she lifted her head and stumbled slightly while catching her footing.

"That dance almost put you to sleep." He grasped both of her hands and spun her around. "This one won't."

She giggled as he then towed her two steps back and then two steps sideways, into the steps of the foxtrot. His eyes were so bright, his smile so big, she laughed again as he spun her beneath their clutched hands. She twirled on her tiptoes, and then at the end of her spin, she slid up next him and, before she realized what she was thinking, planted a kiss directly on his lips.

Lane caught her around the waist and held her there, with his lips pressed against hers. The music played on, faintly. She could hear it beyond the pounding of her heart echoing in her ears.

She looped her arms around his neck, and gasped slightly as Lane's tongue slid between her lips and into her mouth. A bolt as hot and powerful as the lightning they'd taken shelter against yesterday shot through her. Heating everything about her, and increasing that powerful ache in her most private parts.

When Lane ended the kiss, a distinct craving for more had her a bit shaky. So did something else. Her heart. The way it felt. Warm. Happy. Full of...

No. It couldn't be love.

She couldn't be falling in love with Lane.

Couldn't.

That would mean she'd want to marry him. But he didn't want to marry her. He'd said so. Furthermore, if that were to happen, it would mean that Father would get what he'd wanted all along. For her to marry a man he picked out.

Father would say that had been right, and that wouldn't change anything for her sisters. It would make it worse, and it would all be her fault. She could never marry Lane.

Chapter Fourteen

"I—uh—I don't see Henry," Patsy said, stepping out of his arms. "Do you?"

"No," Lane said, pulling his eyes off her to glance around the room. What was happening to him? He'd hardly looked for Henry. He'd been too focused on her. She consumed him, when he was with her and when he wasn't. It was like he felt whole again. There was no longer an emptiness inside him. An emptiness that he'd continued to try to fill by thinking about Naomi and Sarah, by avenging their deaths. But that hadn't been working for some time now. Because of Patsy.

Stepping back, he gave the room a full and solid once-over. Henry was nowhere to be seen. He had to get his head back in place and couldn't do that with her around. Luckily for him, it was time to change that. "It's going on eleven. Time for us to leave."

"Leave? Eleven isn't that late."

"Not to some, but eleven is what time I'd told your father you'd be home." Her father. Lane swallowed at the way his stomach churned. He couldn't be falling in love with her, because that was exactly what William Dryer wanted, and not at all what Patsy wanted.

Wrinkles formed between her eyes. "When? When did you tell him that?"

"When I picked you up and told him where we'd be going." He took her arm. "You hadn't come downstairs yet. He said he'd be waiting up for you, so we need to leave."

She started to nod, then her eyes snapped wide open. "Waiting up?"

"Yes." Did she really expect anything different? This was the same man who'd threatened to send them all to a convent. How had he become so deeply involved in all this? It wasn't like him at all.

"Oh, no!" She shot around him. "I'll be right back!"

She made a beeline to her sister Jane, who was leaning against the piano. He couldn't hear the exchange, but it was animated with plenty of hand gestures and head shaking. A moment later, Jane disappeared in another direction while Patsy hurried toward him.

Lane bit the tip of his tongue to keep from saying that their sneaking out had to come to an end at some point.

Once he saw her eyes, any humor he may have had disappeared. She was petrified. Like she had been in the cave yesterday upon learning the time.

"We have to give them a ride home," she said, nearly breathless. "They'll never make it if they wait for the streetcar, or by running."

"That's fine." He guided her toward the door. "We can give them a ride. Did you tell them where we are parked?"

"Yes. Jane's getting Betty and will meet us outside."

She was visibly shaking. "It'll be fine," he said.

"Not if my father finds out they've been gone."

Jane and Betty arrived at the car as he was opening Patsy's door. They didn't wait for him to open their doors.

"Get a waggle on, Lane," Jane said as she slammed

her door. "Our father's going to have a lather on if we aren't home when Patsy arrives."

"He might already know you aren't there," Patsy whispered, as if not wanting anyone else to hear.

"He's never gone upstairs before," Jane said. "We have to hope he didn't tonight, either."

Lane had never done anything unlawful, but as he started the car and pulled away from the curb, he felt as if he was driving a bank robbery getaway car with stolen loot in the backseat.

There was little traffic, allowing him to arrive on the street to their house in mere minutes. Far enough away from the Dryer home that if someone was looking out a window, they wouldn't see his headlights, he pulled the car over to the curb as the women requested.

Jane and Betty leaped out and ran into the shadows of the trees.

"How will they get inside the house?" he asked as they disappeared.

"They'll climb the trellis."

"Climb the trellis?" His insides buckled. "Is that how you snuck out every night? Climbing up and down the trellis?"

"Yes."

"All the way to the second floor?"

"Yes, and in through the bathroom window."

"You could fall, break a leg, or worse."

"No, we're careful."

Whatever filled him was more than a sense of obligation, or of fear. It was real, and sincere. He reached over and touched her cheek, forced her to turn away from the window and look at him. "Careful? What if one of the boards broke? They are not strong enough for climbing up and down."

"We stay away from the weak boards." She glanced toward the passenger window. "They should be there by now."

He clamped his back teeth together and pulled the car back onto the road. The mixture of emotions rolling around inside him was foreign. Any kind of emotions had been foreign to him for years, until he'd met her.

She was so alive and vibrant. He'd been that way once. Is that what was happening to him? That he was trying to be young and carefree again? No. He was too mature for that. Too mature for any of this. That's what happened. People grew up. He'd been young and alive once, but life, and death, had changed that for him, and there was no going back.

"Patsy, I'm worried about you sneaking out like that. Climbing the trellis," he said, pulling into the driveway.

A sly smile curled up the corners of her lips. "I don't have to sneak out right now."

Right now, because of their pretend engagement, but what about next week, when that was over? He knew the answer. She, and her sisters, had gotten the taste of freedom, and no matter what Dryer threatened them with, the hunger they now had wasn't going to go away.

He opened his car door. "Your father is looking out the window."

She wheezed while sucking in air. "I hope they made it inside without him knowing."

He opened her car door, helped her out and then guided her up the walkway. Her steps were stiff, and her arm beneath his hand trembling. It had been a long time since he'd had a father waiting when he walked someone to the door, and despite his age and experience, Lane wasn't sure what he should do. He didn't know what to expect, either.

Dryer opened the door while they were walking up the steps. The man's expression was always foreboding, so the one he wore now gave no inclination as to what to expect.

Lane kept his hold on Patsy's arm, making a split-second decision that if Dryer blew up, Patsy would be leaving with him.

Turned out that wasn't necessary. Dryer was affable, and his wife appeared excited to ask Patsy about her evening. Before he left, Patsy assured him she'd have an article about Dominica's for him tomorrow.

As he climbed in his car, started it, Lane questioned, once again, what the hell he'd gotten himself into. He'd never thought he'd meet a woman who could tie him in knots the way Patsy had. His mind. His emotions.

Shifting into Reverse, he recalled falling in love with Naomi, and how easy that had been.

A shiver shot through him so fast, he slammed on the brakes, making the car jerk to a stop.

What the hell was he thinking? He wasn't falling in love with Patsy, there was no reason to compare…

His thoughts stilled as he stared at the big brick house before him. The tall white pillars that framed the front porch and extended past the second floor to the roof. The massive white door and white shutters on the windows. The golden glow of light emitting out of the windows on the second floor.

Patsy was in one of those rooms, and a variety of images flashed in his mind. Of her smiling, laughing, dancing, kissing him.

Her lips were so soft, so sweet. Her smile so bright. Her actions so lively and animated.

He shook his head, dispelling the images. None of that meant he was falling in love with her. He'd sworn off love while watching the casket that held Naomi and Sarah lowered into the ground. That pain had been excruciating, something he'd vowed to never be open to feeling again. He was older now, knew how to protect himself from things. Things like falling in love again.

Releasing his foot off the brake, he backed out of the driveway. He needed to find Henry, aid the FBI in any way they needed in order to apprehend Burrows and put an end to this sham of an engagement.

Then he'd be able to forget all about Patsy. Never shed another impossible thought about caring for her, about her.

He huffed out a breath as the truth washed over him.

He wouldn't be able to forget her. That would be no easier than forgetting Naomi and Sarah. That had been different. He'd been able to keep them in his mind through his revenge of seeing Rex Gaynor jailed, and then knowing the man was paying for what he'd done. He'd been shocked when he'd heard Gaynor had escaped because he'd thought that part of his life was over. Settled.

Then, why, when he'd heard that Rex hadn't been directly responsible for their deaths, had he not felt that same level of revenge toward Burrows? The man was evil.

This wasn't about Burrows. The revenge he'd sought after Naomi's and Sarah's deaths was no longer burning inside him. It had dissolved. He couldn't recall exactly when. Years ago, maybe. After Rex Gaynor was sentenced, he was sure of that. But life had gone on. A lot of time since then was a blur because he'd focused on work, on building the *Gazette* into the most popular paper in the state.

That had happened.

He no longer had to work day and night. He could choose what he wanted to write about, to focus on. Ultimately, he'd chosen Patsy.

Why? Because he saw a little bit of himself in her? He hadn't known she'd wanted to become a reporter until later.

He held his breath as something inside him opened up. She'd captured his attention that first night, when she'd dragged him on the dance floor and made him dance like he'd never danced before. Made him live like he'd never lived before.

That's what had been missing from his life for years. The living part, and once she'd opened him up to it, he'd wanted to go right on living. Made up all sorts of excuses so that could keep on happening.

He wasn't after Burrows because of the train accident. He wanted the man captured because of Patsy and had found a way for her to help him to keep her close.

That, all of what he'd done, wasn't fair to her. She hadn't asked for any of this. From the beginning she'd been honest about what she wanted. He was the one who hadn't been. He had to figure out a way to put a stop to all of this.

Now, before it was too late.

Mind set that he could do that, he headed back to the Rooster's Nest. He'd wait all night if needed for Henry to arrive.

Once Patsy was sure her sisters were fine, and that no one was the wiser about their being gone, she sat down to write an article about the restaurant, but the words wouldn't come. Instead her mind kept playing images of Lane. Of talking with him, laughing with him, dancing with him.

Kissing him.

She picked up the paper she'd been trying to write on, balled it up and tossed it on the floor. Being Patsy was so much harder than being Libby ever had been. Libby would never have fallen in love with anyone. She was too liberated for that.

But Patsy. She huffed out a burning breath of air. But Patsy wasn't. She'd fallen in love. What else could it be?

She couldn't love Lane. That would mean everything she'd done was for naught. That her father would get exactly what he'd wanted right from the beginning. And Lane...

Lane didn't want to get married. He'd said so. He was still in love with his wife. Had to be, that's why he wanted to see Burrows behind bars. So all she had to do was not fall any deeper in love with him. She could do that.

No, Libby could do that.

A great sense of relief washed over her.

Convinced Libby could do that, she picked up her pencil, and started to write. She'd just have to be Libby all the time.

Which turned out to be harder than she'd thought.

The moment she saw Lane the following evening, her heart began to race. Ignoring it, she kept her distance as they walked to his car, and was thankful that he didn't seem to mind.

He was corrigible, and praised her about the article for the restaurant, but there was no hand holding, and she'd make absolute certain there was no kissing.

They went to a movie premiere that night, and though it was a wonderful experience, she knew she'd never be able to write an article about it. The entire time the movie had played, an alternate one had played in her head. One that included snuggling close to him in the dark theater, and laying her head on his shoulder. The things Patsy wanted to do, but she was Libby, so she kept her distance.

Thankful once the movie had ended, she nearly shot out of her seat. "Are we going to the Rooster's Nest now?" she asked, hoping that being among a crowd would make everything easier.

"No." Lane stepped aside for her to walk ahead of him between the velvet chairs. "I'll take you home now."

She waited until they were outside, walking toward his car before asking, "But what about Henry? We still need to find him."

"He must have found the information he needed without us. I went out to the cabin today. His stuff is gone."

"Just like that? Without telling us?"

"He's working undercover, so can't tell us."

That could be true, but something about his tone made her ask, "Where are you going, after you take me home?"

"Back to my office. I have a lot of work to do."

"Do you need any help?"

"No."

This was what she wanted, to hold herself back from him, not fall in love with him, because Libby wasn't in love with him, only Patsy was, but it sure made her sick to her stomach.

She still felt that way the next morning, when she arrived at the breakfast table and found her entire family fawning over the article about Dominica's in the newspaper. The one that had her name under the article. Even her father was beaming, and joyous.

"Oh, we are so proud of you, Patsy," Mother said. "So proud."

Patsy tried to act elated, as excited as they all were at seeing her name in the paper, but it just wasn't there.

Happiness. Deep inside her. It might have been if she'd never realized she'd fallen in love with Lane.

She did her best to keep a smile on her face all day, even when Lane appeared at the door to take her out that evening. To another restaurant—where she once again tried her best. This time so she could write another article about the place.

Her concentration became sidetracked when Victoria Lloyd stopped by their table. Afterward, she and Lane came close to having a row.

"Stay close to my side at this place," he said as he opened her car door.

He was referring to a juice joint near the docks. The smell of decaying fish and saltwater filled the air and there were no streetlights to brighten the dark, dank area. "I will."

There was a hint of disgust in Lane's eyes as he took her arm. "I don't like this idea."

"You heard what that dockworker said. If anyone knows where Burrows is, it's the owner of this place."

"Yes, I heard him, and I'd also heard when I told you not to talk to him."

His tone was sharp, but she ignored it. They had just left the Underground Feed Pen, a real two-bit joint that had been so smoky her eyes still burned. The stench of bad booze and body odor was still lingering in her nose, too.

Lane hadn't wanted to go to that joint, either, but back at the restaurant Victoria had said that she'd heard through the pipeline that Vincent Burrows had been at the Feed Pen last night.

Lane had wanted to take her home as soon as they'd finished their meal, but Patsy wouldn't let him. "He wouldn't have told you that," she pointed out. "As soon as he saw you, he clammed up." She had taken a moment when Lane had been stopped by someone he knew to find out any information she could. She'd hurried to the bar, where seeing a man puffing on a cigarette, she'd asked him to bum her one and give her a light.

The man had given her a cigarette, lit it and answered her questions about knowing a man named Burrows while she'd let the cigarette smolder into a butt between her fingers.

"Just don't talk to anyone here," he said.

She planted her heels into the gravel, making them both stop. "If I don't, we won't get the information we need on Burrows."

Lane shook his head.

She nodded. "No one is going to talk to you. Everyone knows who you are. That dockworker at the Feed Pen certainly did. He called you 'that reporter' before he took a hike."

"He probably came here," Lane growled. "To warn Burrows I'm looking for him."

"No, he didn't. He just went to the john. I saw him." She patted the front of his suit coat. "You just stay hidden, let me do the talking." The tweed of his jacket had her looking him up and down. "Take your coat off."

"Why?"

"So you won't stand out as much, and here—" She reached up with both hands and messed up his neatly combed hair. "There, now you'll fit in better."

He frowned at her, but took off his coat. "I won't stand out carrying around a suit coat?" He looked her up and down. "It's you who's going to stand out in this joint."

Flustered, she shook her head, but stopped shy of saying that women were meant to stand out. She pointed to the car that was only a few steps away. "Put your suit coat in the car."

"Why don't we just get in the car and—?"

"We've already had this discussion," she said. "You need me to find Burrows."

"No, I don't."

Her frustration was quickly growing. All this standing around and jawing wasn't getting them anywhere. Lifting her chin, she said, "Yes, you do. We both know Henry is missing, and Burrows is behind it." Henry was missing. He'd admitted that earlier, while being angry she'd talked to the man in the first joint.

Lane shoved a hand through his hair and spun around. He walked to the car, threw his coat inside and walked back. "Let's go."

A quiver of satisfaction made her grin.

"Don't be fooled," Lane said. "I'm only going along with you right now because I know you'll come here on your own if I don't."

That was highly unlikely, but she wouldn't tell him that. This was truly a downtrodden part of town, and without him at her side, she wouldn't be here. Warehouses lined both sides of the dark alleyway, and, besides the smell and darkness, there were noises that had her quivering.

Sounds of people shouting, things clanging and banging, and foghorns blaring as ships floated in from long voyages, carrying various loads of cargo. This was where men went to never be seen again, had been for years, and years, and years.

He steered her between two huge buildings to a door on one of them that had a single lightbulb hanging down from a single board. The bulb flickered as it swayed in the wind blowing off the water and between the buildings.

She could hear the electricity lighting the bulb snap and sizzle overhead as Lane opened the door.

He looked inside before nudging her to cross over the threshold before him. Another single bulb hung overhead, and three doors led off the small area they'd stepped into.

"This one," Lane said, opening the door on his left.

He took a hold of her hand and walked through the door first.

It wasn't like any speakeasy she'd been in, not even the two-bit joints. Smoke lingering in the air was so thick, it created a gray haze that not even the overhead lights could penetrate. There was no music, but plenty of noise. Men, sailors, dockworkers and some whom she didn't want to imagine what they did were talking, shouting at one another, in different languages. Above the hum of conversations, a fast click, click, click came from a big wheel spinning on one wall. The occupants were from around the world from the looks of them and their attire.

When the wheel stopped, shouts grew into a roar, both of elation and disappointment.

Gambling. This was a gambling house. A dice joint.

Other tables, where men were gathered around, playing cards and rolling dice, proved it.

She glanced up at Lane.

He shook his head, silently telling her to not say a word, and steered her toward the bar along the back wall. It was made of plank boards laid across the tops of several wooden barrels. There were no bar stools, no metal footrests.

A woman, with light-colored hair pressed into finger waves and wearing an orange dress that barely covered her breasts, stepped up to the other side of the plank. "This ain't the place to bring her," the woman told Lane.

Patsy shivered at the way the woman eyed her.

Lane slid his hand from the center of her back to the side of her waist and tugged her closer to his side. "We're looking for someone," he said.

The woman let out a hoarse laugh. "Ain't we all?"

"A supplier," Lane said. "For our establishment on the other side of town."

The woman's eyes lit up. "I see." She reached behind her and grabbed a bottle, then overturned a glass sitting on the bar. "Who you're looking for isn't here right now, but I'll give you a sample." She filled the glass from the bottle and then slid it across the bar.

Lane picked up the glass. Patsy wanted to stop him. The glass was far from clean, but he was already drinking the amber liquid.

He set the glass down. "Not bad. Do you know when he'll be back?"

She shrugged. "Couple days. Leave me your information, I'll send him your way."

"Do you have a piece of paper?" Lane asked. "I need to get things ordered right away."

A smile formed as the woman walked to one end of the bar. Returning with a pen and paper, she laid them in front of Lane. "He'll be back no later than the day after tomorrow."

Lane scribbled an address on the paper and handed it to the woman. "Thanks."

The woman leaned over the bar. "You be careful leaving here. A skirt like that draws attention."

Patsy's insides quivered.

Lane nodded and then steered her toward the door. Patsy didn't even consider protesting. This place was not somewhere she wanted to be, nor did she want to talk to anyone. She could feel eyes on her back and they made her skin crawl.

They were almost to the door when a gruff man stepped in front of them. His lips were pulled back into a sneer, showing a mouthful of rotting teeth. "How much?"

Lane stepped in between her and the man. "She's not for sale."

The man threw back his head and laughed. "Then I can have her for free."

Before Patsy knew what was happening, Lane punched the man. Not once, but twice. As the man flew backward, onto a table, Lane grabbed her hand and pulled her out the door.

Once out the second door, he said, "Run!"

Patsy didn't need to be told twice. She took off like a full-grown bear was chasing her down. That man had been as tall as a bear, and his face held enough whiskers on it that he'd looked like one, too.

Lane was running beside her, holding her hand. "Is he following us?" she asked, afraid to turn around.

"I don't know. Just keep running."

She had no intention of slowing down, and didn't until they were at the car.

Lane wrenched open the driver's door. "Get in!"

Patsy jumped in and scooted across the seat before she twisted, looking behind Lane. "I see someone! Hurry!"

Lane started the car while he was climbing in, and shifted into Reverse while shutting the door.

The car spun around and the tires threw gravel into the air as Lane shifted into First and took off up the road. Patsy's heart was pounding and she was gasping for air as she turned to look behind them.

"See anyone?" Lane asked.

"No, but I'm sure I did earlier." It might have been her imagination; it was hard to tell. The place was scariest she'd ever seen.

"Hold on, and keep an eye out to see if anyone follows us."

Clutching onto the back of the seat, she kept her eyes peeled out the back window as the car sped along, tires squealing as they rounded corners. "I don't see anyone."

"Good. Keep watching. If anyone is back there, we'll lose them downtown."

She kept an eye out, but didn't see anyone following them, and by the time Lane pulled the car off a road and parked, he'd taken so many turns and side roads, if anyone had been following them, they'd have long ago gotten lost.

"Where are we?" Patsy asked, flipping around to face forward.

"Lincoln Park," he said.

She recognized the music first, and then spied the big carousel across the manicured grass. "Lincoln Park. I haven't been here for years." When they had been young, they used to come here and have picnics when her grandmother and aunt visited them.

He opened his car door, climbed out and then held out his hand. "Let's take a walk."

She scooted across the seat and climbed out the driver's door. Even at this time of night, the park was full of people taking in the amusement rides, carnival foods and outlandish displays of men and creatures.

"Have you ever ridden in an ostrich cart?" he asked as they started walking through the grass.

"No, but I read the article you wrote about them in the newspaper. Are they as huge as they look?"

"Yes. Let's rent one."

She glanced around, back toward the car. "Are you sure we aren't being followed?"

"Yes."

"Who was that man?"

"One of many who work the docks."

"You mean work at the docks," she said.

"No, I mean work the docks. It's a dangerous place." His expression was serious. "People go missing all the time, never seen again. Not in this country."

"Shanghaied?" That was another article that he'd written that she'd read.

"Yes."

Bits and pieces of the article filtered through her mind, about young men and women who were believed to have been shanghaied. Underhandedly forced onto a ship bound for faraway shores and never seen again. She shook her head to dispel the thoughts, but still had to ask, "Why did that man ask how much?"

"They are willing to pay for specific people, especially young women." He stopped and turned to look at her. "Now you know why I didn't want to take you there, and why you can never go there on your own. No matter what. People have gone missing from the docks since it first became a port."

She nodded. There was no chance of her ever going down there again. But she was interested to know if their trip had been useful. "What address did you give that woman?"

"One that doesn't exist. It's just an empty lot out by the ball park."

"Will you go there, watch for Vincent Burrows?"

"No."

"Why not? We could catch him and—"

Chapter Fifteen

Lane pressed a finger against Patsy's lips. His heart was still in his throat over what could have happened back at that wharf rat hole. This whole thing had to come to a stop. He'd been saying that for days, but tonight had confirmed it. It had gotten too dangerous.

He was sure no one had followed them. Men like that goon were after easy targets and he doubted that anyone in that hole had ever driven a car, let alone owned one. His fast trip through town was to scare her from ever going back. "No," he said.

She opened her mouth to speak, but his finger was still there.

"Vincent Burrows isn't even in town," he said. "The woman at the joint confirmed it."

She eyed him skeptically.

Lane removed his finger and started walking again, having said all he was going to on that subject.

"What are we going to do?" she asked.

"Wait to hear."

"Wait to hear? Hear what? Hear from whom?"

"Henry. For all we know, Burrows could already be behind bars." He highly doubted that, but hoped she believed it. The past couple of days he'd been trying to justify what he was doing. But there was no justification for this. For putting her in danger.

"Mr. Cox!"

He looked up to see George Martin waving at him from behind a small corral. "Hello, George," he shouted in return. "Got a cart we can rent?"

"Rent?" George laughed. "For you, I give cart for free." He then shouted to one of his seven sons in Spanish.

"Can I rent an ostrich to pull it?" Lane jokingly asked as he and Patsy arrived next to the corral.

George, a pudgy and very enterprising man whom he'd written an article about several months ago, laughed harder. "Bird free, too. You put my picture in newspaper, and people come, rent carts, give me much money. You ride for free. Always."

"Well, that's very kind of you, George." He nodded at Patsy. "She has never ridden in an ostrich cart."

"Very fun," George said. "Very fun." Waving them toward a gate in the corral, he continued, "You like very much."

Patsy giggled. "I'm sure I will. I've wanted to ride one since reading Lane's article."

"Good man, Lane," George said. "Good friend."

Within minutes, one of George's sons led two ostriches, pulling a cart with two massive wheels, out of the corral.

"Bee's knees!" Patsy exclaimed. "Those birds are huge! Much bigger up close."

"Yes, they are." Lane climbed up into the seat and then helped her up beside him. "I have to warn you, the ride is a little bumpy."

"I won't mind!" she exclaimed while sitting down on the narrow seat.

Lane took the reins from George's son, and waved at George. "Thank you!"

With little else to hang onto in the simple, two-wheeled cart built light enough for the birds to pull, Patsy wrapped her hands around his arm. "This is so exciting!"

He gave the reins a tiny flip, just as George had taught him while he'd been interviewing the man upon hearing a permit for ostrich rides had been given at the park during a city council meeting. It was an interesting attraction, and he'd learned more about ostriches than he'd ever need to know.

The birds started forward, in their surprisingly smooth gate. It was the cart that made things bumpy because of the long poles hitched to the sides of the birds.

Patsy's laughter filled the air around them as they followed a pathway that wound around the park.

This was exactly why he'd driven to the park, so their last minutes together were fun. Memorable. He had to end the entire fiasco. Now. Henry was missing, and Burrows was behind it. He couldn't chance that happening to her.

He couldn't chance falling deeper in love with her, either. That's what kept happening, day after day, and he needed to end it while he still could.

"I truly can't believe how big these birds are," Patsy said.

"Close to nine feet," he said. "Their wings are too small for them to fly, but they do help them run faster. Up to forty miles an hour."

"Really?"

"Yes, and like horses, they sleep standing up, often with their eyes open."

"Ducky!" Hugging his arm, she said, "Tell me more about them."

"Their eggs can weigh an average of four pounds, and upon hatching, the baby chicks are the size of a full-grown chicken." He searched his mind for more information he'd learned while writing the article about George and his amazing birds, and told her that the eggs hatched within six weeks, that the birds lived for over fifty years and a few other things he remembered as they circled the park and headed back to George's corral.

After returning the ostrich cart, he led her to the carousel, and stood next to her as she rode a painted horse. He memorized the smile on her face, the sound of her laughter, telling himself that would have to be enough for him.

When the ride ended, he bought a stick of cotton candy that they shared while walking back toward his car. There was a wrenching in his stomach, a sorrow, over what he had to do.

"I need to ask you something, Patsy."

She looked up at him. "What is it?"

He had to be honest with her. Completely. "When my wife and daughter died, I blamed myself because I had been too busy working to take care of them like I should have. That's why they went to San Diego. Naomi had been ill, with the flu, and went down there so her mother could help her with Sarah until she was feeling better."

"You couldn't have known the train would have been robbed," she said quietly. "It wasn't your fault."

"No, I didn't know that, and I know it wasn't my fault. I've accepted that over the years. I've accepted a lot of things over the years, some more recently than others. I loved Naomi, and Sarah, and will forever miss them, but they are gone, and nothing I can do will ever bring them back. That includes bringing Vincent Burrows to justice."

"What are you saying, Lane?"

"That I'm going to wait until I hear from Henry, then I'll write the story, and I have to ask you to do the same."

Anger flashed in her eyes. "Are you telling me I'm off this case?"

"I'm not telling you. I'm asking you." He was blundering this. Her father told her what to do and then, therefore, he had to ask her, let it be her decision. It's what needed to be done, but the idea, the thought of not ever seeing her again, was gutting him. "Something could have happened to you tonight, at the docks. I don't want another death on my conscience."

"Lane, nothing—"

"Yes, it could, and I don't want to live through that again."

Her expression softened, and she stepped forward.

His heartbeat became a drumroll. It was pathetic, the way he wanted her, the way he craved everything about her. Fighting it had become the hardest thing he'd ever done.

"What are we going to do, then?"

"Call the whole thing off."

She didn't so much as blink before asking, "The engagement?"

"Yes. But I'll give you time to write a few more articles. I'll tell your father I'm going out of town for a short time. You can continue to write articles and send them to the newspaper. Then, when our week is up, I'll come see your father."

The way she kept her chin up, barely moved, concerned him. He expected more of a reaction from her. "It appears you've thought of everything. Except one thing."

Before he could respond, she looped her arms around his neck.

Then, before he had time to stop her, she kissed him.

Her lips slid across his like a dance, and tasted even sweeter than the candy they'd just shared. She leaned closer, pressing her lithe, perfect body against his. The pounding of his heart increased, and blood rushed throughout his body, throbbing in places.

She used her tongue to tease his lips, run the very tip of it along the seam of his mouth. He fought the desire to give in, but it was no use. His lips parted and he welcomed her tongue inside his mouth.

Her back arched, pressing her breasts more firmly against his chest, teasing his already heightened system.

His hands roamed over her back, up her sides, his palms tingling at the heat beneath the thin material of her dress. He wanted her like he'd never wanted anything. His groin muscles jolted as his thumbs encountered the undersides of her breasts, and then the pebbled hardness of her nipples.

Her hands combed into his hair as a whimper of a sigh left her throat and entered his mouth at the same time she pressed her hips up against his.

He pulled back, out of the kiss, searching for common sense to prevail, but her lips were still next to his, and there was something so intimate, so special about breathing the same air as her, that his mind couldn't think of anything else.

His body couldn't ignore how drawn it was to her.

Capturing her lips again, he drove his tongue inside her mouth and cupped one of her supple breasts. Unrestrained beneath her dress, the weight of her breast filled his palm. His arousal peaked with anticipation and expectation.

The jolt of that was oddly a virtue at that moment, one he needed. It forced him to realize where they were, what he was doing and, mostly, how this should not be happening. Not here.

Not anywhere.

Not anytime.

He pulled himself out of the kiss, and took a step back, gulping air.

Her breasts were rising with her labored breathing as she stepped over and opened the car door. "Take me home."

The ride was quiet, and torturous. Lane tried to explain this was how it had to be, but she held up a hand his way and looked out the passenger window. He considered telling her that he loved her, and would for a long time. That had been hard to admit. Even to himself, but he did love her. Despite believing he'd never love again, despite digging deep and trying to find enough guilt over finding someone to take Naomi's place in his heart. That hadn't happened. There was no guilt. Naomi wouldn't have wanted that. He understood it completely because he would never have wanted that for her, and he didn't want that for Patsy, either. He also didn't want her forced to marry someone for the wrong reason. Which was also why this all had to end. He was still chasing down the killer of his first wife. If that didn't prove to her father that he would never be the husband she deserved, nothing would.

She wouldn't understand that. He barely understood it all himself, but knew it to be true.

At her house, he parked the car. Her father stood at the door, waiting. As usual.

Lane got out, walked around and opened her car door. She looked up at him as she took his hand, let him help her. As soon as she was out, she released his hand. "Goodbye, Oliver."

Head up, she walked to the house.

He closed the door and followed.

"Good night, Father," she said as she walked into the house.

Lane gestured to the open door behind William. "We need to talk."

Patsy made it all the way upstairs and down the hall into her bedroom before the tears hit. She pressed the back of her head against the door and cried until she felt empty. Then she pushed off the door and stumbled through the darkness to the bed.

She shouldn't have kissed him, but she'd had to. She had to know for sure if she was truly in love with him.

She was.

Completely in love with Lane Cox.

Shouldn't there have been a dramatic moment, something that she could pinpoint to say that was exactly when she fell in love with him?

A person would think so, but it hadn't happened that way. Perhaps because every moment she'd spent with him had been amazing. Being with him filled her with dazzling freedom, and incredible adventures.

Sadness filled her. If only he wasn't someone her father had chosen. If only he wasn't still in love with his first wife. If only she was someone he wanted to marry.

Two lights shone into the darkness, and she climbed off the bed, went to the window.

Lane's car backed out of the driveway, then stopped in the street. She couldn't see him inside it, but felt him looking up. At her window. Her fingers started to tremble, then her arms. Her torso. Her legs.

Slowly, his car started moving, driving away, and an incredible sense of loss gripped her heart. Further proof she was in love with him.

Now she just had to figure out what to do about that.

Chapter Sixteen

Patsy lifted her chin and drew in a deep breath before raising a hand and knocking upon the door of the brownstone house. The sound of the ocean crashing into the shore echoed up the hill as she waited, wondering if she should knock again, louder this time.

The click of the knob turning caused her to stiffen, stand straighter and force her lips to form a smile. She had figured out what she was going to do about loving Lane, and that didn't include sitting at home, waiting for the week of their pretend engagement to end.

"Patsy?" Victoria Lloyd frowned deeply. "What are you doing here?"

"I need to talk with you, Mrs. Lloyd, if you don't mind."

"Of course." Victoria opened the door wider. "Come in."

"Thank you." Patsy stepped over the threshold, and followed Victoria across the entranceway, into the room that had held the dance-off she and Lane had won. Her throat tightened at the memory.

The room was full of furniture today. Two maroon

brocade couches, facing each other, and several side chairs.

"Please, have a seat," Victoria said, while sitting down on one of the sofas. "Has something happened?"

She lowered onto the edge of one of the couch cushions, and folded her trembling hands together. Huffing out a breath, she said, "I'm curious to know if you've seen Lane recently."

Victoria frowned. "No. Not since the restaurant the other night, when I saw both of you."

The undeniable anxiety that had filled Patsy when she'd gone to his office, and not seen his car there, filled her all over again. She'd spent all day yesterday confused, even scared, about being in love with him, but this morning, she'd decided that although her father might think he'd chosen Lane for her, he hadn't.

She had.

The night she'd forced him to dance with her. Lane had said he didn't dance, but he had that night. He also said he didn't want to get married, but he must like her. He'd kissed her. Several times. He still loved Naomi, but that's normal. Everyone continued to love people long after they'd died. She still loved her grandmother. Hadn't stopped just because she'd died, but that didn't mean she couldn't love other people. Lane had to know that. Know that he could love her, and still love Naomi and Sarah. She'd expect that, understand that. She'd come to that conclusion this morning, too.

Now, she was prepared to force him to admit that he loved her, too. That's why he'd said he didn't want to go through that again—losing someone he loved.

She didn't want to go through it once, let alone twice.

"Patsy? What's happened?" Victoria asked.

"Nancy Wells said Lane was out on an assignment, and didn't know when he'll be back."

"Perhaps he is." Victoria smiled slowly. "Did the two of you have a disagreement?"

"No." That's not what Patsy would call it. "He did suggest we call it all off."

"Your pretend engagement?"

She gulped in a breath of air, hoping that would keep the tears at bay. "Yes, I didn't know where else to go."

Victoria leaned forward and grasped her hands. "You've come to the right place. And don't you worry, Lane loves you. I could tell that the night I saw you dancing with him at Raymond Klein's party. I know I'm much too old for him, but I loved teasing him. He was so devastated when his wife and child died. I was, too, for him, but that was a long time ago and it's time he learns to live again."

"If Vincent Burrows lets him," Patsy said. "I'm sure Lane is out looking for him."

Lane slouched down in his seat, staring into his drink, like the other occupants in the room were doing. He'd taken a page out of Patsy's playbook, was in disguise.

A grin tugged at his lips. Libby. Liberty. Liberty Bell.

His disguise wasn't as good as hers.

Heaviness filled his chest and he huffed it out. He missed her. Patsy.

Her smile.

Her laugh.

Her lips.

Pushing all that to the back of his mind, he scanned the room.

He'd never gone to this length before to get a story, but this was more than a story. This was his future, and he was taking precautions so that once it was all over, he could court Patsy properly, and ask her to marry him without any shenanigans involved. He was done living in the past. He had a future and wanted it. One that included Patsy.

The FBI was as convinced that Henry and his partner had been shanghaied, and that Burrows was behind it. Two other agents, Les Wilkson and Doug Osmond, were at this seaside gin joint, too. Both dressed like him. In dirty clothes, smelling like fish guts, and looking like the dozens of dockworkers in the room.

He'd spent the past two days following up leads on Burrows and his whereabouts, and tonight, finally, he was a step ahead of the criminal rather than two steps behind. This was Burrows's lair and he was due any moment now.

The door opened, and Lane shifted his gaze in that direction, waiting. Two women walked in. One older. One younger. A flapper. Wearing a black beaded hat and dress.

His heart skipped a beat. He looked away, flustered. Every woman reminded him of Patsy. The little beaded hat on that flapper's head was a lot like the one she'd worn the night they'd attended Raymond's engagement party.

Engagement.

Guilt filled him. He'd told Dryer as much as he could. That he was on the cusp of a major story, one that could get too perilous for Patsy to know about.

Dryer had taken that well. Even offered to help.

A tingle rippled up his spine as he watched the flapper plant a foot on the foot rail beneath the bar as she leaned on one elbow on the wooden top.

That, too, reminded him of Patsy.

Damn it.

That flapper had red hair, not blond.

Clamping his back teeth together, Lane turned to the door again. Where the hell was Burrows? He should have arrived by now.

As if he had no control over his eyes, they roamed back to the flapper. She and the older woman were moving along the length of the bar. Even her walk reminded him of Patsy.

When Dryer had offered his help, Lane had told him he could do that by keeping an eye on Patsy. Twenty-four/seven.

A shiver rippled Lane's spine as the women rounded the bar and walked through a door that opened just then.

Twenty-four/seven.

Damn!

Dryer thought he'd always known where Patsy was 24/7, but didn't. Her father didn't have a clue about her Liberty Bell life.

But he did.

Red hair or blond, that flapper was Patsy.

Leaping to his feet, Lane barreled his way through the crowd, tossing aside chairs and people in his hurry to get to the door that Patsy had just walked through

Commotion ensued in his wake. Dockworkers could be an ornery bunch and it didn't take a lot to get punches flying.

Lane made his way to the door, and shoved aside a bulky goon who tried to stop him from opening it. The goon stumbled into a table, and that's all it took for an all-out brawl to ensue.

Lane shot into the room. Full of shelves and booze, the room was void of people.

"What happened?" Doug asked, arriving in the room.

"Did you see Burrows?" Les asked, right behind Doug.

Lane ran across the room, to another door. "Burrows is here, and he has two women. They went through here."

He should have been prepared for this. For Patsy to keep looking for Burrows. She wouldn't have stopped just because he'd asked her to. No, she'd have kept on looking for Burrows until she found him.

Wrenching open the door, Lane entered a dark and dank hallway. The only light was the one shining behind him. The only sounds were that of the brawl still going on in the gin joint.

Knowing the bouncer would be on his tail soon, Lane searched the darkness.

Where'd they go? They couldn't be that far ahead of him.

"Split up," Lane directed. Going on instinct, he ran forward to the closest door while Doug and Les shot down the hallway, one in each direction.

Lane pulled open the door, and started down a set of stone steps. The walls were built of large boulders, as well. Dampness grew as he ran down the slick, uneven steps. The air was heavy with the musty scents of mold and mildew. Pausing briefly, he listened, certain he'd heard something.

He had.

Voices.

More specifically, a raspy female voice. One he recognized.

Victoria Lloyd.

Damn it. He should have known. Continuing downward, Lane walked on the balls of his feet so his heels wouldn't click against the stones. Footsteps sounded above him. He ran faster, leaped off the bottom step and shot around the corner. Old, rotting crates with faded coffee bean labels were stacked high, and he slid between two rows, listening and watching.

The goon he'd shoved aside upstairs stepped off the stairway and continued forward, past the crates. A string of lightbulbs was draped along the low ceiling, leading through a stone archway.

Warehouses like this lined the wharf, dating back to long before California was a state. The wooden structures aboveground had been replaced, rebuilt, but those underground had withstood time, weather and man, including numerous fires that had leveled the area more than once in the past century.

Lane stayed hidden amid the old cargo crates and made his way toward the archway that the goon had entered. Edging his way along, he had his ears pricked, focusing on deciphering sounds beyond distant foghorns and the thud of the goon's footsteps.

Carefully, he peered around the corner of the archway. More crates. These ones new, with colorful labels of sugar and corn, and in the center of the room was a massive still.

The goon didn't pause as he walked around the big copper burners, pipes and holding tanks toward yet another door.

Sounds entered when the man opened that door. Traffic, ships, people.

Lane shot out from behind the wall, and crouching down, ran across the room as the man walked out the door. More crates lined the walls here. These ones were stacked five tall, and full of whiskey bottles, but still labeled sugar and corn.

Easing open the door, Lane saw the goon walking up a ramp that led to a loading dock for both trucks that would deliver cargo by land and the shipping containers that would be pulled onto the big ships heading out to sea and foreign ports.

Hugging the wall made of heavy logs to withstand the force of rushing water crashing into the rock seawall not far away, Lane ran up the hill.

It was as if a hand grasped him around the neck, squeezing the air out of him, when he got his first glance over the ramp wall. Moonlight beamed down on a head of blond hair like a stage show spotlight.

Burrows had a hold of Patsy, and the goon whom Lane had followed was running along the pier, toward them.

Lane had no idea what possessed him at that moment. He had no gun, no weapon of any sorts. All he knew was the woman he loved was in the hands of a killer.

With a growl that came from the very bowels of his being, he shot up the ramp, and ran toward the pier.

Patsy tried everything she could think of to break the man's hold. She twisted and kicked and slap, but Burrows had her in an iron grip, so tight she could barely breathe.

Her struggles were futile, but she kept trying. As soon as she and Victoria had walked through the door behind the bar, two goons had grabbed them, hauled them downstairs and then out to this pier, to Burrows. Who'd laughed when he'd grabbed her and started dragging her down the pier. They were being shanghaied. Just like Lane had written about.

The man she loved.

The man she'd never see again.

She almost thought she heard his voice, shouting her name, beyond the ship horns bellowing and the black water slapping against the sides of the concrete pier. That was impossible. Still she twisted her neck, trying to see behind her as she thought she heard him again.

Her heart leaped for a hopeful moment, at the man running toward them. That hope shattered. It wasn't Lane, but another one of Burrows's thugs. They were all as ugly and mean as him. Victoria had called the tavern and said she needed to talk to Burrows. He'd called back hours later, said to come to the tavern. Then, when the thugs had grabbed them and hauled them to the pier, he'd said he was going to get rid of them once and for all. Just like he had Rex Gaynor and the Federal Reserve agent on the train. The one he'd been following for months, looking for the right moment to steal the old bills being transported. Along with his partner Billy Phillips.

Burrows jerked her arm so hard she couldn't stop the wail of pain that shot out of her mouth. He jerked her again, spinning her around so they faced the man running up the pier.

"What?" Burrows shouted to the man.

His head was right next to hers, and she squeezed her eyes shut at how his shout made her ears ring.

Another shout made her eyes snap open, and her heart leaped again at the sight of Lane running behind the man. Two men were running behind him.

She opened her mouth to shout his name, but in the very instant, Burrows released her, shoving her backward. Stumbling, she reached out, looking for something to grasp, but was hit by a barreling force.

Her feet left the ground and she went flying, over the edge of the pier at the same time shots rang out.

"We have to swim for it!" Victoria shouted.

Patsy didn't have time to say she didn't know how to swim before she hit the water. Panic engulfed her mind as quickly as her body sank into the black water. She flayed her arms and kicked her feet, but it didn't help, she just kept sinking, lower and lower.

She was going to drown.

Fear filled her.

She couldn't breathe.

Couldn't see.

This wasn't how she wanted her life to end.

She didn't want her life to end.

Kicking harder, she tried to make her body move, find the top of the water. Find air. Her lungs were on fire. She had to take a breath. Had to breathe.

Something grabbed her and she fought against it, tried to get away. She couldn't. Whatever it was that had a hold of her was shoving her through the water.

This was it.

The end of her life.

A moment later, her head shot above the water. She gasped, coughed and sucked in air. And water. She spat it out, and, realizing that something still had a hold of her, she started kicking, pushing at it.

"Breathe, just breathe. I got you."

Her entire being froze with disbelief. "Lane?"

Water filled her mouth again as she sank. In an instant, her head was above water again.

"I got you, honey," he said. "Don't fight the water, just relax. We're almost to shore."

She was on her back, his arm was around her, under her arms, and she stretched her neck, needing to know that it was really him. That she wasn't dead, imagining things.

It was dark and water splashed in her face. "Is it really you?"

"Yes, it's really me."

An amazing, soaring joy filled her so completely she didn't care that she was in the water, that she didn't know how to swim. She flipped around and wrapped her arms around his neck.

Her lips found his, and they sank beneath the water. She didn't care.

His hands grasped her waist and propelled her upward, until their heads were above water again. She didn't stop kissing him. Wouldn't ever stop kissing him.

"Come on, you two, get out of the water before you both drown."

Patsy pulled her lips off Lane's at the sound of Victoria's voice.

"She's right," Lane said. "Hold on to me."

"I am," Patsy said, and would hold on to him forever.

"Come on!" Victoria said, waving from the top of the rock wall that kept the sea from rolling into the warehouses. "I'll help you up."

Lane swam her to the wall, and helped her get her feet on rocks so she could climb upward. He was right behind her, and Victoria grabbed her arms as soon as she was within reach.

"I didn't know you couldn't swim," Victoria said, pulling her into a hug. "But it was our only hope of getting away."

Fuzzy-headed, Patsy asked, "What happened?"

"Your fiancé came to your rescue," Victoria said. "Our rescue."

Lane climbed up on the rocks and steered both her and Victoria off the rock wall and onto the ground. "What are you two doing here?"

Patsy bit her lip, and swallowed. "Trying to stop Burrows from finding you."

"It's my fault," Victoria said. "I called him. Told him I needed more whiskey. I thought we could trap him at my house, but he told us to come here instead. I had my derringer, but his goons took it away from me."

"That was foolish," Lane said. "Very foolish."

Looking up at him, Patsy asked, "How'd you know where to find us?"

"I didn't," Lane said. "I was in the gin joint when you walked in." He pointed toward the pier. Police cars, with red lights flashing, were lined up along the ramp that led to the pier. "The FBI was there, too, and federal prohibition agents."

"Did they catch Burrows?" she asked.

"I assume so," Lane answered. "But he wasn't my concern. When I saw you going over the edge of the pier, all I could think about is that you don't know how to swim."

"You saved my life," she whispered. He had. She'd have drowned if not for him.

Lane cupped her face with both hands. "I love you, Patsy Liberty Bell Dryer. More than I've ever loved anyone. More than I'll ever love anyone."

Her heart welled to ten times its normal size, leaving her with barely enough breath to say, "I love you, too, Lane. More than anything or anyone."

He kissed her then. A long, incredible kiss that left Patsy nearly floating on air. The red lights still flashing brought her back to earth. "Burrows did kill Rex, he said so," she told Lane.

"I know," he said.

She bit down on her bottom lip, before telling him, "He'd been following an agent, waiting to steal the old bills being transported. That's why he blew up the passenger car, to kill the agent."

"I know," Lane repeated.

She loved him so much and didn't want to cause him

pain, but he needed to know the truth. "He was responsible for Naomi's and Sarah's deaths," she said quietly.

He cupped her face with both hands. "I know that, too. And I know he'll pay for it. What I want you to know is that all of that, the train accident, Burrows, Gaynor, Naomi and Sarah, that's all in my past. I'm focused on the future now. A future that I want to share with you. If you're interested."

Happiness filled her as she nodded. "I'm interested. I'm very interested."

Once again, his kiss left her floating on air.

She was still floating on air an hour later, when Lane pulled into her parents' driveway.

"Ready?" he asked.

She nodded and kissed him on the lips, briefly because another car pulled in the driveway next to them. Victoria had insisted upon driving Mother's car home. They had used it to go to the gin joint, and it needed to be brought home, but—

Patsy sighed. "I do hope Victoria knows what she's in for."

"Don't worry about Victoria," Lane said. "If anyone is able to hold their own with your father, it's her."

Her father was out the front door and down the steps before Lane had even opened her car door. As soon as she stepped out of the car, Father made a comment about her looking like a drowned rat every time Lane brought her home.

Considering it was the second time he'd brought her home dripping wet, she laughed, which seemed to shock her father.

"Hello, William," Victoria said, interrupting anything Father may have been ready to say. "It's been awhile."

"Victoria Lloyd?" Frowning, and looking confused, Father asked, "What are you doing here?"

Victoria held out the key to Mother's car. "Returning your wife's car, which was just used in busting a notorious bootlegger, among other things." As she dropped the key in Father's hand, she added, "I really could use a drink. You have one, don't you?"

"Of course, come in," Father said, waving at the open door.

Once Victoria had entered, Father said, "Go change your clothes, Patsy."

She was still wearing the black dress she'd borrowed from Victoria, but it was no longer dripping wet. Just covered in seaweed. Smiling, she tugged the jacket Lane had given her out of the backseat of his car tighter. "No, I'm fine, thank you."

Lane stepped in behind her, and said, "I thought you promised to keep an eye on her, William."

Father appeared to still be finding his tongue when Victoria said, "I'm waiting for that drink, William."

Mother guided them all into the living room, while Father went to his office. She, Lane and Victoria were all seated on the sofa when he returned with a tray of drinks. He didn't offer her one, but she didn't hold that against him. She was too happy to hold anything against anyone.

Except Vincent Burrows. She hoped he was getting exactly what he deserved. Patsy had to bite her lip at the differences between Lane's tale of the evening, which was fact-based, and Victoria's overly embellished version.

"Patsy, darling, are you sure you're all right?" Mother asked. "That sounds like a harrowing tale."

"Yes, Mother, I'm fine." She looked at Lane. Because of him she was fine. "I believe I just had my first lesson in being the wife of the best reporter in the state."

"Well, now," Father said gruffly. "If this is the sort of thing that—"

"You're the one who picked Lane out for me, Father." Patsy wrapped both hands around his arm.

"Yes, well—"

"And I'm so glad you did," she added.

Lane smiled at her, and then, despite her parents' sitting right there, he kissed her forehead. "You need to go take a bath, and I have an article to write for tomorrow's paper."

Patsy didn't protest, she did smell awful, and after saying goodbye to him and Victoria, she turned to walk up the steps.

Father took her arm. "Patsy."

"I am marrying Lane, Father," she said. "That's all there is to it."

"Well, maybe you should take some time, think about it."

He sounded meek, mellow.

She grinned. "I already have." Then, she stretched on her toes so she could kiss his cheek. "Thank you. There isn't a finer man on this earth than Lane Cox."

She hurried upstairs, where her sisters were eagerly waiting to hear about everything that had happened. Even though they had been listening from the staircase.

"I'm sorry I kept you from sneaking out tonight," she whispered as they entered her bedroom.

"We had to know where you'd gone," Jane said. "I can't believe you took Mother's car without permission."

Patsy flung open her closet door. "I had to."

"Because of the story?" Betty asked.

"No, because of Lane," Patsy said. "I love him." She handed a dress to Jane and then walked over to her chest of drawers.

"What are you going to do with this?" Jane asked, looking at the dress.

Happiness bubbled inside Patsy. She plucked out her underclothes and shut the drawer. "I'm going to put it on, right after I take a bath, so I no longer smell like seaweed, and then I'm going to climb out the bathroom window."

Chapter Seventeen

Lane had been at the office for less than half an hour when he heard tapping on the glass front doors. After giving Victoria a ride home, he'd gone to his apartment, bathed and put on clean clothes before coming to the office, knowing he'd be here half the night.

Burrows had followed his uncle to California years ago, but his uncle sent him home because he couldn't be trusted. Rather than going home, he'd heard about the Federal Reserve collecting old bills and learned about the train shipment. After blowing up the train and killing Billy Phillips, he'd followed Gaynor, but Rex had been arrested before Burrows could kill him. Turned out, Burrows and Billy had been working together and Rex Gaynor had been the third person. Rex didn't know that, or know that it was him whom Burrows was supposed to kill. Burrows had found the money Rex buried and took it back to New Jersey, until being ousted by his family for dirty dealings. He'd have been killed if he hadn't been a family member of the mob syndicate out there.

He'd returned to California to start another bootlegging business. He'd offed Gaynor because upon his return, he'd heard Rex was claiming someone else had blown up the train and was afraid Rex might be able to identify him. That Billy might have told Rex about him. In the meantime he'd stolen a shipment of Minnesota Thirteen and had been using that to convince people to invest in his business and buy his product, but when Victoria had realized she wouldn't get her money back, because his whiskey was so bad and once they tasted it, no one would buy it a second time, he tried to off her, too. He was in the midst of stealing another shipment of Minnesota Thirteen, which he figured was easier than making his own whiskey. All in all, Burrows's bootlegging business backfired on him as much as his train robbery had. A criminal always returned to the scene of the crime. That's what got Burrows caught.

It's also what got Henry shanghaied. When Burrows had discovered Henry was on his tail, he'd captured Henry and his partner, knocked them out and put them on a ship bound for the east.

The tapping repeated.

Lane tossed down his pencil and stood. He was never going to get this story done in time for tomorrow's edition. A story that may be the biggest in LA history.

"I'm coming!" he shouted as the tapping sounded again.

The only light on was the one in his office, and the streetlights outside the door, which was how he saw Patsy.

He jogged past the filing cabinets and the long front desk to unlock and open the door. "What—?"

"How about…?" She held up a hand and drew a line in the air with her thumb and forefinger. *"Residents Can Sleep Soundly Again. Notorious Gangster Arrested."*

He laughed. "A headline? That's why you're here?"

She stretched onto her toes and planted a kiss on

his lips. "Yes. If you don't like that, maybe you'll like *'Famous Reporter Assists FBI in Arrest of Bootlegger.'*"

He laughed again, and enjoying her game, asked, "How about *'Flapper Liberty Bell Saves City'*?"

She giggled. "I don't think that would be a good idea."

"Not ready to give up your false identity yet?" He peered out the door behind her. "Did you steal your mother's car again?"

"No, the streetcars are still running. It's not midnight yet."

"But you did sneak out."

She didn't nod or shake her head, just looked at him as if he should know the answer to that.

He did.

"How are you going to get back home?"

She turned around, and locked the glass door. "You can give me a ride when we are done writing the article."

He should drive her home right now, but the printing crew would be in by 5:00 a.m. and he needed his story done, completely edited and ready for print. Knowing her, as he did, she'd just sneak out again, probably beat him back here. They'd have to talk about that once they were married.

Married.

The idea thrilled him.

Because he loved her just as she was.

He took a hold of her hand. "Come on. You can work on the headline while I work on the story."

"Ducky!"

Once in his office, he looked at her. "But first, I thought you agreed to stop working on the Burrows case."

She grinned. "No, you asked me to stop working on the case, but I never answered."

Technically, she was right. "It's a good thing I love you," he said.

Looping her arms around his neck, she kissed his chin. "Yes, it is."

He kissed her, long and lovingly, the exact way he'd wanted to for days. Then, knowing he'd never get any work done this way, he let her loose and glanced around, looking for a task to assign her to. There were several typewriters in his office, stationed at different locations. Having more than one came in handy while working on more than one story. "Do you know how to type?"

"Yes, I just don't have one at home."

Marvel filled him. "You are perfect, you know that?"

She giggled. "Yes, I do." Sitting down behind a type-writer, she picked up a piece of paper to feed into the roller. "Now, get a wiggle on, we have a story to write. I'll type up tonight's events while you write the back-story, and then we'll put it all together."

The two of them were so in sync, the story practically wrote itself. She was excellent in bouncing off ideas as to how to put things together, and in remembering small details that made the story even more perfect. Between the two of them typing, and editing, it wasn't yet mid-night when he finished reading the final copy. Aloud.

"That's perfect, Lane. Perfect." Standing beside his desk, she rubbed her arms. "Parts of it gave me goose bumps."

"It is perfect." He set the paper on his desk. "And the *Gazette* will be the first paper to break the news."

She handed him another slip of paper. "What's this?"

"Just a flier to remind all taverns to check any alcohol they may have recently purchased. I know you already wrote an article about it, but a reminder might help spread the information. We don't want people getting sick. I typed it up while you were editing the article."

She walked behind him and rubbed his shoulders. "I thought maybe we could mail it, or have it delivered to the speakeasies. I'd hate to have someone get sick when we could prevent it."

"I like that idea. A community service notification." He leaned his head back. Her hands were doing wonders on the tension in his neck. "Once we are married, I'll let you do this every night." Several other things that they would do once they were married entered his mind.

Leaning down, she whispered in his ear, "We don't have to wait until we are married."

He tightened specific muscles against the heat throbbing in his loins. The past two days, he'd been focused on catching Burrows, but she'd never left his mind. Neither had the future they would have together. He glanced at his desk drawer, the one holding the single piece of jewelry he'd purchased this morning.

He spun his chair around, grasped her by the waist, and planted her on his lap. "I never imagined that this would happen, Patsy, that I would fall in love again. You caught me off guard, and showed me how to live again. It's like you saved my life."

She brushed his hair back with one hand. "You did save my life, Lane. And I'm not talking about tonight." She grimaced slightly. "When you saved me from drowning."

That was just one of the things he loved about her. Her honesty.

"You saved my life before then because you saved my dream. I would never have had the guts to truly become a reporter, not without your help," she said seriously. "But it's more than that. You believed in me. You

made me believe in myself, you made me strong and…"
She shrugged. "I can't even explain it, other than to say
you made me whole. Asking you to dance with me that
night at the Rooster's Nest was the best thing I ever did."

He rubbed the underside of her chin with one knuckle,
knowing exactly how she felt, because she'd done all that
to him. "I think that's when it happened."

"When what happened?"

"I fell in love with you."

She shook her head.

He nodded. It had taken time for him to figure it all
out, but like any good story, he eventually got to the bottom of it. "That's why I never denied the rumor about us
being engaged, and went along with your father's plan. I
was already in love with you. My heart knew that. It just
took my head a bit longer to figure it out."

She giggled. "I couldn't stop thinking of you that
night, or any night since then. Or any day."

"I couldn't stop thinking about you, either, and haven't.
You are on my mind day and night, and will continue to
be." He touched the side of her face. "I know I'm a few
years older than you and—"

"Age doesn't have anything to do with love, Lane.
We all love people who are older than us and younger."

She was right about that, like so many other things
she'd made him understand. "Naomi would have liked
you." That had been something else he'd realized. "And
she'd be happy that you made me live again."

A tear slipped out of the corner of one of her eyes.
"She would have?"

"Yes, she would have." He held his breath, preparing
for this moment. He was nervous. Because he loved her
so much. "I have something to ask you."

"What?"

He reached over and pulled open the drawer with one hand, while looking her straight in the eye. "Will you marry me, Patsy? Not because of rumors, or your father's selection, but because I love you and I will love you for the rest of my life."

She squeezed her eyes shut as she nodded. "Yes, I will marry you." Opening her eyes, she smiled big and brightly. "Any time. Any place. I'd marry you right now if I could."

He held his hand out, with the box sitting in his palm.

"Lane," she gasped.

"Open it."

She did and gasped again. "It's gorgeous."

"It's a sapphire to match your eyes, but if you don't like it, we can exchange it."

"I love it."

He took out the ring and slid it on her finger. "I love you, Patsy."

She pressed her lips to his before saying, "You make me so happy, Lane."

"You make me happy." He kissed her forehead, and knowing he had to stop before he couldn't, added, "I can give you a ride home now."

A teasing gleam appeared in her eyes as she lifted a hand to the bodice of her dress. His blood started pounding harder as she undid one button, then another.

"Not, yet, Lane."

Her whisper was like an enchanted melody. The actions of her hands, unbuttoning more buttons, had him mesmerized.

"It's warm in here," she whispered. "Don't you think?"

She was seducing him. He should stop her. A groan formed in the back of his throat, and the knowledge that he'd been trying to stop her from one thing or another since they'd met rolled around in his mind.

He hadn't been able to stop her then, and even if he could now, he didn't want to.

She shrugged the blue material of her dress over one shoulder, then the other, letting it fall away, exposing a silky, translucent white camisole. Her nipples were prominent little nubs.

He brushed a thumb over one of them, watching as her lids fluttered shut. She arched her back, and he leaned down, licking the nub.

Her fingers combed into his hair, as she arched against his mouth, wanting more. He took the entire nipple into his mouth, tasted it, suckled it. She urged him on, begged him to not stop.

He slid his hand beneath the silk, pushed it up, out of the way, and then settled his mouth on her other nipple.

Pleasure rippled through him, the ecstasy of their petting so intense he abandoned any thoughts of stopping.

This, the sharing of their love, had been building between them for days, and neither of them would be satisfied until it was achieved. He lifted his head, found her mouth and kissed her while rising from the chair.

Lane carried her across the room, with their mouths locked, their tongues teasing, tasting, enhancing the desires encompassing them. The leather couch in his office had been used as a bed before, on those nights when he'd been too tired to walk across the parking lot, but tonight would be the first time he'd used it for pleasure.

Gently lowering her feet to the floor, he pushed the bunched-up dress over her hips, let it fall to the floor and then slid the camisole over her head. She was so beautiful, so delicate.

With a throaty laugh, she pushed down the silky, short

pants, and kicked them aside while boldly unbuttoning his shirt.

"Life with you is such an adventure," she whispered. "I can't wait to experience this one."

He ran his hands down her sides, over the supple, warmth of her skin, her hips. "You are an adventure."

She pushed his shirt open, sliding her hands over his chest, down his stomach. Then giggling, whispered, "I like being an adventure."

"I love you, Patsy."

Patsy knew at this moment, her world was completely full. Anything she'd ever want stood right before her, declaring his love. The reality of that made her eyes burn with sweet, joyous tears. There, naked before him, where nothing could be hidden, she declared, "I know you do, and I love you, Lane. So very much."

He kissed her gently, caressed her sweetly, and when the time came to lay her down, he softly whispered, "It might hurt at first."

His kindness was only one of the things she loved about this man. "I don't care." She didn't. She wanted this union of their bodies, of their love, more than she'd wanted air to breathe while being submerged in the ocean this evening.

He'd saved her life tonight, but truth was, he'd saved her before then. The very night they'd met, he'd saved her from the boring life of captivity she'd been attempting to escape from for years. With him, she'd discovered who she truly was. What she was truly capable of.

Mostly, loving him.

Her body hummed with anticipation as he laid her down on the sofa. Eager, thrilled to be alive, to be with him, she parted her legs as he settled himself above her.

As he slid inside her, she gasped, not at the snap of pain, but with welcome. The freedom, the abandonment she'd loved experiencing while with him, was as alive and well inside her as all the other sensations he was providing.

He whispered his love for her in her ears, kissed her passionately and caressed her skin all while taking her on their greatest adventure to date. It was as if her very soul came to life and performed a wild and passionate dance, making her pant for air, as the music inside her sizzled.

Just when she was sure she couldn't experience anything greater, his magnificent, firm, lush body turned rock hard as he drove inside her firmly, and remained right there as her dance came to a brilliant crescendo.

Afterward, as they lay there, arms and legs still entwined, breathing heavily, Patsy had to give credence to the joy bubbling inside her. "Now, that, Oliver, was one hell of a dance."

Hours later, as they ran across her backyard, Patsy twisted and pressed a finger to her lips due to the snap Lane had made by stepping on a stick.

"Sorry," he whispered. "I'm not as good at this as you."

"I told you that you didn't have to walk me to the house."

"Yes, I do. I won't sleep until I know you are safely inside."

She shook her head and hurried toward the trellis on the back of the house. There, she stopped and turned around, face up for him to kiss.

He shook his head. "Up you go."

"You aren't climbing up with me!"

After glancing upward, to the second floor, he reached behind her and touched a wooden board of the trellis. He kissed her then, a quick peck. "No, I'm not. I'll break those boards for sure. But I'm standing right here until you are in that window."

She was already certain that he would do just that. "I'll be fine. Go home."

"I will. Once you are inside." He shook his head, touching the boards again. "You know this is an accident waiting to hap—"

She cut him off with a kiss. A long one that made her wish they were back in his office. Then, before he could protest again, she grabbed a hold of the trellis and scrambled up the wall with the skill of someone who had been doing it for a long time. Because she had been.

After flipping in through the window, she turned around, leaned out of it and blew him a kiss.

He acted as if he caught it, which made her smother a giggle. She pretended to catch the kiss he blew to her, and waited until he'd disappeared into the trees of the backyard before she left the bathroom and hurried down the hall to her room.

There, tucked in her bed, she dreamed of the future, of being Mrs. Lane Cox.

The smile that put on her face was still there when the sun woke her the following morning. She hummed a jaunty tune as she floated along the hallway and down the steps, and even paused to brush a kiss on her father's cheek upon arriving in the dining room.

"Good morning," she nearly sang.

"What's good about it?" he grumbled. "The newspaper hasn't arrived yet."

No longer intimidated by his gruffness, she planted her hand on her hips. Defending her soon-to-be husband, she said, "Lane had to write the feature article after he left here last night. I'm sure the paper will be delivered as soon as possible."

"Well, if a man can't even produce his own newspaper in a timely manner, maybe he's not fit for this family."

"Yes, he is," she said. "You handpicked him, remember?"

"I could always change my mind."

Two weeks ago, she would have been worried by that. This morning, she merely shrugged. "I won't change mine."

Her mother walked into the room, carrying a cup and a pot of coffee. "Good morning, dear. Change your mind about what?"

"Marrying Lane," Patsy answered. Then, as long as they were on the subject, she said, "Mother, I truly don't care about the how, when or where of my wedding. All I care is that it is Lane that I'm marrying, so how soon can we make that happen?"

Still gruff, and frowning fiercely, Father said, "If you're in such an all-fire hurry, why don't you just elope?"

"William!" Mother exclaimed. "Don't say such things."

"That may be the grandest idea you've ever had, Father," Patsy said, just as a knock sounded on the front door.

"Who can be here at this time of the day?" Mother asked.

"Probably the newspaper boy," Patsy said as Father marched past her.

It wasn't the newspaper boy, but the owner himself. Patsy had to restrain herself from running across the room when Lane entered with her father.

Forcing her legs to walk toward him, she asked, "What are you doing here so early?"

He handed her a newspaper. She glanced at her father, who also had one. Taking the paper from Lane's hand, she read the headline: *Notorious Bootlegger behind Bars.*

Smiling up at him, she nodded. "I like that. Simple and to the point."

Lane pointed beneath the headline. "Read the byline."

Aloud, she read the tiny print, "By Lane Cox and Patsy Dryer." It was such a tiny thing compared with all that had happened, but the fact that he'd included her name on the article made her love him even more. Without a care as to who was in the room with them, she looped her arms around Lane's neck and kissed him.

He kissed her back, too.

Epilogue

Oh, hurry up!

Eyes closed, Patsy knelt at the altar as the priest droned on and on. Had she known it would take this long for her and Lane to become husband and wife, she'd never have agreed to the church wedding her mother insisted upon. She'd already waited a week.

The longest week of her life.

As if he'd heard every thought dancing around in her head, Lane laid a hand on top of hers. It had been a long week, but at least she'd spent hours with him during each one of those days, and as soon as the priest proclaimed them husband and wife, she'd be spending all twenty-four hours of every day with him.

Please, Lord, he can say amen at any time now.

Lane squeezed her hand again.

Finally, the priest stopped and then, after she and Lane stood, and faced the congregation, he pronounced them husband and wife.

Patsy wanted to jump for joy, but settled for releasing much of her happiness in a shared kiss before they walked down the aisle together, hand in hand.

Mother had insisted upon coffee and cake being served

after the ceremony, so that's where they went, into the basement of the church, where they would need to stay for an hour.

That's where Patsy had drawn the line. She had agreed to everything else, including the long white wedding dress complete with a veil, but once the ceremony was done, she'd firmly insisted that she and Lane would remain at the church for one hour. No longer. Otherwise it would be dark before she got to show him her surprise.

Dozens upon dozens of people were there, including the two FBI agents who had been with Lane the night Burrows had attempted to shanghai her and Victoria.

After the men offered their congratulations, she turned to Lane. "Has there been any word on Henry?"

Lane shook his head. "No, but the FBI won't stop looking until they find him."

"Burrows still hasn't told them what ship?"

"No," Lane answered. "He probably doesn't even know. The thug who'd hauled Henry aboard didn't know the name of the ship, or where it was headed." He kissed her forehead. "Don't worry. Henry's tough. He'll be fine."

Their conversation ended as other guests approached. Patsy was cordial to all, but kept one eye on the clock, and precisely when one hour was up, they left the church, beneath a shower of rice being thrown as they ran to Lane's car.

"You certainly have been impatient today," Lane said, laughing as they drove away.

"I have a surprise for you," she said.

He glanced her way. "I have a surprise for you, too."

She hadn't expected that. "Where?"

"At the *Gazette* building."

They would have to go there first, because once they

got to her surprise, they wouldn't be leaving. "Can we go there now?"

"Yes, that's what I'd planned."

She kissed his cheek, then laid her head on his shoulder. "Good."

The *Gazette* office was closed for the wedding, and as he unlocked the door, Lane said, "Close your eyes."

"Nothing is going to jump out and bite me, is it?" she joked.

"No."

Eyes closed, she let him lead her into the building, and already familiar with the space, she knew they were in front of his office door when they stopped.

"Open your eyes," he said.

She did, and pressed a hand to her mouth at the freshly painted door.

Lane and Patsy Cox
Proprietors
Reporters

Tears of joy filled her eyes. "Thank you," she whispered.

"No, thank you," he answered softly. "I not only got a wife, I got a business partner." He kissed her. "A life partner."

Taking her hand, he led her back toward the outside door. "Tell me where we need to go so you can show me the surprise that's been making you so impatient all day."

"Not impatient," she insisted. "Just excited. But, I really, really love your surprise. That means so much to me. So very much."

"You mean so very much to me," he said, kissing her as they arrived at the car.

Once he was behind the wheel, she directed him where to go. As the drive took them closer to Hollywoodland, he asked, "Are we going to your father's house?"

"No, you'll turn up there. It's a gravel road on the right."

"I don't remember a gravel road."

Anticipation was tickling her insides. The road had been overgrown due to not being used, but that was no longer the case. "It's there. I'll show it to you."

Having driven on the road several times over the past couple of days, she knew exactly where it was and pointed it out for Lane to turn on a short time later. He cast her a curious frown.

He recognized the area, but didn't say anything.

Neither did she.

He drove until the road ended, at a run-down cabin in the woods. The very one they'd walked to and found Henry living in.

"Why are we here?" Lane asked.

"Turns out that my father owned this land, and I asked him to give it to us for our wedding. It's too hilly to develop, but for someone who used to camp out as a boy, it would be a nice getaway."

"Patsy, that's very thoughtful of you."

She shrugged. "I know it's hard for you to get away from work, and this way, when we do have a chance to *sneak* away, we won't be that far." She opened the car door. "I had the inside fixed up. Come look at it."

They walked hand in hand to the door—the new door that closed tightly, and locked. She opened it, and waved a hand. The men her father had hired had done a beautiful job of reinforcing the structure, and her mother and sisters had helped her furnish it with a large bed and an icebox full of food. She figured that's all the place needed for now.

Other than the large sign she'd painted and hung on the back wall.

She knew the moment Lane saw it.

He laughed and picked her up, carried her over the threshold.

Stopping in front of the sign, he looked down at her, and winked. "It's perfect."

She nodded in agreement as they both looked at the big wooden heart, and the names she'd painted inside it.

Oliver and Libby

* * * * *

*If you enjoyed this story, why not check
out these other great reads by
Lauri Robinson*

Married to Claim the Rancher's Heir
In the Sheriff's Protection
Diary of a War Bride

*And be sure to read the
Brides of the Roaring Twenties series*

Baby on His Hollywood Doorstep
Stolen Kiss with the Hollywood Starlet